F SCOTT ANDISON

DEATH
OF THE
REPUBLIC

ISBN: 1461001188
ISBN-13: 9781461001188

In memory of two of the best storytellers I ever knew -

Alexander Bruce Andison 1946 – 1965

Alexander Lamb Andison 1921 – 1989

Prologue – Vindicate Me, O God

Throngs of his supporters sang, shouted and screamed *Onward Christian Soldiers,* the campaign's theme song, while they waited for their candidate to appear. Some were crying, others overcome with elation. All were seized by an almost religious fervor that had defined his quest for the White House. Gradually the cacophony softened as the crowd began to lose steam. Reverend Robert Strong stood in the wings, waiting. Waiting patiently for the right moment to arrive. His wife, Doris, stood by him, gripping his arm, caught up like the crowd with excitement. She urged him to go on stage, but still, he waited.

Then it appeared – a brief lull as the audience took a collective breath - the moment he had been waiting for. Smiling knowingly at his wife, he gently loosened her iron clasp and strode confidently onto the stage. The crowd erupted once again at the first glimpse of him emerging from behind the curtain, every soul present cheering as one at the top of his or her lungs. After a few seconds of standing in the middle of the platform, soaking up their adoration while attempting to look humble, he moved forward to the microphone, ready to give his concession speech.

"My friends, my friends...Please, if I may...

(Cheering and applause)

"Thank you. Thank you.

(Cheering and applause)

"My friends...please...

(Cheering and applause)

Rev. Strong held up his hands, motioning to the crowd for quiet.

"I would like to begin by reading Psalm 43:

Vindicate me, O God, and plead my cause against an ungodly nation;
O deliver me from the deceitful and unjust man!
For You are the God of my strength; why do you cast me off?
Why do I go mourning because of oppression of the enemy?
O, send out Your light and Your truth!
Let them lead me; let them bring me to Your holy hill and to Your tabernacle.
Then I will go to the alter of God, to God my exceeding joy; and on the harp I will praise You, O God, my God.
Why are you cast down, O my soul? And why are you disquieted within me?
Hope in God; for I shall yet praise Him, with the help of my countenance and my God.
Alleluia.

"These words, these words of God, my friends, they offer us hope. Hope that one day we may set up the Lord's tabernacle at the very heart of this great nation. Hope that next election our faith will prevail.

(Cheering and applause)

"Although we are beaten today, we are not vanquished. Although we are vilified and castigated in the media, we remain undaunted. Although our family and friends endure accusations, slander and even threats of death, we remain committed to our cause.

"We have hope in God. We have faith we will prevail.

"But today, my friends - today the nation has spoken. I want to congratulate the President on his election and pray he leads our country bravely and with purpose.

(Boos and jeering)

"Now, please...please. Let there be no mistake. I have great respect for the President and intend to support him in the next four years in any way I can in helping fight this great depression that has shaken these United States of America to the core. The President is a devout Christian and a good family man. It is our duty to pledge allegiance to his leadership and administration. As I have said repeatedly throughout the campaign, we support many of the initiatives proposed in the President's platform.

"Whatever our political leaning – Republican, Democrat or Independent - we need to work together to make America strong once again. Whatever our beliefs, each and every one of us lucky enough to call themselves citizens of the United States – the greatest nation in the world's history – owes it to one another to put our differences aside. Whatever our racial background or religious beliefs, we must work together. We must work together for America.

[Cheering and applause]

"And talking about working together, I want to thank each and every one of our Coalition of Christians supporters across the country and all of you here tonight for the countless hours you've devoted to this campaign. I want to thank my brothers and sisters in the Baptist community who supported our mission. I want to thank the millions of Catholics who saw our common belief in Jesus as more important than affiliation to a political party. I want to thank my friends within the Latter Day Saints community, the Pentecostals and all the folks from other Christian denominations who found it in their hearts to support our cause. We are united in Jesus. We are all brothers and sisters. We are all family.

[Cheering and applause]

"All of you who know me, know how important family is to me. I want to thank my wife, Doris, and my two beautiful kids, Marcus and Angela, for standing by me through everything. For their love and support and their prayers. For putting up with the endless hustle and bustle that is all part of this great democratic race to lead the most powerful nation on earth. And I want to thank my brother-in-law, Colonel Sherman Gale, for all the support in putting together what we consider to be the most blessed campaign ever. Our only regret is that my little sister, Sherman's late wife, couldn't have been here tonight to see how much we have accomplished and how far we have come. I just know she is looking down on us from heaven tonight and smiling.

[Cheering and applause]

"My friends, tonight we must give thanks, praise Jesus. The Coalition of Christians has come a long way in the last four years and so has America. There are lots of good news stories out there and millions of people who are starting to live their dream again. Not everything is as bad as you see on TV. Our progress on civil rights and economic transformation is promising. We implore the press: *Focus on our similarities and not on our differences.* Try to show where things are working, not just where they are broken or corrupt. Don't hide away the problems, but try to show the solutions as well. *Try to be more balanced.*

"Now, speaking about the press, it has chosen to depict us from the beginning of the campaign as an insignificant, religious-right fringe group that is mired in evil. But that just isn't true. You know that it isn't true. *God knows that it isn't true.*

[Cheering and applause]

"First, we are not insignificant. Last time I checked this evening, it looks like we received almost one in every four votes cast. And this was not from just pockets around the country. We see our support coming from virtually every corner of this wonderful land.

[Cheering and applause]

"Second of all, we are not right-wing. We are conservatives. We believe in preserving traditions that have served us well in the past – that's all. But we are not right-wing.

[Cheering and applause]

"And finally, finally my friends, we are certainly not evil. Not me, not my wife, not my kids, not our supporters. We are not evil – we are Christians. *Praise God!*

[Cheering and applause]

"Yes my friends, we are Christians, like almost eighty percent of all Americans. And eighty percent - *that's what I call a majority.* A Christian majority that will, in the end, support our cause – a majority that will come to see *our* dream as its own.

"Today our coalition is rejected by an 'ungodly nation', but we must find strength in our Lord, through our dear Savior Jesus Christ, to fight on for what we know is right. What we know is our right to claim as Christians.

[Cheering and applause]

"When you remember this day sometime in the distant future, when you are telling your children and your children's children how hard you worked, how much you prayed, how determinedly you fought, you'll remember that you were witness to it — *that you were the very foundation shaping its destiny* — the very re-birth of our great nation. For what you have seen here today, what you have been part of, is the beginning of the end for the old Godless ways of the past. It is only a matter of time until these United States formally embrace Jesus. God *will be* manifest in our Constitution. *While today we are humbled, tomorrow we will prevail.* God bless you all, and God bless America."

(Cheering and applause)

———

Caroline Shapiro turned off the TV, shaking her head. She found it hard to believe the numbers. While it was no surprise that the Democratic candidate had won, Strong's showing across the country had been impressive - to her, almost scary.

"At least I know what I'm going to write about now," she said aloud to herself as she sat down to hand-write the first draft of her syndicated column for newspapers across the country. Although her popular TV show, *It's My Dime*, took most of her time and made most of her money, she steadfastly pumped out six short articles a week, donating the money she made to a writer's foundation she supported. Though a household name as a result of her on-camera work, she never forgot her humble origins as a small town newspaper journalist.

She wrote quickly and with purpose, using, as always, her trusted Mont Blanc fountain pen. When she was done she sat back and read the results:

One Big Surprise Deserves Another

We thought nothing could beat the 2008 election when Barak Obama became the first Afro-American to win the presidency.

What could happen in this election of 2016 to surprise political pundits who've seen it all?

How about Independent candidate Reverend Robert Strong - that's right, Reverend - last week taking six states and winning 33 Electoral College seats? How about Strong garnering almost twenty-five percent of the national vote, with indication of broad base support across the nation – a mere eight percent less that the second place Republican candidate?

Representing the Coalition of Christians movement, Strong's showing is making even the most jaded Washington correspondent sit up and pay attention. Undaunted by his third place finish, and the continued accusations in the press that he represents a hidden, right-wing agenda, Strong continues to hold rallies across the country which are drawing huge crowds.

So what's the appeal? Why is this charismatic preacher from Wyoming making such a splash? Well, for one thing, he's just oh so personable, with movie star looks and a congenial, easy-going manner. To top it off, he's charming, funny, humble and, after all, haven't we turned the quest for the White House into an overblown popularity contest?

Take a deeper look at Strong and you'll find a great orator. Where Obama was very adept at speech making, Strong can only be described as inspired. Preaching in church from the time he was seven, Strong commands a presence that evokes attention, admiration and ardour. The spoken word is used by the Reverend in the most engrossing manner. To say he mesmerizes a crowd does not overstate the effect.

It is also impossible not to note that Strong has an effective message of moderation and conciliation that appeals to many Christians, and not just fundamentalists. His work in the South to forge ties with the Baptists paid off by delivering him Alabama and Mississippi. His olive branch to the Catholic Church gained him millions of votes in large States like Florida and California. His moderate but common sense pan-Christian theme appeals to young and old alike.

There is one final ingredient to explain the phenomenal showing of this religious, political newbie. The good reverend is backed by brother-in-law Colonel Sherman Gale, purported to be one of America's richest men. It is estimated that Gale managed to contribute and raise more than $300 million for Strong's campaign. And there doesn't seem to be an end to the money any time soon.

Keep your eye on Reverend Strong over the next four years. He could make things very interesting next time around. In the meantime, we'll be watching and waiting to be surprised in 2020.

1 - Message From God

He stood on a craggy outcropping of rock, looking down at the still-dark canyon floor that lay far below. The rising sun at his back cast its yellow, acid-clear light. Shadows of the billowing clouds overhead moved slowly over the vast expanse of striated, ochre-red cliffs, speckling the landscape with patches of sunlight and shadow. It was truly awe-inspiring, and the exact spot where it had happened eight years ago. The very place where God had spoken to him.

He had stood here for hours now, waiting. Waiting for the divine presence to come back to him. Praying God would grace him with certainty of what he was to do. He had come up here on his own last night before sunset, wearing nothing but a light windbreaker. He had stood all night in the cold - shivering, waiting and praying. Still there was nothing. His limbs screamed in agony but he ignored them. His stomach ached with hunger but he denied his need for food. The muscles in his legs began to quiver and knot up but he refused to sit down. Sweat fell from his brow as the morning sun gained strength and beat down hot upon his broad back, yet he kept alert, watching.

Suddenly, it was not God but dizziness that overwhelmed him. He could feel his consciousness leaving his body and the sensation of falling forward. He was jarred to his senses by a strong hand grabbing his shoulder and pulling him back from the precipice.

"Dad!" yelled the voice behind him. Though startled, he immediately collected himself. "I'm OK. I just got a little woozy."

"Well, you haven't eaten anything or taken any medicine since lunch yesterday. It's no wonder you're feeling woozy. You really have to watch your blood sugar level."

Colonel Sherman Gale winced. He hated talking about medications and blood sugar levels. He hated that his body was becoming old and weak. He refused to acknowledge that he would be seventy in just a little over a year. He had staved off the effects of old age well into his mid-sixties, but now - now it was getting so much harder. After standing all night he could hardly move. There was a time when he could have stood for two nights without batting an eye, but it was clear those days were long gone.

"I don't need a lecture. I've been praying all night for direction from the Lord. I can't let my weakness get in the way of that."

"I know, sir. That's why I came up here to find you. I knew this is where you'd be. But you could have died..."

The Colonel looked at his son and the worried expression of concern on his face. He was right. Who knows what could have happened if his son hadn't caught him before he fell.

"How long have you been here?" he asked the younger man suddenly.

"From just after midnight."

"Well then, K.C., I'd say we both could do with an old-fashioned Wyoming breakfast!" the Colonel responded, laughing and putting his arm around his son's colossal shoulders and squeezing him hard.

"I'd say I pretty much agree, Dad!" his son said, "I could definitely go for a big feed right now!"

As they walked toward the trucks, K.C. could see that his father was laboring.

"You sure you want to drive back? You could come with me and we can send somebody to pick up your truck later."

"Naw, I think I'll be fine, son. You follow me and I'll pull over if I have to."

———

K.C. watched his father's truck come to an abrupt halt in the driveway outside of the family's sprawling ranch house. He was still tense from trying to keep up with his father's mad cap pace back from the canyon. He pulled up his truck beside the other one and hopped out.

"Have a little trouble keeping up?" jawed Sherman.

"Like always, Dad, like always," K.C. replied shaking his head as he walked by his father and towards the front door. The older man put his head back, laughed heartily and grabbed his eighteen-year-old son ruggedly. K.C. couldn't help smiling at the rough treatment. He was glad his dad was feeling better and acting his usual brash self. It scared him when he saw him show any signs of weakness or age. Ever since his mother had died nine years ago, his father had been his mainstay. It made him panic when he thought he might lose him, too.

While Sherman was a solidly-built six footer, his son was almost half a foot taller and weighed in at a well-muscled 250 pounds. K.C. turned around quickly, grabbed his father and lifted him off the ground.

"Now that's my boy!" Sherman grunted as he was hoisted into the air.

K.C. laughed and put his father down. As he did so, the two looked directly into each others' eyes.

"I'm just scared sometimes, Dad," K.C. confessed, "I'm worried about losing you. And then up on the cliff..."

Sherman thought before he answered. K.C. deserved the best answer he could give.

"Maybe that was the sign I was looking for, son. The fact that you were there to save me. It has to be part of God's plan. I think God wants me to explain to you what I've been working on for the last eight years. I think he knows I need help and has shown me how to get it."

"You know I'll help anyway I can," answered his son with honest conviction.

Sherman just smiled and put his arm around K.C.'s shoulders as they left the front foyer and made their way towards the kitchen.

"Let's go see what Lotti can fix us up for breakfast. Then we'll talk."

———

They walked into the kitchen to find Lotti deep inside the walk-in refrigerator. After a couple of minutes she came out holding a carton of eggs, a large rasher of bacon and some oranges.

"I heard you two coming and knew you'd be looking for grub. Now you go get washed up proper and I'll have this ready in just a few minutes."

"How do you know what we want?" Sherman teased their amply proportioned cook.

"I know it better than you do yourself, Sherman Gale. For goodness sakes, I've been cooking for you since you got out of the army more than 25 years ago. Before you met your blessed wife, God rest her soul."

"That is true," said Sherman, "From before I knew either Patricia Anne or God."

"So you just get on out of here and let me go at it. I'll give a shout when it's done."

Sherman Gale turned and left as ordered but his son lingered.

"Lotti, have you seen Faith?"

"Oh yes. She's already been for a ride. She cut a bunch of wild flowers to put on your sweet mama's grave. I think she's up there now."

"Thanks, I'll go check after I've cleaned up."

"Alright, sweetie," she replied and added, "Say, is your pa OK? He's been fierce preoccupied of late."

"I know he's got a lot on his mind. Now that I'm finished school I can give him more of a hand. He told me that he wanted to talk to me after breakfast about what he's been doing. I just hope I can really be of some help."

"You are, always. Your sister and you are so precious to him."

"Yeah, but I just hope I can *really* be of assistance. He has such important business to do."

"Well, off you go on your important business and I'll see you in about 20 minutes. Here's a fresh baked biscuit to tide you over!" she said, lobbing a hot bun out of the pan she was extracting from the oven. He made the catch with flair and headed happily out of the kitchen, devouring the warm morsel in two bites.

———

A freshly washed K.C. made his way up the gentle slope behind the house to the top of the hill where their mother was buried. Even from a distance, he could see his sister's long, flaxen hair shining in the morning sun. As he approached, he saw she was kneeling down in front of the grave. The colourful bunch of flowers she had picked lay neatly at the foot of the monument marking the spot. Her hands were pressed together, held up in front of her face. It was obvious she was praying.

K.C. walked up to the grave and stopped just behind his sister. He didn't want to disturb her so he remained silent, standing and watching. After a few moments, she turned around and looked up at him. She was crying. Tears streamed down her face but even her heartfelt anguish could not conceal her dazzling beauty.

"Oh Sis, please don't," he said, dropping to his knees and wrapping his large arm around her small frame. She gave way immediately, turning and hugging onto to him tightly.

"It's just that I can hardly remember her, and what I can remember only makes her seem farther away," she sobbed.

"I know, Faith," K.C. said tenderly, "I know how much it hurts. But for Dad's sake, let's try and be strong. He has so much responsibility right now. We have to try and help."

"Where were you two last night?" she asked, changing the subject, "I could see that you were both gone."

"Dad went back up to the canyon. I went up after him to make sure he was alright."

"Anything? Did he get anything?" Faith knew that the canyon was where her father had been spoken to by God. She also knew that her father had been back many times since but had never felt the divine presence again.

"I think he got some sore muscles and a very hearty appetite," K.C. quipped. He didn't tell her about having to catch him before he fell. It would just have worried her more.

"I wish God would talk to him again," she replied, "It would make things so much easier."

"I don't think God cares about making things easier for us," K.C. replied, "I believe He has a totally different perspective because He is infinite. One year or a hundred years is all the same to Him. We can't lose faith because God doesn't give us what we want when we ask for it."

"Yes, I know you're right, it's just..." she started and then paused.

"It's just what?"

"Oh, it's really nothing important. Let's go down and get breakfast. I think I'm all done crying for today."

"That's good, because both Dad and I need to see your beautiful, smiling face."

She blushed as they rose, embarrassed but flattered by her big brother's attention. They walked arm in arm as they made their way back to the house. She had wanted to tell him but she just couldn't right now. She didn't know if he'd believe her. She didn't know if she believed it herself. God had spoken to her — directly to her — on several occasions over the past year. She wondered why God was so silent to her father.

———

When brother and sister stepped into the kitchen they found their father sipping on a large mug of coffee and chewing a warm biscuit. He was watching Lotti intently, enjoying seeing the swift efficiency of a true master in action. In under the twenty minutes she had estimated it would take her, Lotti had cooked the bacon, whipped up a stack of golden-brown flapjacks, fried some not-quite-ripe tomatoes and was just now turning the eggs over in the crackling, sweet fat of the frying pan upon which they fairly floated.

"Man that smells fantastic!" burst an enthusiastic K.C. as he walked through the door, startling both his father and the cook.

"Land sakes, you're loud!" complained Lotti with a big smile on her face, "Good thing for you I'm getting deaf."

Faith ran over to her father and gave him a big hug.

"Hey, sweetheart, up on the hill again?"

Faith nodded and hung on to her dad harder. K.C. and Sherman Gale exchanged knowing looks. Watching all of this was Lotti, who took matters into her own hands by shooing all three of them towards the breakfast table.

"Lotti, are you joining us this morning? After cooking up this feast you surely deserve it…"

"Now, Colonel, you know I'd like to but I have so many chores left and they take me so much longer to do now."

"You know, we have discussed getting you some help."

"Help. I don't know what you mean by help. Remember that little Vietnamese gal that you brought in to "help"? She was a real disaster and just caused me to do a mess of extra work. I'm still looking for some of the setting I think she stole. No, thank you, sir, I don't need no help."

It had been more than ten years since they had tried bringing someone in to give Lotti some time off. The idea was evidently as appealing to her now as it had been then.

"OK, OK, you win," Sherman acquiesced, "But please, won't you sit down and eat with us?"

"Well, when you put it that way I expect I can't say no. And if I do say so myself, those flapjacks are particularly tasty this morning."

They all laughed as they sat down to breakfast.

———

K.C. pushed away from the table, having eaten his fill. Lotti had a look of disbelief on her face.

"I can't believe one human being can eat so much in one sitting," she said, half in wonder and half aghast, "You realize you just downed a dozen flapjacks, six eggs and about a pound of bacon?"

"Not to mention the three grilled tomatoes and the biscuits," his sister teased.

K.C. laughed, holding his stomach in satisfaction. He looked over to catch his father's attention but found Sherman Gale deep in thought.

"You OK, Dad?" his son asked.

"Oh, yes, yes of course. Sorry, I was just somewhere else," he replied, "That was really one great breakfast. Thanks so much, Lotti. Now let's help with the cleanup."

"No, No. I want you folks out of here and doing whatever it is you all do. Just leave Lotti here to do what she has to do. That's all I ask."

With that Lotti shooed them good-naturedly out of the kitchen. When they were safely outside in the hallway, she shut the door on them forcefully.

"Well, I guess it's our house, but her kitchen!" Sherman said.

They all shouted their thanks for breakfast once again through the closed doors, responded to by Lotti shouting, "Now git!" They couldn't help laughing as they made their way down the hall to the den.

"Well, honey," Sherman said, addressing his daughter, "K.C. and I have some serious talking to do, so we'll catch up with you later. Are you going into town to help with the pageant setup?"

"Yeah, of course. I was hoping one of you could take me so I can practice driving."

K.C. nodded affirmatively that he could do that.

"But Daddy, I really think there is something I should tell you. Tell you both. It's really got me worried and I don't know what to do..."

"Why of course, Faith. Come on in and tell us what the matter is," Sherman replied, putting his arm around his daughter and guiding her into the spacious den. Faith sat down in one of the large leather chairs while her father and brother sat on the divan directly across from her. She fidgeted as they looked at her expectantly.

"So what was it that you wanted to tell us?" asked her father tenderly, interrupting the silence. Faith sat looking at them with her large blue eyes and a strange smile on her face. They both knew from experience that pushing her would result in stubborn silence. All they could do was gently encourage her and wait. She played with her beautiful golden locks that tumbled from her head and shifted several times before clearing her throat as if ready to begin.

"Well, I guess it started just about a year ago," she began, "and it's happened three more times since then – including last night."

"What happened, Faith? You know you can tell us anything. Please don't be afraid."

She looked at them with anguish, but even with her face creased with despair she was gorgeous. Her looks reminded Sherman so much of his late wife that it made him feel his daughter's anguish all the more. Faith closed her eyes as if resolved to finally release her burden.

"God talked to me, Daddy. Some of the things He said make sense, but some I don't understand. If it's not God then I must be going crazy because it's so real. And the feeling, the feeling is just, just..." She was at a loss for words.

"Overwhelming. Like everything wonderful and horrible at the same time," her father ventured.

"Yes, yes that's it!" was her reply, "It feels too much!"

Sherman Gale and his son sat looking at Faith, not sure what to say. It was the right thing to do because Faith continued.

"At first I didn't know what to think - but when it happened again - and then again..."

"What is God telling you?" asked K.C., breaking his silence.

"The first time He told me not to be afraid. The second time He said to keep faith and ..."

"And?" prompted her brother.

"He brought me the presence of Mama. I could feel her K.C., feel her touch and smell her smell. Do you remember?"

Shaken, K.C. replied, "Yes, I remember. I do remember."

"The third time He told me to prepare. And last night He gave me a message for Daddy that I couldn't understand."

Sherman Gale sat forward and looked hard into his daughter's eyes.

"What was the message Faith?" he asked.

"It's why I thought I had to tell you. In case it is true and that God has chosen to talk to me. He told me that you had to do it – to use the sword if necessary. He said the time is now. That's all, Daddy. I don't know what it means or if it's of any use, but that's what the voice said."

"The voice of God," Sherman Gale stated with certainty. "The message is very clear, Faith, and very important. It's why I was up at the canyon. Asking my question of God. And he sends me a message from an angel and saves me with an angel too. I can see I have to tell you both now. He has shown me that I need both of you to succeed. I tried to keep you from it while you were young but the time has come – God has said so Himself."

———

"Now then," began Sherman Gale, "you both know that just after your mother passed away I was visited by the Lord. What you don't know is what the Lord revealed to me. It was more than just a voice and a feeling – it was a vision and it was disturbing."

He paused, cleared his throat, and looked at each of his children in turn as if deciding what to say. Finally, a look of resignation came over his face, and he continued.

"Who am I to judge what you should or shouldn't hear? I am not worthy as a vessel of the Lord's word, Faith. I'm glad He has chosen you instead."

Both his children protested, but Sherman silenced them at once by holding up his hand.

"I think I have to start way back when I was a young man, just about your age K.C. I think that's where I have to begin, because what I'm going to tell you only makes sense when you know where I've come from – what happened to bring me to this place.

"The day I finished school I enlisted in the army. I couldn't wait to get out of my home. My mother was an alcoholic who brought home most of the money doing cleaning jobs and my dad was a small time hood who was in jail at least as much of the time as he wasn't. I guess I was what they now call 'abused'. Dad used his hands and Mom used anything she could get her hands on. That's why you haven't really ever heard about them."

Both Gale's children were clearly shocked. They had of course been told that their grandparents had died, but had no idea what kind of family their father had been raised in. He stopped briefly, letting it sink in.

"As you can imagine I had a pretty harsh upbringing, and because of that I grew up physically tough and emotionally calloused. When I was accepted into the army, I was ecstatic. Rules, regulation and regime – I just loved it. I was strong and fit and eager. I was sent to Vietnam right out of training. I killed my first man before I turned nineteen. I stayed in the Marines and saw action in every US military campaign up to 1990, when I retired with 25 years of service. I am proud of the service I did for my country but I am not proud of many of the things I did over the years. God was not in my heart then and I have asked for His forgiveness so many times. Your mother told me I was forgiven but some of the memories haunt me. I'm telling you this so that my vision will make sense to you. You need to know."

Neither K.C. nor Faith wanted him to stop. He had never talked about a time before their mother or a time when he had not known God.

"When I got out of the Marines I was hell-bent on making as much money as I could. And I did really well. Better than I, or anyone else, thought I could. It was all going along as planned until I met your mother. She changed me forever. She helped me find Jesus and my way to our Lord. Every year I was with your mother increased my belief. It was like she healed my soul and made it whole. I learned to love God through loving your mother. It was a feeling that I had never felt before. Then she brought you two miracles into the world even though doctors told us it would never happen and my belief in a higher power became even stronger.

"But when God took your dear Mama from us, it shook my faith to the core. I almost gave up, I was so lonely with despair. I tried not to show you kids or others around us that I had doubt, but I did. I even thought about ending it all. That's what I was doing up there at the canyon when it happened. I was standing on the edge. I wanted so much to jump – to end the pain."

Sherman Gale broke. His children had never seen him like this before and it frightened them. They both instinctively rushed to his side, comforting him. His back heaved in spasms as he held back his tears and tried to continue. Finally he could.

"This is so hard to tell you but I know I must. I know it will change how you look at me."

Gale paused yet again, trying to gain composure. After what seemed forever, he continued.

"So I was looking down at the bottom of the canyon, when suddenly a bright light appeared. It was golden and bright beyond belief, but it did not hurt my eyes. As I watched the light draw closer and closer I could see an angel dressed all in glowing, white robes. The angel was floating up from the canyon floor on the carpet of light until he was standing right in front of me in mid-air. I fell to my knees in awe!

"Then the angel spoke, but in a voice so high and clear it sounded like music.

'God has chosen you as His Christian Soldier, to establish a Christian leader whom true believers can follow at the approaching End of Days. When pestilence is strewn about the earth and retribution against God's true believers is delivered by the hand of the Beast, they will need a sanctuary on Earth where they can be safe. For Christians of the world, you must make a place where they can gather. You, who have been blessed, have caused much suffering in the world.'

"As the angel said this, up from the depths of the canyon flew the screeching, bodiless souls of every person I had ever killed. Their faces stood out as they flew past me. Some of them came so close I could feel them. Most were men of fighting age, but some were women and children and old people. The face of one woman stood out. I remember, because her face will haunt me forever. Oh sweet Jesus, how could I have been such an agent for evil? I could feel her anguish and pain. I can still feel it now and can hardly live with the memory."

Sherman took a deep breath, his head now buried in his hands.

"I fell on my face and begged the angel to show me no more, but he commanded me to stand and listen.

'Redeem yourself in God's eyes. Serve Him and Christ in this holy quest. You have the knowledge and the means — both given to you by God. Serve him now and prepare.'

"And then the angel was gone and I was left alone."

There was silence in the room. Sherman sat, head still in hands. K.C. stood up and looked out the window. Faith stayed by her father, her left hand on his shoulder. She was the first to speak.

"Daddy, I still love you and I forgive you. I know God does too. It was a different time. You were a different person."

K.C. moved back towards where his father and sister were sitting.

"Father, please listen to Faith. We know what you are, what you've been to us. I forgive you. Please, please forgive yourself. I know Mama would have – I'm sure she did."

Sherman nodded but couldn't respond. K.C. sat down and put his arm around his father's shoulder. In doing so, he found Faith's hand and held onto it tightly. And then the three of them sat there, silent, trying to gain strength from each other's love and their faith in Jesus.

Finally Sherman took his head out of his hands and stood up with resolve.

"That's why I've been working even harder this time to get your uncle elected President - because I failed God last time. But even after all my hard work and the work of thousands of others I'm afraid to say it doesn't look good. I know now it won't happen this election unless something truly extraordinary is done to change things. So that message you got last night, Faith, it reaffirmed my will to carry out The Plan I'm going to tell you about. The Plan will change everything. It will guarantee we elect our first truly Christian president. Now get comfortable, both of you, because this is going to take some time."

2 - Unexpected Visitor

The small delivery truck made its way up the long driveway to the palatial ranch house. The windows of the vehicle were wide open and gospel music could be heard blaring from inside. This afternoon, Ned Cooper, one of the trusted hands in the Church, was delivering and installing an upgraded heat pump unit for the Gales. The truck reached the security gate and was motioned forward by the guard. Ned inched forward and turned down the music.

"Hey, Ned," the guard grunted, "Who ya got with ya today?"

"Some poor coolie just off the boat from China, Fred. Strong as an ox, but doesn't speak a word of English."

"Well, I better check his pass just the same. You know how particular the Colonel is..."

"Yup, I sure do," Ned replied taking the document from his passenger and handing it, along with his own pass, to the guard, "Here ya go."

After a few seconds of scrutiny the guard scanned the passes and returned them to Ned, indicating with a nod that they were free to proceed.

"Thanks Fred. God Bless."

"Praise Jesus," the security man replied.

———

The installation went smoothly. Ned's helper did all the heavy lifting and fetching, leaving Ned to focus on the technical stuff. He'd become an expert at installing the units since working on The Ranch's new housing project. Ned had done well over five hundred units himself, so could pretty much hook one up in the dark. As they were packing up their truck for the return back to town, the front door opened and K.C. and Faith stepped out, followed by their father. They all seemed surprised to find Ned there. Ned's face lit up as he moved to engage them.

"Oh, hello, Ned," opened Sherman, "Guess you were putting that new heat pump in?"

"Oh, yes sir, Colonel," fawned Ned, "It should be much better than the old one. The way it works is incredible. See it just…"

"Ned, I do apologize, but Faith and K.C. need to get going and I'm catching a ride with them," Gale interrupted. "Maybe next time you can run me through the technical details. We really do appreciate your doing it."

"Well, sure, Colonel. Of course I understand, sir. It's a true honor to work for you and your family, sir. I consider it a real privilege."

"Well, I don't know about that." Sherman Gale paused and looked hard at Ned's helper. "Who's this?"

"Name's Chen. Christian refugee from Nanjing. I hear the Chinese government is cracking down again."

Chen shuffled a bit as Sherman looked him over studiously.

"Let's see your hands," Gale demanded of Chen.

Chen looked confused and it was clear he didn't understand. Sherman Gale held up his own hands to show him what he wanted and Chen, understanding, mirrored the action. Sherman pulled both of Chen's hands forward so he could get a good look at them.

"Just what I thought. This man is a martial arts expert. See what they can do with him over at security. I think we're wasting some talent getting him to lift and carry."

Chen looked like he was still trying to understand what was going on. Sherman said goodbye to Ned and joined his children waiting in the truck.

"What was that all about, Daddy?" asked Faith from behind the wheel.

"Just wait, honey, I really have to make one quick call."

He picked up his phone - an ultra secure satellite-based handset - put his thumb on the reader and said the word 'security'. Seconds later he began talking, with no salutation or introduction.

"Listen, I want you to check out an Asian guy I'm sending over with Ned Cooper. Run a full backround on him and keep him secure until he clears. Got that?" Sherman listened for the expected reply, then said, "Excellent. Over and out."

"Gee, Dad," K.C. began, "Who do you think that guy is?"

"I don't know, son, but he just didn't smell right. Remember I told you that the government is trying hard to figure out what we're up to? We've already exposed several spies who've infiltrated The Ranch. Maybe this guy's for real, maybe he's not. We'll know soon enough."

———

Ned and Chen drove back toward the ranch's main town with the radio blasting once again. This time Ned was happy and was singing along. He could tell everyone he had seen the great man and they would crowd around asking for details. Chen looked, as always, to be completely out of touch with what was going on. He sat there grinning, trying to follow the words.

"Not that it means a thing to you," Ned said, addressing Chen, "but I gotta stop by my place on the way to drop you off. Left some tools I'll need this afternoon. After that I'll run you by the security office like the Colonel asked. Imagine you being an expert at anything!"

Ned laughed and Chen laughed too, making Ned laugh even more. Ned was still smiling when he pulled up in front of a lonely cabin just off the main road. He jumped out leaving the van idling. He indicated that Chen should wait, then disappeared quickly inside the cabin on his quest. A few minutes later Ned reappeared to find both the truck and Chen gone. He wasn't smiling anymore.

———

A security team found the truck abandoned in a gully at the end of the road about five miles from Ned's cabin. They began tracking immediately with the help of dogs and helicopters.

Steve Thomas, Chief of Security, was personally directing the search, and was confident they'd subdue the intruder before he got off the property and onto the main road. The route their quarry had taken was incredibly rugged and dangerous and would make for slow going.

But after only twenty-five minutes, the news came over the radio. A lone man was seen running towards the highway and had been picked up by a waiting car. A helicopter was still tracking the car, but catching and bringing back the perpetrator was going to be almost impossible. Soon it was reported that the car was lost in a shopping mall parking lot near Casper. Now,

Thomas found himself heading out to meet the helicopter that had just touched down. He was thinking about what to tell a very severe-looking Sherman Gale glowering at him out of the window of the slowly descending chopper.

———

Derrik Chu, alias Chen the Chinese refugee, sat in the front passenger seat beside his partner Kyle Anderson, who was at the wheel. They had just pulled into the mall's underground parking lot and were waiting for another company car to pick them up.

"Man, that was fricking freaky! That Gale has a sixth sense or something."

"Did you get any of the bugs planted? That was the whole point of getting near Gale's place."

"Well, a couple on the outside, but I'd guess they won't be working for long. Sure as fuck they'll do a full sweep of the perimeter after I ran like I did."

"Want some gum?" Anderson asked.

"No, I don't!" Chu exploded, "Come on man, don't you think it's strange that he could pick me out like that?"

"Well to be honest, no I don't think it's strange. You make the worst goddamned Chinese refugee I've ever seen - you look like a linebacker and you can't speak one word of Mandarin or Cantonese. You're lucky somebody didn't start talking to you."

"They did! On the first day, but I pretended I was deaf."

Anderson laughed and Chu joined him.

"Anyway, all told, I'm surprised they didn't catch on sooner. It gives me some hope that they're not as smart as everyone seems to think they are."

"Well, fuck you!" Chu replied in feigned anger.

And they both laughed again and waited.

———

"I'm telling you, Colonel, it wasn't like nothing we ever saw before. The man moved more like a puma than a person. My guys on the ground saw him go up a sheer rock face that stopped the dogs cold. We just couldn't contain him," Steve stammered.

"Well, we just had a visit from one of the best, that's all. We should have spotted him long before he got so close to me and my family. He could have killed us all if he had been assigned to do it. Now I want you to try and track down who this guy was. We have his picture and prints so it shouldn't be too hard. Pull out all the stops. And get up to the house and give it a special sweep. I'd bet anything he left some bugs planted, and they'll be good ones."

Sherman Gale was furious. At this point in his plan, secrecy was absolutely necessary. He had gone to such excruciating and painstaking detail to make sure nothing leaked out.

"I want to know where this man was and what he had access to. I want a dossier that tracks that son of a bitch right up to the moment he hightailed it off The Ranch. And I want it by tomorrow morning. Is that clear?"

"Yes, sir. Very clear, sir. By tomorrow morning."

But Sherman Gale ignored the reply. He was staring out at the open landscape trying to collect his thoughts. They were going to have to move more quickly than he wanted. It was only a matter of time until a breach of some kind occurred.

Thousands of people lived on The Ranch and literally hundreds came and went each day. The government had slipped agents in before and they'd do it again – and sooner or later they'd stumble across something. It was act now or miss the opportunity.

It was God's will.

He prayed that everything was ready.

3 - Briefings

Agents Chu and Anderson sat at the large conference room table in the Denver Field Office waiting for the meeting to begin.

A thin, surly-faced man in a tailored Italian suit entered the room and sat down purposely close beside Chu. Without looking up, Chu could tell it was the red-headed, sharp-nosed Adrian Hinks, SSA in charge of the office in Casper. Hinks had a sneer on his face and was audibly sniggering.

Chu couldn't help it. He knew he shouldn't, but he just couldn't help it.

"So, what are you laughing about, Hinks?" he demanded.

"Nothing, Chu, nothing - except I heard you lasted about twenty minutes in there before you got chased out."

"Hey, at least I got out. Not like your buddy Petersen."

Petersen, who had successfully infiltrated Gale's operation for almost a year, had been found two weeks ago, drowned upstream of The Ranch. Most of the information on the inner workings of The Ranch had come directly or indirectly from him.

The smile wiped off Hinks face and Chu realized at once he had made a mistake.

"Fuck you, Chu! Man, that should be your name, you piece of shit. He was a good agent and friend. And he leaves behind a wife and two young kids..."

Chu felt his face flush. He hated Hinks' guts and he hated having to do what he had to do now.

"Sorry to hear that, Hinks. And you're right, I shouldn't have made that crack."

Hinks just stared straight ahead. Chu looked over at Anderson for support, only to find his partner shaking his head with a look of severe disapproval on his face.

The young agent sunk down in his seat, put his head in his hands and wished for the thousandth time he could just let things go.

It seemed to take forever for the meeting to begin. When the meeting did convene, Chu found himself tuning out. It was the same old crap they'd gone over at the last meeting. They knew that something big was being planned but they didn't have any details. There was some indication that the research laboratory Gale recently built on The Ranch was involved. There was a confirmed report that Gale had illegally ushered three experts in biological warfare into the country from Russia. Robert Strong, still running far behind the Democratic candidate, was resorting to biblical prophesies involving plague and pestilence...

It was when Hinks was giving his summary on the surveillance operation at The Ranch that Chu finally sat up and paid attention. He heard about the unsuccessful attempt to plant bugs in and around Gale's home. He winced as he heard how his cover was blown and the details of his ignoble scramble to safety. Not waiting for Hinks to finish, Chu interjected, appealing to ASAC Jenkins, who was chairing the meeting.

"Excuse me sir, but that's not what happened. Gale suspected something about me – he didn't realize I was an agent. If he'd been sure, I wouldn't have had any chance of getting away. It was in my report."

"Your report was the worst piece of crap I've ever seen," Hinks hissed, responding directly to Chu. "Twenty-two words in total. That's what you gave me. What am I supposed to do with twenty-two words?"

"I tried to keep it simple so you'd understand it, but I guess I failed. You're so fucking stupid you couldn't even get that right!"

"You son of a bitch!" screamed Hinks as he turned to face Chu, leaning over him menacingly.

Chu gave a supercilious smile taunting him, and that's when Hinks made a big mistake and took a wild swing.

In a flash, Hinks was on the floor, pinned. Chu held two fingers beside his neck and was threatening to break it.

Everyone in the room knew enough not to physically intervene. It was ASAC Jenkins who broke the tense silence and restored a sense of order.

"Well, I guess the meeting's over. Next scheduled meeting is in two weeks, same time. If you've finished Mr. Chu, I'd like to see you in my office immediately."

———

"His name is Derrik Quincy Chu, Special Agent FBI," read Steve Thomas. He stopped abruptly as he noticed a look of puzzlement on Sherman Gale's face.

"Quincy? Where the hell did he get that moniker?"

"Seems that both Agent Chu's parents watched a show called Quincy during the 1980's..."

"D.Q. Chu," remarked Gale, almost to himself, "Parents have the strangest notions about naming babies, don't they?"

He had hated the name Sherman when he was young. It had been the root cause of many a childhood scuffle. Steve Thomas was nervous and clearly looking to please his boss. He eyed

Sherman Gale for permission to continue. After a few moments of reflection Gale nodded for his Security Chief to go on with the briefing.

"Chu was born in San Diego in 1988, which makes him thirty-two. His father was half White, half Chinese; his mother, the daughter of post World War II Japanese immigrants. His father was a Navy man. He was killed on a tour in the Gulf when Chu was eleven years old. Chu's mother, a teacher, moved back home to Sacramento to live with her father shortly thereafter. Chu's mother is a devout Christian. Chu attended church until he was eighteen. He was even a choir boy for five years. Chu has a younger sister, Frances, who lives in Seattle. She's a teacher, as well."

Thomas looked up briefly and saw that Gale was still fully engaged.

"Is this the kind of detail you're looking for Colonel? I could skip over some of this stuff if you want."

"No, this is perfect. Just what I want. Please continue."

"Yes, sir. Well, let's see. Chu's grandfather ran a karate school and taught him for years. The old man was a demanding teacher and it seems Chu was an exceptional student. Won lots of tournaments and contests. There was a falling out between the two when Chu decided to go to college instead of staying and taking over the karate school. Got into Stanford on a partial scholarship. Worked evenings and weekends to make money. Then he got involved in Extreme Free Running in a big way. Made several You Tube videos that became quite well known. At one point, he was considered one of the top free runners in the world."

"Free running success led to academic mediocrity. Chu lost his scholarship in third year. Hopes of getting into Law school vanished. He started doing a lot of partying which involved drinking and smoking pot. Nothing more toxic.

"Barely finished his undergraduate degree. Ended up being recruited into the FBI at a job fair. He's been with the Bureau since college graduation. Lots of commendations and merit pay increases, but word is he doesn't really fit in, and he's had one disciplinary suspension with probation."

"And what was that for?" interjected Gale with real interest.

"Got into a harangue with his superior. She was sleeping with one of the female agents on the team. He got sick of the favouritism and publicly called her out. Led to a big blow up with him punching holes in the wall. She got demoted and suspended. He got suspended and put on probation."

"And since then?"

"A few minor incidents. He's a hothead for sure, but seems to be a good agent."

"Well I like the sound of him. He has good moral fibre and a strong sense of justice."

"He also works for the FBI and was trying to bug us."

"It was his job. You said yourself you never saw anybody move like him."

"That's for sure, Colonel."

"And I think it's about time we took the FBI head on, don't you? Let's just ask them what they're up to."

With an unsure look, Steve nodded agreement. He could see Colonel Gale had already made up his mind.

———

Emmett Jenkins looked over his desk at SA Chu sitting slouched in front of him. He put both arms on his desktop and leaned forward, moving to the edge of his chair. Derrik Chu slumped down further in his.

"Mr. Chu, you put me in a very difficult situation. I've overlooked quite a few issues in the past because of your commendable performance, but this latest stunt..."

"I know, I know, sir. I'm just so frustrated about fucking up the bug planting operation. We worked hard to make it in there and then got nothing. Then Hinks mouths off."

"Well, that wasn't your fault. Nobody was fingering you in any of the reports I read."

"I don't care about the reports. I do feel responsible and I know others think so as well. But it's not just that that's eating me. I mean, it's all backwards, isn't it?"

"What do you mean 'backwards'?"

"Well, I didn't sign up to push papers around and read operations manuals. I wanted to do real stuff – like the kind of stuff I saw in the movies. The FBI chasing down bad guys. Pursuing them no matter what it took. Now I'm running, but I'm running away from the bad guys. They're chasing me! We live in fear that Gale's lawyers will come after us. They're making us sweat and they're the bad guys. Do you see what I mean by all backwards?"

"Yeah, I do see what you mean, but so what? It's the world we live in. We have to do our jobs in spite of all the crap. It always comes down to this with you, doesn't it? Do you want to see a copy of the OPR report from a few years back?"

"Sir, you know we've talked about that. The SSA I 'lost it' with got sanctioned for giving favours to the agent she was sleeping with and for harassing me."

"But you were also found to be taking horrific shortcuts with paperwork. Look, there are constraints we deal with and processes we've established to handle problems that arise. If you can't hack that then maybe you really do have to think about finding a new line of business."

ASAC Jenkins sat back in his chair allowing the weight of his words to sink in. Chu sat, eyes downcast, looking at his shoes. After more than a few minutes he finally broke the silence.

"I do want to stay with the Bureau sir. So whatever discipline OPR comes up with I'll take, if they don't let me go outright."

"Who said anything about the fucking Office of Professional Responsibility being involved?"

"I, I just assumed."

"Hey, Hinks took a swing at you. I'll be talking to him later."

Jenkins couldn't help smiling. He liked Derrik Chu, even though he was a true pain in the ass. At least Chu cared. So many of them these days didn't really give a shit and were only going through the motions.

"So, you're not going to write this up?"

"No - no I'm not. But I am going to reassign you."

"OK. Where to now?"

"Well, Mr. Chu, it seems that a certain Colonel Sherman Gale has asked for a private meeting with you to be set up asap. So let's see where that meeting goes and then talk about where you're going to end up."

This news came like an electric shock to the young agent. He was going to ask a question but thought better of it when he saw that Jenkins was hard at work on his computer. He got up to leave, but paused.

"You know, sir, this is probably out of line and I know agent Hinks is in charge of The Ranch operation, but I just don't trust him. It's just a gut feeling. Nothing I can point to specifically..."

"Between you and me, I don't trust anybody. Except you, Mr. Chu - you I trust."

Chu looked both surprised and pathetically pleased.

"Yeah, I trust you to be a bonehead," he added acerbically, going back to his work.

Chu's face fell as he hurriedly left the ASAC's office.

As he walked down the long, deserted corridor, Jenkin's echoing laughter reverberated all around him. But Chu didn't really notice. He was deep in thought, wondering why Sherman Gale would want to see *him*.

4 - Cat and Mouse

Going through the last security check, before reaching the sprawling ranch house Sherman Gale and his family called home, went much smoother than Chu had anticipated. If the guard recognized him, he didn't show it. He simply indicated that Chu was expected, asked him to surrender his gun and opened the gate. After complying with the request, Chu drove the black unmarked company car up the long driveway. It felt a lot different to the last time he had visited here riding alongside Ned. The memory of blaring Christian music flooded his mind and made him smile. So much of the music was familiar to him, garnered from years and years of going to church. He had to admit he liked a lot of it. It was energetic and positive.

A large, impassive-faced attendant in front of the main entrance directed him where to park the car, waited while he did it and then ushered him to the door. His escort watched attentively as he rang the doorbell. Chu could see he was armed. Within seconds the door was answered by one of the prettiest young women SA Chu had ever seen. It startled him, as he'd been expecting another henchman or two. The girl's enormous, crystal-blue eyes stood out but her slender figure, delicate features and waste-length, golden-blonde hair wowed him, too.

"Oh, hello," she said almost gleefully, "You must be Agent Chu. Pleased to meet you."

With this, she stuck her small hand boldly out, expectantly. After a moment of hesitation Chu took it and they shook briefly.

Her child-sized hand all but disappeared in his but her grip was surprisingly firm and conveyed strength and authority.

"Daddy's expecting you. If you come this way I'll show you to the conference room. Ooh, con – fer - ence room! Sounds *so* official, doesn't it? By the way, my name's Faith. What's yours?" Her voice was high and melodious with the trace of a strange lisp. He answered, his voice sounding rough and uncultured by comparison.

"Uh, Derrik."

"Nice name. Why did you come here before as Ned's helper? That was you, wasn't it?"

Her eyes opened wide and she smiled sweetly, exhibiting no apparent guile as she waited for his response.

"Well, yes, but it's kind of complicated and has something to do with me being an FBI agent."

"Like doing spy stuff? That sounds really cool. But why spy on us?"

She looked at him directly for a few moments. He was at a loss for words. Without waiting for an answer, she turned and almost skipped off down the long hallway. They turned left and right several times before Faith spun around suddenly to face him. Chu pulled up quickly to avoid running her over but came within inches of her. So close in fact that he could smell the sweet fragrance she emitted.

"Well, we're almost there, so you're going to be off the hook from answering any more of my questions. I'll just talk to Daddy later, you know, and find out, anyway."

"I'm sure you will, Faith. I bet you get pretty much everything you want."

Her eyes flashed with anger before she caught herself. But for a second Derrik Chu could see this was no ordinary seventeen-year-old.

"Are you saying you think I'm spoiled?" she pouted in mock anger, jutting out her jaw and defiantly putting her hands on her hips.

"I'm not saying that at all. I was just thinking that it would be hard to say no to you. That's all."

"Oh, that's sweet," she cooed, looking up at him coyly before turning and bouncing along happily, leading the way again. After going down a wide flight of stairs they arrived at the conference room. She knocked loudly on the over-sized door and then used a security fob to enter. Chu followed closely, not knowing what to expect.

"Here, Daddy, I brought you your FBI agent like you asked. I grilled him but he didn't crack!" she chided. Colonel Sherman Gale laughed as his daughter moved quickly to his side and hugged him affectionately. There were two other men with the Colonel at the large table. One was Gale's son K.C., who Chu recognized; the other was Steve Thomas, who he didn't.

"Thanks, my little Inquisitor, and welcome to The Ranch again, Mr. Chu."

Before Chu could respond, Gale continued.

"This is my son, K.C.," he said, indicating the burly, smiling young man on his left, "and this is my Security Chief, Steve Thomas. As you can see by Steve's countenance, Mr. Chu, he is not happy to see you here. If truth be known, I think Steve would like to shoot you!" They all laughed except Steve.

"I'm not partial to trespassers, especially the Feds," Thomas growled.

"Please, Steve. Let's show our guest a little respect. Remember, I invited him here – this time." And they all shared another round laughter with Steve joining in this time. When the laughter subsided, Sherman Gale got back to business.

"Now if you all could please excuse us, I have some important matters to discuss with Mr. Chu. Mr. Chu, would you like to stretch your legs and take a walk?" It was not a question but a command. Chu smiled to himself and wondered what would happen if he said no. But he didn't. He accepted the invitation and soon found himself walking up the hill behind the ranch house with his host.

They walked in silence until they reached the top, where Colonel Gale stopped and stood, surveying the land around him. For miles around, as far as the eye could see, were shimmering, undulating fields blowing in the wind. The yellow light of harvest time, with its long, deep shadows, dominated the landscape. It was beautiful.

"All around us, as far as you can see in any direction, that's The Ranch. More than 300,000 acres," he said moving his hand in a sweeping motion, "You can't see one bit of what we call '*the outside world.*' From here, you can also see my wife's final resting place," he continued, pointing anew to a small knoll about two hundred feet from where they stood. He paused, not for drama, but because he was genuinely moved. Chu didn't know if he should say something or not. One thing his grandfather had tried to teach him was patience. Sometimes it would take his grandfather days to get something out. Chu waited, pushing down his impulse to speak.

"I'm sorry, Mr. Chu. It's been more than eight years but I still miss her so. Faith is the spitting image of her mother, you know. I'm so blessed that she left me children. It was so difficult and she was so brave. I have to talk about my wife because she was the inspiration for all the work I've done. I made a promise to her and to God and I mean to keep it. I just want you to understand that."

"You know, today The Ranch has a population of more than 20,000, and we're totally self-sufficient. Totally. Food, energy, medical, security, education... There's no crime, everyone is housed, nobody is unemployed. It's not heaven on earth, but it's as close as you can get."

Chu looked confused, wondering why Sherman Gale was telling him all of this. Most of it he knew already. Gale read his guest's state of mind to perfection.

"I suppose you're wondering why I'm rambling on so. I know you're a man who likes getting to the point. A man of action!"

"Well sir, to tell you the truth, I've been wondering why you wanted to see me ever since I was first told about the meeting."

"You have been very patient, Mr. Chu, and that impresses me. Can you stay patient just a little longer? There's something I want to show you." They walked across the top of the hill towards a large barn that Chu assumed was used for horses. Sherman Gale reached the open door of the barn and walked in. Chu followed, several feet behind.

As he entered the barn, two dark figures dropped down on either side of him. A third man, hooded and dressed in black, sprang out from behind a stall. Chu dropped to the ground, sweeping his leg forcefully, breaking the leg of the assailant on his right. The one on his left threw a kick at Chu's head, which he warded off automatically, countering with a crushing blow to the solar plexus as he rocketed up from the ground. A final, lightning-quick heel kick to the head of the third man ended the confrontation. It was over in less than three seconds.

A wild-eyed Chu glared at Sherman Gale who was standing twenty feet away, smiling. As Chu moved towards him menacingly, several men dressed in suits came out from the shadows, each with a gun in their hand. In a flash Derrik Chu ran up the wall, into the rafters and was gone.

———

From his hiding spot, Chu could hear clapping, followed by the loud voice of Sherman Gale calling out to him.

"Bravo. Bravo. Very impressive Mr. Chu. Very impressive indeed. Now please come down from up there. My associates have all gone. You really have nothing to worry about, I assure you."

"I wasn't worried, I can *assure you* of that," responded Chu dropping down almost silently about ten feet behind where Gale was standing. Gale spun around to face his angry guest who looked determined to get an explanation.

"I am sorry, Mr. Chu. I really am. I was told you were good but I just had to see for myself. Remember I asked for your patience? I know I'm asking for a lot, but could you bear with me a little longer?"

Chu shrugged his shoulders. What else was there to do but go along with the charade? At this point he didn't see that there was really much choice.

———

They were driving at breakneck speed down the gravel road that led from the Gale homestead to town. Gale was concentrating hard on the road. Chu leaned over to take a peek at the speedometer and saw that they were travelling at more than ninety miles an hour.

"It's all right, Mr. Chu. I'm used to driving on gravel. I love the way it slides."

And with that they hit a slight turn, and Chu could feel the truck sliding sideways and the rear end kicking out wildly. Gale adjusted the wheel quickly back and forth and the truck stabilized. He threw back his head and let out a whoop, followed by a hearty laugh. Chu felt his stomach drop and hoped they didn't have to go much further. After a few minutes of driving in silence Gale suddenly spoke.

"Do you believe in God, Mr. Chu?"

The question came out of the blue. Stalling for time, Chu pretended he hadn't heard the question.

"Pardon me?"

"God. Do you believe in God or are you an atheist?"

"Well, I'm not sure what I believe," he responded, searching hard for words and fighting the queasiness that engulfed him. "I do think there is something beyond this world but I'm not sure."

"So you do believe in a higher power?"

"Yes, I guess you could put it that way."

"So how about Jesus? Do you believe in Jesus?"

"I believe that Jesus did live and that he was a very special person."

"But you don't believe He was the Son of God?"

"No. No, I don't. I used to when I was young, but not now."

"The prodigal son," Gale stated thoughtfully. "I'm pleased by that, Mr. Chu. Very pleased. As I'm sure you'll be pleased to hear that we're nearly there!"

Less than two minutes later they hit paved road on the outskirts of the flourishing Christian community that was rapidly consuming more and more of Gale's land. Chu had read that the influx of people wanting to live on The Ranch was so great, it had to be carefully controlled. Gone were the early days when tents and makeshift shacks were commonplace. Hard work, water, sunshine and Sherman Gale's deep pockets had transformed the once dusty shanty town into a thriving, modern community. Thousands of hopefuls made application to come to The Ranch, but only a few hundred lucky ones were picked each year. Their profile, education and skill sets determined their eligibility for 'immigration', but it was the personal interview that tested their faith.

When they pulled into the parking lot of a low lying industrial building, Chu recognized it at once from surveillance pictures he'd seen: the laboratory where they suspected Gale might be producing a deadly virus. The place at the very heart of their investigation.

Sherman Gale watched Chu closely as the agent studied the building.

"I'm guessing you're familiar with this place?"

Chu feigned uncertainty but failed to impress.

"Come now, Mr. Chu. No need to insult my intelligence. I know you folks think that something sinister is going on in there. That's why I brought you. Come on, let's stop playing 'silly bugger' and go inside."

The security to get into the building was impressive. A man-trap controlled entry to one person at a time.

"Please follow me, Mr. Chu," Gale said, walking over to a pad next to the control door. He placed his thumb on a reader and stated his name. The door opened and Gale went into the gateway. After a few moments of processing another door opened at the far end and Gale disappeared inside. Derrik Chu copied what his host had done and to his surprise the outer door opened for him too. Once inside, he could see that the unit was a combination metal detector and sniffer. Air jets blew all around him checking for traces of unknown elements. When the door opened on the other side he was greeted by a guard with a wand. Sherman Gale stood beside the guard, smiling as Chu was checked out.

"Even I have to go through this rigmarole every visit. Kind of an enhanced airport experience, wouldn't you say? But as you can see, we're very careful about security. We used your fingerprints and voice sample to give you access. I hope you don't mind."

"I don't suppose I'll be authorized to enter tomorrow," quipped Chu. Gale laughed choosing not to respond. Instead, he turned around and headed down the corridor in obvious expectation that Chu would follow. They didn't go far before they reached a glass enclosed meeting room. Inside a team of people in white lab coats was sitting around the table waiting for them.

———

"In summary, uh, the research being conducted at the lab is mainly targeting, I mean, targeted at cervical cancer - its detection, treatment and prevention. We're, um, proud to have the most advanced cervical cancer detection kit on the market today. And as you heard from Dr. Struthers, Gale Labs is receiving a very prestigious award for the work her team has done using adult stem cells to reverse the progression of even advanced cervical cancer..."

Dr. Richmond paused, unsure of what to say next. While he was the lead scientist at the lab and his credentials were impressive, he was a terrible public speaker. He was also very nervous, as he always was when Sherman Gale was around.

Gale just sat there looking hard at the scientist. Richmond had planned to say more but one look at the Colonel's face and the words evaporated from his mind.

"Are you finished Dr. Richmond? Because if you are, I've got a few things I want to add."

Gale was impatient, almost angry, and his tone conveyed this message.

"Of course, Colonel, of course," stammered Richmond, submissively sinking back into his chair.

"The important thing to note here is that we're doing good things at the lab. That's what we'd like your bosses at the Bureau to understand. What I wanted you to understand, Mr. Chu, is that we are Christians who don't fear and loathe science. We embrace it. We think that God wants us to enrich our lives through its application. To use it as a tool for His purpose. Now do you have any questions before we call adjournment?"

Chu could tell the way he said it that Sherman Gale didn't expect or welcome questions.

"Yes sir. Just a couple."

"Well, Mr. Chu?"

"Are all the staff who work here Christians?"

"As I think you know, all residents of The Ranch have accepted Jesus in their hearts — or at least purport to," Gale said, looking sarcastically at Chu as he said it, "So yes, the folks around the table and all the others who work here are Christians."

"Dr. Richmond, could this lab be used for virus research?"

"Well, it's certainly equipped for it. In fact, a great deal of work is being done here with a viral strain that is a known causal factor in cervical cancer."

"But could you change or alter a virus at this lab?"

"What I think Mr. Chu is trying to ask," interjected Sherman Gale, "is whether or not we are conducting germ warfare experiments here Dr. Richmond. Isn't that right Mr. Chu?" Dr. Richmond looked horrified, as did the majority of people around the table. Sherman Gale was bemused.

"Really, Mr. Chu. Must you insist on being the proverbial bull in a china shop? Go ahead, Dr. Richmond. Answer Mr. Chu's question."

"We could do anything with the equipment at this lab. It's one of the best of its kind in the world. Now, what we don't have is the people with knowledge and experience doing that kind of research. That's by far the most important thing: the people."

"With that, Mr. Chu, are we done?"

"*One* more question, sir."

Gale's countenance darkened again. Chu could see that he struggled not to lash out. He could understand that.

"I thought you said a couple of questions. That usually means two."

"Yes, sir. But my last question is, where can I find a washroom?"

"A washroom?" he laughed. "I'll take you there directly, Mr. Chu. Dr. Richmond, thanks to you and your colleagues for the briefing."

When he came out of the washroom Sherman Gale was nowhere in sight but Chu could hear him talking with someone nearby. He looked to his right and couldn't help noticing a door with large red letters on it boldly stating: Controlled

Area — No Unauthorized Admission. Chu moved to the door quickly to investigate and discovered to no surprise that it was locked. He could still hear Gale talking so he moved towards the sound, checking out the contents of several deserted office cubicles on the way. As he got closer to the voices he could clearly hear them talking, obviously nearing the end of their discussion. Chu knew he didn't have much time, but checked one last cubicle. He recognized in a flash that there lay two Russian reference books and scientific journal in plain view. He wanted to get a closer look but he didn't have time. He could hear Gale saying his farewells and beginning to walk down the corridor back to the washroom. Chu leaped from behind the cubicle and began his apparent nonchalant saunter in the direction his host was returning. Gale seemed surprised to see him, so Chu offered explanation.

"Oh, hi. Sorry. I heard your voice so tried to find you. Got a little lost in this place though. It's pretty confusing."

"Like a maze," Gale admitted, "You really need to stick with somebody who knows their way around."

He looked at Chu sideways as they walked down the hall towards the exit, but could read nothing. Chu simply smiled and wondered what lay ahead next.

———

On the ride back, Chu was invited, and had accepted the offer, to stay at the Gale's for dinner. He figured the meeting had gone on all day so it might as well go on into the evening. He was sure the office would be wondering what was going on. Jenkins was probably pulling out his hair by now. Chu himself was still trying to figure out the angle. Why was Gale taking so much time with him? There had to be some reason.

Faith and K.C. joined them for dinner, which proved to be a feast. Chu hadn't eaten so much and so well in a long time. Now the four of them sat around the table, drinking coffee and picking at the remnants of dessert.

"Sir, that surely was one of the best dinners I've ever eaten! My compliments to the chef."

"I will pass along your kind remarks to Lotti, who, as always, has truly outdone herself!"

Heads around the table nodded in agreement. Dinner conversation had been polite and had stayed at a surface level. They had talked a great deal about Faith's school and her volunteer work and had a lively exchange about high school football. Now there were awkward moments of silence and the conversation started and stopped without flow.

"Well, kids, if you'll excuse us, Agent Chu and I have a couple of things to discuss." Sherman Gale stood up and motioned Chu towards the door.

"Nice meeting you both," Chu said, standing up in compliance.

"Yeah, you too," responded K.C.

"Maybe see you again soon," added Faith, shining him a radiant smile. At a loss for a response, and slightly red faced, Agent Chu hurried out of the room, closely followed by his frowning host.

———

They were sitting, facing each other on opposite sides of the large conference room table. Gale broke the silence.

"You know, of course, that I'm managing my brother-in-law's campaign?"

Chu nodded.

"Well, I'm expecting a significant increase in threats against him and his family, so I would like to hire you to work with the team assigned to protect them."

"Pardon me?" Chu raised his voice in disbelief. "You're offering me a job?"

"I saw what you can do. One of the best I've seen, and I've seen a lot. You would be a great asset."

"And what's in it for me? Leave my career and the Bureau?"

"It's not like you've had a picnic there, son. I've seen the reports. I know you resent all the bureaucratic bullshit they throw at you. You come work for me and you'll never have to fill out another form."

"You think I'd give it up just for that?"

"No, no I don't. How about a guaranteed ten year contract at more than double your current salary, a generous per diem for the days you're working, a car that you can choose, a new place for your mother and grandfather..."

"What! What did you say about my mom and grandpa?"

"We'd build them a new house in one of the developments we're working on in Sacramento. It'd be in the Church's name, of course, but it would be theirs for as long as they live."

"I'm not sure she'd accept the offer, even if I did take the position."

"Well, she sounded pretty excited when I talked to her about it this morning."

"You talked to my mother?"

"Yes. She said the location would be a lot closer to her work. You know, the money you send them helps, but it really isn't enough. She's been thinking about selling, but values are so distressed."

Chu didn't know what to think. Gale sat across the table from him, grinning and waiting.

"I'm a bit taken back here, Mr. Gale. This was not something I even remotely thought we were going to talk about."

"I appreciate that son. So if you want to mull it over, please feel free. And please, I'd prefer you call me Colonel."

"No, I don't need to mull it over. It's just not going to happen. I wish you'd left my poor mom out of it. I can't believe you'd get her hopes up."

"Just trying to help."

"Well, you don't need to. I can send more money. Thanks for letting me know that, at least. But as for the job offer – thanks, but no thanks. The Bureau might not love me, but I love it."

"Well, I'm disappointed son, but I understand the sentiment. Once a soldier, always a soldier. But I'll warn you, I'm used to getting my way. So if you change your mind..."

"I won't. Now, sir, if that was all, I think I'd like to go now."

"To debrief Jenkins?"

"Maybe I'll go home first and get some sleep."

"No, you'll go and report in like the book says, even though you resent it. Like any good soldier. Just remember, Mr. Chu, I'm used to getting my way."

5 - Reassignment of Duty

Agent Chu sat across the table from a clearly agitated Jenkins and an extremely unhappy Hinks. The latter wore a sneer so pronounced, it was laughable. Two other men who Chu didn't know sat near the end of the table on his right. They hadn't spoken a word, or been introduced.

"So Gale gets a few guys to try and beat the crap out of you, then just shows you around the lab we've been trying to get into for three years, takes you home for dinner with his kids and finally offers you a job. Does that just about sum it up?"

"I guess. Except you forgot the thing about the Russian books I saw."

"Right. Russian books in the secret lab."

"I don't know if I'd call it secret, sir. They seem to be working on cancer research. Specifically cervical cancer. The kind that killed his wife."

"So you told him you didn't want the job? Sounds like you're starting to think this guy's OK."

"Well, he's not the monster I had him pegged for. He's very human. Loves his kids. But, like I said already, I told him I wouldn't work for him – even though the promise of no paperwork was very tempting..." Chu winced when he thought about all the forms he would need to fill in before he could call it a day. It was already nearly midnight and he was feeling beat.

"We've already confirmed he talked to your mother this morning. They were on the phone for more than half an hour. What was that all about?"

"I haven't had a chance to talk to her, but from what I can gather it was part of the pay package. If I came to work for him they'd build my mom and grandpa a new house."

The elder of the two unknown men at the end of the table, a big man of middle age, raised an eyebrow. In an instant Chu could see that this guy was superior in rank to Jenkins and was about to speak.

"Mr. Chu, my name is Roger O'Reilly. I work for the Secret Service and I'm directing the government security teams assigned to protect Robert Strong." Chu nodded in acknowledgement but didn't say a word.

"We received a request this morning from Robert Strong's office for you – you specifically – to be assigned to Strong's campaign. Mr. Jenkins here has already agreed."

"So you see why we're interested in the job offer. It would appear that Colonel Gale was going to get you on his page no matter what." O'Reilly paused, a little theatrically, and waited for the information to sink in. Chu thought this drama was so old school, but the ensuing silence, as always, grated on his nerves, compelling him to speak.

"The last thing he said to me was that he was used to getting his own way."

"You can bet on that, Agent Chu. You can certainly bet on that. Now, if you don't mind, Jenkins, we'd like to brief Chu here before he reports in tomorrow. He's got a lot to absorb before we let him into that tangled little nest." Jenkins got up to leave but Hinks remained seated.

"If I may, sir," Hinks began with deference, "I'd like to stay for the briefing as well. I'm the FBI's lead agent for surveillance on The Ranch, so it might be very helpful to..."

"Sorry, Sparky," O'Reilly interjected, "the information is given on a 'need to know' basis only."

"And I *'need to know'*," Hinks all but shrieked. O'Reilly looked to Jenkins for assistance, which Jenkins translated as a jerk of his head aimed at Hinks, signalling to the perplexed agent that he should clear out.

"Like I said, you have to leave. Sorry, Agent Hinks. I don't make up the rules." Jenkins left quickly with Hinks close behind. From the back, Hink's neck could be seen to be scarlet red, his ears burning.

———

Chu opened the door to his apartment just before sunrise. He was exhausted. The briefing had gone on and on until his head was spinning. In the end they cut it off when he started nodding off every five minutes. The plan was that he'd go home and get some sleep, then be picked up at 5:00pm and taken to the airport. O'Reilly said the briefing would continue on the plane ride to Dallas where Strong was currently campaigning.

Chu ate a piece of toast and wolfed down almost half a tub of yogurt. After a quick shower he literally crawled into bed. He was so tired he couldn't think straight. It was just before seven, so he figured it was safe to set the alarm for three. That done, he placed his head on the pillow and got ready to be engulfed in sleep.

But something was on his mind. He couldn't quite think what it was until he looked over at the picture of his parents at his bedside.

"Mom," he said out loud sitting up and remembering that Gale had talked to her. He jumped out of bed and headed for the answering machine. Sure enough he could see on the call display that his mother had called no less than six times. It was a bit early but he knew she would be up – so he picked up the phone and dialled home. After two rings, the phone was picked up on the other end.

"Oh, Derrik," she said almost breathlessly, "Thank goodness you've called. I'm just so confused...I could hardly sleep last night."

"Yeah, Ma, that's why I made the call. I would have sooner but I've been in meetings since Sherman Gale called you. Look Mom, I'm sorry, but I just couldn't accept the job. For good or bad the FBI is the place I want to be."

"Yes sweetheart, and Colonel Gale realizes that. He said he was impressed by the way you turned him down. He said it doesn't happen very often."

"What? Just wait – you mean he talked to you after I said no to the job?"

"That's right. He phoned last night and said you'd had a wonderful dinner together."

"I can't believe it! So he phoned just to say that."

"No, he wanted to let me know that we could still have a new place if we wanted it. He said I should check with you to see what you think."

"Well, I don't know what to say. What's your feeling?"

"Oh, I most certainly would like to do it. This place is so run down, and with the bedrooms upstairs it makes it really hard for your grandpa. He's going to be ninety soon, you know."

"Yeah, I guess that's a consideration."

"Anyway, the Colonel said you might have some objections to the offer. You don't, do you, honey?" Chu paused before he spoke trying to get the words right.

"No Mom, not a problem. I just don't like the idea. And it's such a substantial gift I'd have to clear it through the Bureau."

"Yes, yes of course, dear."

"I don't know how big an issue it will be, but if you're sure you want it, then I'll ask." Chu couldn't quite believe his own words, but his mother seemed convinced.

"The Colonel said it was an act of Christian charity to reward me for being devout all my life."

"Well, that's great, Mom but I'm just not sure what his intentions are. I don't really trust him. And could you please stop calling him 'the Colonel'? He retired from active service years ago."

"Oh, dear. Well, that's what he told me to call him. You know, Derrik, he's very impressed with you, even if you're not impressed by him. He said I should be very proud - that you're one of the best he's ever seen. He said your father would be proud, too."

This was too much for him. He wanted to scream but he knew his mother wouldn't understand and he couldn't explain it to her. So he just sat there holding the phone in silence.

"Are you still there, honey? Are you OK?"

"Yeah, fine, Mom. I gotta go now, but like I said, I'll ask and see what they say. I'll be in touch as soon as I know."

"So you think it's OK to start doing some design work? The Colonel, I mean Mr. Gale, said we could customize things quite a bit."

"I think that would be fine, Mom," he said with resignation, "and I'll let you know as soon as I can what the word from on high is."

After goodbyes he headed straight for bed. But now, he didn't seem so tired. His mind kept mulling over the question: Why was Sherman Gale trying to put him in his pocket?

———

The car arrived promptly at 5:00 to pick him up. A feeling of dread came over him when he saw it round the corner and slowly pull up to the curb in front of his building. Like something out of a movie, two men in sunglasses got out. One stayed with the car while the other made his way to the front entrance. Chu took his two carry-on cases and headed out the door. A concerned agent was just pressing the call button outside the apartment for a second time when Chu exited the elevator. A look of relief came over the man's face when he saw Chu approaching.

"Thought you might be running late," he blurted when Chu opened the door.

"Just thought I'd come down and save you the effort of coming up. I saw the car pull up."

"Guess it's a little conspicuous, huh?" the man replied laughing.

"Just a little. Say, you guys Secret Service?"

"Yup, I'm Dobbs and my partner is Stevenson."

"Pleased to meet you. Where are we going?"

"Plane leaves from Cheyenne, so that's where we're headed. We have just over two hours so let's get a move on."

"Check, chief," Chu responded, but his sarcasm was totally wasted on Dobbs who was hurrying back to the curbside. Stevenson was already in the car with the engine running when they reached it. Immediately after Chu climbed in the back seat, he gunned the engine and took off, squealing the tires loudly. Chu sat in the back seat and rolled his eyes as they sped away.

——

As they screeched to a halt on the airport tarmac, Chu breathed a sigh of relief. He loved speed but the trip down had been almost frightening. Taking calculated risks was one thing, but driving as fast as they did down to Cheyenne seemed unnecessarily foolhardy. His companions seemed caught up in the drama and almost savored each frantic manoeuvre he felt could only be described as stupid.

His relief was short-lived. As soon as he jumped out of the car he spied a grim faced O'Reilly waiting for him. Chu went to thank the two agents who drove him down, but Stevenson had already tromped on the gas and was spinning the tires as he raced away. O'Reilly attempted a smile as the car turned a sharp corner and nearly spun out of control.

"Idiots," O'Reilly said disdainfully, shaking his head, "Now if you're not too rattled, let's hop on board and continue the briefing. You're scheduled to be introduced to Reverend Strong in four hours and we need you prepared."

"Yes, sir," Chu responded, "Ready as I'll ever be."

——

"How about I sum up what I've got so far, then you fill in the blanks? I just don't think that starting from square one has much benefit," Chu said hurriedly, trying to avoid the Secret Service man reading from the thick tome he held in his hands.

"Yeah, OK. We can start that way if you want," replied an uncertain O'Reilly as he closed the briefing book he was about to refer to.

"Right. Well, first off, we have several groups involved in running security for Strong. In total, the team has twenty people. You Secret Service guys have seven people, there's Gale's security team of twelve, one of whom is a CIA operative, and now there's me. We have a minimum of three people attached to Strong twenty-four hours a day. Daily roster sheets with assignments are passed out every morning at seven by Gale's man, Tony Wheeler. Wheeler is an officious prick who makes everyone's life miserable. You hate his guts and wish you were in charge. And finally, the last thing you need is a snotty-nosed punk like me from the FBI adding to the confusion." O'Reilly stared at Chu impassively, but two of his colleagues nearby couldn't help smiling.

"You're a real smart ass, aren't you Mr. Chu? I'm not sure you realize the importance of the work we do."

"Maybe not, but I'm right, aren't I? Did I leave anything out?" O'Reilly stared at Chu intently. He appeared to be thinking carefully about his next words.

"Look, I'll cut to the chase. I've already got so many wild cards I have no control over, it's making it impossible for me to do my job. If you do pick up anything, all I'm requesting is that you share it with me. I'm not asking that you don't inform your bosses – that's up to you - I'm just asking for you to let me know as well. I'm flying blind here and I don't like the way it feels."

"OK. I see where you're coming from. I appreciate your candour."

"And I see I can count on yours," O'Reilly replied, smiling for the first time. "Is it really that obvious that I can't stand Wheeler?"

"Well, I had to read between the lines, but not very hard!" Chu laughed.

"I'm going to have to work on that."

"But I'm really looking forward to meeting the dickhead!"

And they laughed together and shared organizational horror stories as they sped towards Dallas and the beginning of a new chapter in Chu's life.

6 - All in the Family

It was past ten when O'Reilly and another agent escorted Chu to the Strong's suite on the 24th floor. They walked in silence down the long corridor to a room with two agents guarding outside. One nodded at them and turned to knock softly. Before they reached the room, the door opened, waiting for them to go in. At the door O'Reilly and the other man stopped short. Chu hesitated and looked at O'Reilly for direction.

"They said they wanted to meet you alone," stated O'Reilly in a matter-of-fact manner, although he was obviously annoyed. Chu just raised his eyebrows and stepped inside, to be greeted by a matronly-looking woman in an apron. Chu was immediately introduced to Robert Strong and his wife Doris. They were warm and sincere, which took him aback. Soon he found himself on the couch drinking green tea, sitting across from the presidential candidate and his aspiring first lady.

They looked different from all the pictures he'd seen of them. He was a little smaller in stature than Chu had pictured, but even more elegant. That was the only word that Chu could come up with to describe his host. He looked as if he was dressed to sit down with a late night TV host, styled impeccably. Fifteen years her husband's junior, Doris Strong was slim, average-sized and average-looking. But that's where the average ended. While she shared her husband's calm, compelling demeanor and perfect sense of style, it was her warm and sincere manner that appealed to Chu immediately. When she smiled, her eyes lit up, showing fine lines which indicated that this was their natural state.

"We find this really relaxes us after a long day – and doesn't keep us awake. We need all the sleep God blesses us with these days!" began Strong, referring to the drink they all held in their hands and trying to ease into the conversation.

"I don't drink enough of it now. I used to as a kid at my grandpa's karate school, but I switched over to coffee in college. Probably not a good idea."

"Well, Agent Chu, you know that we didn't invite you here to discuss green tea. My brother-in-law tells me that you are probably the best agent the government has, and I need you to do something for me. I need you to protect my wife and me. Sherman tells us there have been numerous and specific death threats against both of us. We haven't even shared this information fully with Mr. O'Reilly. You must understand that we can't entirely trust the government at this point."

"Then why me? Reverend, I work for the FBI. If I'd taken the job that was offered to me I can see how it makes sense – but I didn't."

"We know all about that. But Sherman says he trusts you to do the right thing. That you won't let us down. He said he'd stake his life on it."

"It's not just for Robert and me, Agent Chu," interjected an imploring Doris Strong, "It's the children I worry about. If anything was to happen to me or Robert, it would kill them. You know, they're back home under lock and key, under constant 24 hour guard. It's like they're in prison. You can't believe some of the threats we've been sent, even against them." She broke down, and a look of concern came over the Reverend's face as he did his best to console her. After a few seconds he looked up at their guest.

"Derrik - do you mind if I call you Derrik?"

"No, not at all."

"Well, Derrik, we realize that this isn't the kind of duty an active person like you would request, but we're asking you to please help us."

"I will do whatever I can to help."

"What Sherman prescribed is that you stay with us. Basically live with us for the next few weeks until the election. Go where we go, eat what we eat, sleep when we sleep."

"Well, uh, I wasn't expecting that."

"Is it a problem? You'll have your own bedroom and en suite and we eat pretty well."

"No sir, it isn't a problem. I'd be honoured."

"Well, that's good. And you know there are some benefits. Like your mom's new place."

"If it gets okayed," replied Chu, reddening noticeably, a little surprised Strong was aware of the detail.

"Oh, I'm pretty sure it will. Anyway, the point is there are some benefits to taking this on. We don't want it to be just one way. We'd like you to think of us as part of your family."

"I know it's kind of corny to say that I'm just doing my duty – but the truth is, that's the way it is for me." Chu almost choked on his words as he said them. Inside he was contemptuous of being assigned to what amounted to babysitting.

"I don't think it's corny at all Derrik," said Strong's wife, "I think it's very sweet and commendable." And with that she stood up and gave Chu a warm smile.

"Well, I'm off to bed now," she said to her husband. "Don't be long, darling."

"No dear, I'm right behind you." he replied, getting up from the couch. Chu stood up to join his hosts.

"Your room is down there," Strong said, motioning to a corridor off the living room. "Help yourself to anything in the kitchen – there isn't much in there right now, but you're welcome to whatever you can find."

"Thanks, Reverend Strong."

"Please call me Robert…"

"And me Doris," his wife chimed in from the master bedroom.

"And tomorrow morning we'll see you at eight for breakfast and then it's off to church. Thank goodness for Sunday morning sleep-ins!"

"Goodnight, Mr. Strong…I mean Robert," Chu said stammering, "…and Doris," Chu added, raising his voice in an attempt to reach his hostess's ears. It would have felt more normal if he had called them Mom and Dad. Feeling very strange and out of place, Chu fetched his two cases and carried them to his bedroom. In the morning, he resolved to try to get out of this duty. But for now, all he could think about was getting some much-needed sleep.

———

It took him a while to orient himself when he woke up the next morning. After a moment of panic, he remembered he was in a hotel room in Dallas. It was 6:30. Still time to shower and get dressed before the 7:00 briefing.

The briefing was a bust. Neither Tony Wheeler nor O'Rielly made an appearance, so Chu didn't have anybody to complain to or request a reassignment. The only thing he learned was that he was accompanying the Strongs to church later that morning, a place he had avoided for years and wasn't looking forward to. It seemed to him that things were just getting worse and worse.

When he returned to the suite, breakfast was already on the table. Robert and Doris were both seated at the dining table and beckoned for him to join them.

"Sorry I'm late," Chu said as he reached the table and went to sit down. He noticed there were two additional places set.

"No problem, Derrik," replied Robert Strong. "We're still waiting on my niece Faith to join us. I understand the two of you have already met."

"Uh, yes. Yes, of course. At The Ranch the other day. It seems like a long time ago now."

"Time is funny, for sure. Anyway, she should be here any second." As if on cue there was a knock at the door which the housekeeper, who Chu now knew was called Nancy, promptly answered.

"Hi, Auntie and Uncle," sang Faith as she entered the room, hugging and kissing each of them as they arose in turn to greet her. Then, turning to a standing Chu with her hand outstretched she added, "And hello, Agent Chu. I told you we might be seeing each other again soon!"

"Well, you were right," he said, shaking her hand and re-experiencing her surprisingly strong grip. She laughed as she sat down, primping ever so slightly in an apparent effort to get comfortable and look her best. Chu followed course, but kept his eyes on the empty plate in front of him. He found it helped not to focus on the girl.

"Faith is coming to church with us this morning and will be spending a few days on the campaign helping out. She's an excellent public speaker, you know, and the crowd really loves her – especially the young people," Doris explained.

"I'm not surprised to hear that," responded Chu, a little too enthusiastically. He could bet that at least a million teenage boys, Christian or not, had seen her picture and been smitten. She was also pretty and nice enough to be adored by teenaged girls as well. Faith blushed appropriately and her aunt and uncle smiled.

"I mean, I can see that she's very accomplished for her age, and that would certainly evoke admiration," Chu stammered trying to dig his way out of a hole, but it just made them smile even more. He couldn't believe his own words – *evoke admiration*!

"I'll help you out here, Derrik," offered Strong. "Let's agree it's safe to say that anyone looking at Faith is going to be hard pressed not to see God-given perfection."

"Uncle Robert!" Faith implored, "Please!"

"Yes, Robert, please," said Doris, "Can we please have grace? We're starving!"

———

The ride to church in the car was a little bit longer and a lot more uncomfortable than Chu had anticipated. Doris was interested in finding out a little more about their protector, so started fielding questions that had a way of getting out a lot of information. Faith followed the conversation, fascinated, while Robert busily prepared the sermon he'd been asked to preach.

"So Derrik, I should have asked last night if we're imposing on you too much. I mean, your girlfriend is probably going to have a thing or two to say!"

"I don't really have a girlfriend right now," he responded awkwardly, "I guess since college I just haven't had much time." In fact he hadn't had a girlfriend for longer than Chu liked to admit — even to himself. Pauline, his long-time college girlfriend, chose graduate school and, shortly thereafter, one of her T.A.s over him. After being officially dumped, he'd been devastated for more than a year. Then he'd gone through a period of sleeping around — for a bit. But it just wasn't for him. He wanted commitment but was deathly afraid of getting hurt. A perfect recipe for staying single and celibate.

"So it's alright to just leave your place for more than a month? I can't believe it!"

"No, really, it's fine. I'll give the landlord a call if I have to." He thought about it. There was no cat to feed. No goldfish bowl to fill. Not even a plant to water. He could just leave and it didn't matter when he came back.

"And all you do is work? Doesn't that get a little tedious?"

"For the most part, although in the past I did do a lot of Free Running." He could see by the look on her face that Doris had no clue what he was talking about.

"Sometimes it's referred to as Parkade because a lot of it happens in parking garages." The fog of bewilderment he could see was not lifting.

"So what exactly do you do?"

"Well, the style I use is to just run. Run wherever you want, as fast as you can."

"So it's running."

"Yes, but not exactly. Let's say I'm running and I get to a wall."

"Yes."

"Well normally you'd go around it, right? Yeah, well, when you're free running you run right over it. Even if it's fifteen feet off the ground."

"Oh, my!"

"We even run up into old buildings and jump down from three stories. It's wild!" Chu could see he was losing her. Faith was still interested, but Doris just couldn't fathom it.

"And your mother knows you do this?"

"Yes, she does."

"And she approves?"

"Well, no. Not exactly. I think she accepts it now."

"Oh."

"I mean, I don't do it much any more."

"No. Why's that?"

"Since the accident."

"You were hurt?"

"Yes, and the Bureau was pretty upset too."

"Are you going to elaborate?" Doris asked with concern.

"Well, I guess I was practising on the roof of the LA office when I slipped and fell through a skylight."

"Did you break anything?"

"Just my arm and leg and a couple of ribs – *and the skylight*." He paused before adding in response to the look of horror on Doris' face, "I *was* wearing a helmet."

"I just don't get it. I'm sorry but I don't know why on earth you would want to do that. I tell you, Derrik, I'm going to pray to the Lord in church this morning that you come to your senses and stop doing it altogether. Your poor mother!"

Chu looked so dejected, Faith couldn't help it and started to giggle.

"Just watch one of my You Tube videos when we get back and you'll see – it's not as crazy as it sounds. Some of my clips have had lots of viewings." His earnest appeal to her aunt made Faith laugh until tears ran down her cheeks. Her laughter was infectious, and soon all three of them were at it.

"All right, all right. I'll watch one of them when we get back – if you promise you don't get hurt in it," replied Doris catching her breath.

"Hey, can you heathens keep it down? I'm trying to pen some words to inspire the faithful," Reverend Strong joked, "But you know, this has given me an idea. I think I'll take a different tack now. I definitely *will* take a different tack." Doris, Faith and Chu looked at each other like they didn't know what he was talking about and laughed some more as Strong jotted down notes in the backseat of the limo. Chu was glad the attention was off him for the moment and was thinking they could use an interrogator like Doris Strong at the Bureau.

———

They were tightly packed together in the front pew. Robert Strong had the aisle so he could get up easily when the time came for his contribution to the service. Doris sat beside him, next was Faith and then Chu. Tony Wheeler was there directing security around the Strongs. At least Chu thought it was Wheeler because of the way he ordered people around, and the dirty looks he had given Chu every time he had gone by, which had been quite often. The display was noticeable enough for Faith to nudge Chu and whisper in his ear.

"I can see Mr. Wheeler is a real fan of yours."

Chu just smiled and nodded his head in agreement. He found sitting so close to Faith very distracting. It was bad enough sitting with her pressed up to his side, but when she whispered in his ear with her hot, moist breath he could feel his body's involuntary call to action. The aroma of her breath lingered, so thick he could taste it. Faith didn't help matters by continually fidgeting and trying to get his attention. Chu was relieved when the service started and he could focus on what was happening at the front of the church.

When it was time for Reverend Strong to preach, people could be heard shifting around so they could get a glimpse of the great man as he stood up and approached the pulpit.

Robert Strong ascended the stairs slowly and with grace. The church fell silent as he stood, waiting to deliver his words to those gathered.

"Worship is a serious business," he began, "It doesn't entail a great deal of laughter." He stood, looking serious and stern, as some people in the pews nodded their heads in agreement. Others had puzzled looks on their faces. Some frowned.

"And I think that's too bad!" he continued, almost shouting out in defiance. "Laughter is said to be the best medicine, and sometimes it's the only thing that makes us stand back from all our problems. It reminds us that our daily trials and tribulations are nothing in comparison to the suffering of millions around the world – that they are nothing compared to the suffering endured by our sweet Savior. We are all so blessed in this country, we should be laughing all the time! Joyous that the Lord has provided us with freedom. I know times have been hard for many of you these past few years, but think of how the early Christians suffered and ask yourself if you would be willing to die for your faith as they did. We should all be laughing every day in every part of this great nation because we can worship freely. We should sing praises to the Lord for blessing us. I recall words from Psalm 126:1-3, 'When the Lord brought back the captivity of Zion, we were like those who dream. Then our mouth was filled with laughter, and our tongue with singing.'"

A half hour later when the service was ending, Chu was surprised that he had actually enjoyed it. Much as he hated to admit it, he used to love the pomp and ceremony of the service. The singing, preaching and group worship gave him a sense of belonging to something bigger than himself. Now as people filed out of their seats and thronged by to congratulate and to be seen congratulating the presidential candidate, the security detail was in high alert. Chu watched, ready in the event of an incident. As he moved with the Strongs toward the door, Wheeler stopped him with a touch on his shoulder and a nod to join him in the corner. Both men kept an eye on the Strong party as it stopped forward progress to deal with yet another group of must-see people.

"O'Reilly briefed me this morning about your coming on board. I just want you to know that I'm totally against this harebrained scheme and have sent a communication to the Colonel saying just that. O'Reilly's not keen on it either, you know." Before letting Chu say anything, Wheeler continued talking, his face screwed up like he smelled something bad.

"Now Reverend Strong and Miss Gale are going to a breakfast rally and you're going to accompany Mrs. Strong back to the hotel. The Reverend will be back there around 13:30 hours. Got that?"

"I assume you're Wheeler. We haven't really been introduced," Chu replied superciliously.

"Yeah, you got that right, genius. Now, just try and stay out of my way and we'll get on just fine." And with that, Wheeler turned and was gone, leaving Chu to re-join the group as it made its way outside to the awaiting cars.

—

"So, did you enjoy the service, Derrik?" enquired Doris Strong as they raced back towards the hotel in a black limousine. Only one escort vehicle accompanied them as the majority of security had followed the candidate and his niece to the rally.

"Yes, I really did, Doris," he answered, using her given name reluctantly. It just didn't seem right to him, being so familiar with these famous people, but they had insisted.

"You feel a little out of place, don't you Derrik?"

He paused before answering, and she patiently waited for him to formulate his thoughts.

"I guess, because being with you feels so much like family - like being in the family I always wanted. Your husband is a larger-than-life hero. And his preaching today was amazing. To think that he just made that up as we drove. And you, you're just so amazing, too...but..." Doris Strong just smiled, gently encouraging him with her eyes to continue.

"I don't know what I'm trying to say, but I guess it's just that I didn't join the Bureau to do this. I don't see how I'm doing any good. And nobody wants me here, aside from you and Robert."

"And Sherman..." she added.

"And Sherman," he conceded, "But that's another thing. To be honest, it just doesn't make sense that he'd want me to do this. I really shouldn't say this, but I was on the team gathering information about him and his activities. He's the subject of an ongoing Federal investigation."

"Well, I don't know about that. I've certainly had my differences with Sherman over the years but I can assure you, he feels you're the best and that your being here will make a difference. He doesn't do things that don't have a purpose."

"Well, Wheeler and O'Reilly sure aren't fans. And you know, I don't blame them. The last thing I'd want if I was them, is a guy with special orders hanging around, getting in the way."

"Well, Mr. Wheeler is a bit controlling. Sherman's already sent him a note telling him to keep his shirt on. And O'Reilly is a good man but is very frustrated. I think they're just jealous because you're getting all this quality treatment. You should really feel very privileged you know!" she said laughing.

Chu had to laugh, too.

"Yeah, I guess it could be worse."

"So why don't you see how it all goes in the next few days and see if you get used to it. Oh, and I thought of another person who wants you here."

"Who's that?"

"Why, Faith, of course. She seems very eager to get your attention."

Chu turned red. He wasn't expecting this. Doris Strong had a way of sliding things in.

"I don't know what to say," he stammered.

"Well, it's pretty ordinary for a girl her age to want to be noticed, but I hope we can agree that any kind of intimacy..."

Chu didn't wait for the words and broke in sharply.

"I would never even consider it. I'm not saying that I haven't noticed her, but I'd never, ever..."

"I didn't think so, Derrik, but I felt I just had to bring it up. Faith is a very determined young lady and she really seems to like you."

"Well, to be honest, you don't have to worry, because I find her a bit overwhelming," he laughed.

"I find her overwhelming, too, Derrik," she replied, laughing in kind, "And sometimes even a little frightening."

7 - Into the Limelight

The rest of the ride back to the hotel gave Doris Strong the opportunity to tell Derrik Chu how she and her husband met, what she had done before they met and what she had done since they met. It was a nice story. She said it was only fair that he know a little more about her and her family, given that she'd been briefed on the intimate details of his life.

She also told Chu about some of the differences she'd had with Sherman Gale and her unease with her husband leaving strategic political matters almost exclusively up to him.

"Robert is a truly good man - an excellent husband and father, an extremely gifted clergyman - but he is not a politician. He believes in the people who are advising him, and that allows him to focus on delivering his message of Christian unity - something he strongly believes in, as he does in changing the Constitution. For him, it's no more complicated than that."

"But it really is more complicated than that, isn't it?" Chu stated flatly.

"Yes, a great deal more complicated. And sometimes I think Sherman Gale is more interested in being God than in doing His work. I swear, I do."

They pulled up to the curb in front of the hotel, closely followed by the escort car. The two assigned agents jumped out quickly and secured the area. One of them nodded to Chu as the driver came round to his door and pulled it open. Chu hopped out and was followed quickly by Mrs. Strong.

They were making their way across the wide entrance when Chu heard the high-pitched scream of a motorcycle. Instead of gearing down, it was revving up, a fact that came to Chu's immediate attention. He instinctively searched with his eyes in the direction of the noise. He could make out a figure speeding towards them. The motorcyclist had something strapped to his torso. It looked like a life jacket but was bulkier. The man was screaming something and clutching what Chu assumed was a detonator. There was no time to react.

The man and the motorcycle shot up the driveway straight at them. Chu took one quick look around and made a decision. He grabbed Doris forcibly and launched himself at the oncoming bomber. Chu's feet struck the driver in the chest so hard, both driver and bike shot off at a sharp angle. Driving his legs back with all the force he could muster, Chu used the assailant's chest to catapult both his charge and himself backwards towards the shallow pool that ringed the entrance of the hotel. As he was flying through the air, Chu saw the motorcycle light up in a bright flash just before they hit the water.

After a few seconds that seemed like forever under the water, Chu stuck his head up to find burning devastation, twisted metal and broken glass everywhere. Only when he determined it was safe did he pull the candidate's wife to the surface and check to see if she was alright. She was sputtering, shaken and in a slight state of shock, but she was in one piece, with only what appeared to be minor injuries. Chu picked her up quickly and carried her up to the room for medical attention.

The two agents with them were dead, along with a bicycle courier and two businessmen unfortunate enough to be at the front of the hotel when the bomb went off. Scores were injured – mainly from the broken glass. Their driver had escaped death by jumping into the back seat of the car, but had been badly burned. The motorcycle bomber and his bike had all but disintegrated. Emergency crews, police officers and agents from at least four organizations buzzed around the hotel lobby and corridors like flies, spilling out onto the blackened grand entrance gaping in wonder at the devastation. As he held her in the elevator, dripping wet in his arms, Chu looked down with concern and she smiled back.

"You saved my life. Now that counts as doing something doesn't it? Although Robert might have a problem with the bruises that I'll no doubt have tomorrow. If you weren't saving my life Mr. Chu, I would say you were being extremely fresh!"

———

Two hours had passed since the incident. Chu sat in the room with O'Reilly and another agent he didn't know. They'd been at it for more than an hour.

"So, I'm a little confused. Exactly when did you realize that there was something wrong? Before you got out of the car or after?"

"Look, O'Reilly, we've been over this already. I got out of the car after one of the agents gave me the OK. Doris followed me out. We took a few steps..."

"A few? Like two or three, or maybe five or six? Or maybe ten?"

"What the fuck? What's it matter? Who cares how far we walked?"

"Because the pool you landed in was exactly twenty eight-feet from the curb! How the fuck did you end up in the pool if you only took a few steps?"

"Look, O'Reilly, I told you already. I grabbed Doris and just sprang at that nut. We bounced back about twenty feet in the air. You say it was twenty-eight, then okay. What the fuck! I already told you this – you just don't believe it. Why not ask Doris?"

"I have asked 'Doris'," he said, playing up the pronunciation of Doris, obviously ticked off that Chu kept referring to her by first name, "and she really can't remember. It's all a blur to her except that you saved her life. Of that she is positive."

Both men were exasperated. Chu's story didn't ring true, he had two agents dead and the only living witness was in critical condition in the hospital. Chu was about to break the silence with another protest when there was a knock at the door. An agent entered and spoke softly in O'Reilly's ear. She stood back and looked at him, not sure what he'd do with the information.

"Well Mr. Chu, it seems that we have a very good security camera recording. They asked me if we want to look it. Interested?" O'Reilly was acting like he held a trump card. Something that would prove once and for all what really happened.

The image of the front entrance came up on the TV screen. You could clearly see the limo pull up and the escorting agents securing the site and giving the OK. They all watched, entranced as Chu and the agents looked off screen at the approaching motorcycle. What followed was unbelievable – it looked more like a circus trick than an escape from a deadly explosion. When the explosion did take place it brought them back to reality.

"Can we see that again please. This time, slow it way down."

Several more agents and staff came into the room to watch. It was even more incredible seeing it unfolding in slow motion. O'Reilly shook his head in disbelief.

"I have never seen anything like that, Mr. Chu. I owe you an apology. When you told me what happened I just didn't think it was possible, but I was wrong. And I have to agree with Mrs. Strong now - you are a real hero!"

Chu felt uncomfortable. Being disbelieved was really annoying but being praised somehow felt much worse. Chu's ears burned.

"Can I go now and see how she is?"

"Yeah, you got carte blanche, my friend. The sun shines brightly out of your ass, so you can do pretty much what you want. The big guy wants to see you, too."

"Reverend Strong?" Chu asked expectantly.

"No, not him. I'm talking about Colonel Gale," a somewhat aghast O'Reilly responded, "He's on his way down here from The Ranch as we speak."

———

Chu was sitting on the couch drinking green tea with the Strongs when Sherman Gale and Tony Wheeler were announced. Gale looked almost angry. Wheeler looked worried.

"Thank God you're alright, Doris. What a scare," Gale said with little emotion.

They all stood up to welcome the newcomers and Gale embraced his candidate's wife with a shallow hug. As they settled into their seats, it was Robert Strong who began the conversation.

"Thank goodness you and the Lord sent us Derrik. Doris is certain she'd be long gone if it wasn't for the resourcefulness of this young man!"

"I told you he was the best. Have you seen the video? They patched it into the plane on the way down. I'm sure we could get them to run it in here."

"I'm not certain I want to see that right now, thank you Sherman," responded Doris. "I'm just not up to it. Once is enough. And those poor people who died..."

"I quite understand. A little shell shocked, are we?"

"Yes, I suppose so."

"So be it then, another time. Anyway, it was certainly one of the most amazing things I've ever seen. Your grandfather taught you well, Mr. Chu. I'm sure he'd be very proud." He paused, letting the words sink in before adding, "I was going to wait for the Bureau to tell you, but the approval has come through for us to build the new home for your mom and grandpa."

"That is good news, *Mr. Gale*. It'll make them very happy. Thanks. I really don't know what else to say."

Gale was noticeably put off by Chu addressing him as 'mister'.

"Glad it worked out, son. Very glad," he said almost absentmindedly, turning his attention to Strong. "Now, the way I see it, Robert, this young fella should stick with you both even closer now. I'm not sure if you know this, but they apprehended another man in the parking lot outside the breakfast rally this morning. When he realized it wasn't possible to make it inside, he tried to blow himself up right there, but the detonator failed. From what we can gather, both men belong to the same homegrown Muslim extremest group. Just another example of how the weak-kneed policies of the current administration allows this infection to thrive and grow."

There was an uncomfortable pause in the conversation. Robert Strong and his wife exchanged looks before Robert responded.

"Well, if you're talking about extremest groups, I agree, Sherman, but if you're referring to Muslims in general, I have to take issue. We can't blame Muslims for the attack today, just as we can't blame Christians for the Oklahoma City massacre."

"We'll keep having this conversation, Robert, and I'll keep trying to convince you. It's in the very nature of the Muslim religion to be violent. It's really just a glorified cult. They're dangerous and they're already at war with us, whether you like it or not."

"Patricia Anne didn't believe that, Sherman. Doris and I were talking about this only the other day. She didn't share your..." Strong paused, looking for a less confrontational term to use than the one on the tip of his tongue, "...disdain for the Muslim religion. She tried to look for the underlying unity, the common bonds..."

"There's no need to bring up Patricia Anne's name!" Gale exploded as he rose to his feet. "I won't have her name mentioned in the same sentence as those heathens. Patricia Anne wanted a Christian United States as much as I do! Maybe even more."

"As we all do, brother. As we all do, praise God," Strong replied, standing up and reaching out to place his hand on Gale's shoulder.

Gale looked at Strong with weary eyes as he brushed off the extended arm. The Reverend shrugged slightly and continued, "We all want that, Sherman. But we also have to respect people's basic human rights. And one of those is freedom of religion – no matter what the majority believes."

"Well, I'm not going to get into a debate about it now, but I'll just say it's too bad they don't see it that way in places where they're in the majority."

Chu and Mrs. Strong stood up, as it became apparent that Gale and Wheeler were not going to sit down again.

"Anyway," Gale began, regaining his composure, "I'm just glad Doris is alright and that the campaign seems to be unfolding according to plan. I've got some loose ends to tie up back at The Ranch, so unfortunately I'll have to take a rain check on the dinner invitation."

———

The meeting had been called in haste as a result of the emergency. As soon as he entered the room it became obvious to Chu that the meeting had been underway for some time. Tell-tale signs of this were papers and empty coffee cups on the table, wrappers on the floor and jackets hung behind chairs. The way they looked at him when he came in made it obvious that he had been one of the major topics of conversation.

People leaned forward in their chairs so that Chu could make his way to an empty seat at the far side of the table from the door. Chu never would have chosen the spot but it was the only one available. Space in the room was tight, as the table was two sizes too big for the room.

Before he could sit down they resumed discussion.

"Like I said, if we leave him here, we need agreement for better information sharing. We have an agent down here but we're getting nothing back. It's bullshit, plain and fucking simple."

It was Hinks talking. Chu deduced he'd been sent down by Jenkins to represent Bureau management. Others present included O'Reilly, Wheeler and an attractive woman about his own age with raven black hair.

"Please, Agent Hinks, we could do without profanity," Wheeler said blankly before adding,"but I do agree information should be shared."

"Guess it was really up to me," admitted O'Reilly, "We just got so caught up with the incident and I forgot. I did discuss reporting at one point with Agent Chu..."

All eyes focused on Chu and he felt on the spot. He wasn't sure what to say, so he waited.

"Well, let's just say we don't want to rely on Mr. Chu to pass along information. His track record is pretty bad."

"Fuck you, Hinks. Can't you let the fucking thing go?"

"Please, Mr. Chu, let's remember our profanity," chided Hinks, "There *is* a lady present."

"I don't give a shit! I'm sure she's heard a lot fucking worse. I'm not going to sit here and have you slag me, understand? Just let me know what the protocol is and I'll follow it like I always do. Fuck me, I haven't been given any fucking information about who I'm reporting to or how or when or in what fashion I'm supposed to report. And I've really had one hell of a day, so you can fuck yourself!"

After some seconds of silence it was Tony Wheeler who got things going again.

"OK, OK. Guess we have some history, huh guys? Well, let's put all that behind us and figure out how we're all going to work together, and we're going to have to figure it out fast. O'Reilly, is the Secret Service going to replace the two men you lost? We're already interviewing another driver and have three more agents we can deploy."

"I've already put in a request for replacements as well as a couple more, if that fits with your plans, Tony."

"Yeah, sure. We can use all the help we can get. Now, Agent Hinks, I'm going to suggest that the Bureau assign another person down here. That way O'Reilly and I can liaise with them, as Mr. Chu's unique working arrangement doesn't allow regular reporting."

"I'm already authorized by Jenkins to fill that role."

"And you think you can make peace with your famous colleague here?" Wheeler asked in earnest, "We can't afford to let personal grievances get in our way."

"Yes, sir. I think I can do that," Hinks replied quickly.

Wheeler looked over at Chu, who appeared disinterested, staring down at the table.

"And you, Agent Chu. Is that going to work for you?"

Chu couldn't believe it. Having to work with Hinks was the last thing he wanted to do.

"Fuck, whatever. I can make anything work."

Chu raised his eyes to find the unknown woman looking directly at him. He tried to read her expression but failed. He did notice though, that she was truly stunning. Not in a conventional way, but there was something about her. Her eyes, a bright blue-green, penetrated through him. High cheekbones and a slightly crooked nose caught light like a canvas. In the entire time she was in the room she had said nothing, responded to nothing and given nothing away.

———

Hinks stayed to discuss logistics with Wheeler while the mystery woman slunk out of the over-tabled room and made a rapid escape down the corridor. O'Reilly walked with Chu in the direction of the elevator.

"Who's she with?" Chu pointed with a nod of his head toward the figure disappearing into the stairwell.

"CIA. Some kind of linguistics wiz. I'm not sure why she's here. Like I told you, we know the CIA has somebody on Wheeler's team but we're not sure who."

"She didn't look like CIA."

"What the hell do CIA look like?" O'Reilly challenged.

"I don't know. Not like that," he said, laughing and shaking his head, "Just not like that."

As they reached the elevator, something Wheeler had said came back to him.

"Hey, O'Reilly, why did Wheeler refer to me as Hink's famous colleague?"

"You'll see. And it's sure got everyone around here scurrying."

Puzzled, Chu got into the elevator to go back up to the Strong's suite.

"Aren't you getting in?" Chu asked.

"No, I've got a lot more work to do. Evidently we have a leak to track down. Sounds like you're going to have a pretty nice dinner, though. It was ordered specially for Colonel Gale, so it'll be nothing but the best. Enjoy."

O'Reilly gave him a mock salute as the doors closed, leaving Chu shaking his head and wondering, as he was whisked upwards.

———

The door outside the Strong's suite was now guarded by three agents. As he approached them they could be seen whispering to each other and nodding. When he reached the door the closest one looked at him with a smile of recognition.

Once inside, Chu could see that the Strongs' bedroom door was closed. He assumed they were in there but he really didn't know. He thought about going into his room when suddenly Nancy appeared exiting the kitchen dressed in an apron. His presence startled her and she gasped, holding her hands up to her mouth. He was about to apologize when she cut him off.

"Oh sir," she began almost breathless, "that was such a brave thing to do! We're all so grateful you saved the missus. God bless you. Bless you, praise the Lord!"

By this time Nancy was holding onto Chu's arm, almost supplicating herself to him. Chu didn't know how to respond, so he used an old cliche.

"Just doing my job, Nancy. And I'm really glad nothing happened to Mrs. Strong, too."

"And the pictures on the television - my goodness, its hard to believe you could do such a thing. A real miracle, that's what I say!"

"They have pictures on TV?" Chu asked, bewildered.

"Yes, somebody leaked the security camera video and now it's everywhere," explained the smooth voice of Robert Strong from behind them, "You're a real celebrity now."

"Oh, Reverend Strong, I was just praising God and this young man!" Nancy said, still clutching onto Chu's arm.

"Yes, thank you, Nancy. Your feelings are shared by a great many, including me."

She nodded, smiling widely as she slowly loosened her grip on Chu.

"Now is everything ready for the dinner? I understand Faith and her brother are still coming?" asked Strong.

"Yes sir, as far as I've heard."

"And my mother and the children?"

"Yes, them, too."

"Alright then, Nancy. I will leave it in your hands, of course. Were we planning on using serving staff tonight?"

"If we can get them cleared through security in time. They're being a lot more picky now - even made me take apart my groceries. If they don't make it in time, I'll stand in."

"That won't be necessary, I don't want you doing that. We don't need servers, do we Derrik?"

"I've got by without them up to now."

The response made Robert Strong laugh.

"That's the first time I've laughed today and it's the perfect response. We'll serve dinner to ourselves tonight, Nancy, if you will do us the kind honour of preparing it."

"My pleasure, sir. We have some very fine ingredients," she beamed, "Looks like dinner at seven."

And with that, Nancy bustled happily back to the kitchen.

"How is Mrs. Strong doing, sir?"

"You mean Doris?" Strong replied chuckling.

"Yes, Doris. How is she doing?"

"Very well indeed, thanks to you! She's looking forward to seeing the children more than ever now. And you know, I wasn't kidding about your being a celebrity. Just turn on the television and see."

Chu walked over and picked up the remote. Seconds later, a news banner lit up the top of the screen. It read: Assassination Attempt Thwarted. He switched around and found that all major channels were glued to the story.

"Wow," Chu contemplated, "so they have actual footage of the incident? I wonder if it's the same one they showed us at the debriefing."

"I'm not sure, but stop here. This is the one they've been playing."

It didn't take Chu more than a second to recognize the video.

"Yeah, that's it. I wonder who leaked it?"

"I'm sure there's a lot of people trying to figure that out. That's not all, either. Because your name is known, people have done searches and found your running videos. They've received a record number of hits – that's what you call it, isn't it? A hit? Anyway, Doris and I were just watching a segment on TV that said so."

"Gee, I hope this doesn't hurt you or your campaign in any way."

"On the contrary, my boy, on the contrary. You can't buy exposure like this. We are the focus of the nation for the next couple of days, and the more people who watch and see what we represent, the more who'll vote for us. I'm sure of that. And Brother Sherman is out there pumping away, telling anyone who will listen that he repeatedly warned the government of the danger we faced, and that only he had the foresight to get the FBI's top agent to protect us. Both statements have proven to be absolutely true."

Chu made as if to protest but Strong held up a hand to stop him.

"Now look, son, I would rather no attack happened at all, but given that it did, it's done nothing but good for the campaign. Now, I suggest you go into your room and get tidied up. Our guests are showing up in just over an hour. I think you'll like my mother and I'm sure the children will get a thrill out of meeting you!"

———

As soon as the children came into the room, Chu saw an immediate change in Doris Strong's demeanour, as if her spirit had suddenly been supercharged. He didn't get emotional very often, but watching her embrace the children made tears well up in his eyes. After several minutes of family hellos, during which time Chu stayed well in the background, he stepped forward and was introduced. In quick order Marcus and Angela had bodily dragged Chu to the computer and now had him cornered, calling up his running videos off the Net.

Faith and K.C. arrived minutes after Grandma Mary and the children. As soon as they entered the room, brother and sister could see their impatient younger cousins egging Chu to hurry up.

"Hey, I want to see them, too!" cried Faith, ignoring her hosts' welcomes and running to look over her cousins' shoulders.

"I'm in!" chimed K.C. tipping his hat to the elder Strongs as he moved quickly past them to join his sister.

"Well, for goodness sake!" said an exasperated Grandma Mary, "We might as well all watch together."

"Good suggestion, Mother," Strong said, turning to the corner and adding, "Derrik, just put it up to the big screen."

Chu looked confused, not knowing how to do it. He felt like his hands were twice their normal size as everyone watched in anticipation.

"Here, let me, if you want," offered Marcus.

"Yeah, sure. Please," Chu replied, taking his hands off the keyboard with relief.

Marcus proudly took over and in seconds a picture flashed up on the TV in the living room. Chu had never seen any of his videos on a screen that big.

There were five of them in all – complete with music and credits. He thought they'd get bored after the first but they wanted more. And they seemed to be enjoying it. K.C. led the way, hooting and hollering every time Chu or one of the other runners completed a trick, with Faith, Marcus and Angela contributing with gusto. Doris and Mary could be heard saying 'ooh" and "goodness" and "oh, my" a great many times. Robert was laughing loudly. Even Nancy came in and sneaked a look while the food cooked.

When they were finished, K.C. was the first to offer his reaction.

"That was the most awesome thing ever!" he proclaimed, "I wish we'd had somebody like you on the football team last year – we might have won State. Did you ever play?"

"No, K.C. I was too busy helping my grandpa run the karate studio after school. It would have been fun, though."

"Well, my boy. I think you are absolutely crazy doing what you do, but I think what you did for Doris was just wonderful. You're on my favourite person list," proclaimed Grandma Mary, getting serious.

"I second that!" piped in Angela, giving Chu an enthusiastic and unexpected hug. Everyone laughed and offered their own version of congratulations and gratitude at the same time. Chu was overwhelmed. He'd never experienced anything even remotely like this.

Robert Strong put his hand on Chu's shoulder and smiled, looking down at him.

"I want you to know how much I appreciate what you did. I feel we have been blessed by God to have been sent such a guardian angel."

Chu tried to reply but couldn't find the words to express what he was feeling – which was a jumble of happiness, pride and belonging.

———

The dinner went on for a full two hours and was enjoyed immensely by all. The company, which had kept up lively and loud conversation from appetizers to entrees, was taking a quiet break from its collective revelry. One of the main topics of discussion that had escalated to hilarity centred around the amount of food K.C. could eat. Grandma Mary had begun the commentary and soon everyone had picked up on it. K.C. had second, third and even fourth helpings of the dishes offered. He now sat with a satisfied smile on his face, hands clasped over his stomach, slouched back in his chair.

"Say, what's for dessert?" he asked, and was immediately answered by a chorus of groans and laughter.

Enjoying the attention K.C. played it up by pretending to be confused by all the furor.

A still laughing Chu got up and started gathering plates. He'd watched during the meal as others brought a continual stream of food from the kitchen. When he tried to help he was told to sit down, as he was a guest. Doris was just about to insist Chu desist when her husband gently held her by the elbow and shook his head slightly. Chu didn't notice the exchange and continued to gather dishes. When he had amassed an impressive stack he made his way carefully into the kitchen.

"Well, Nancy really out did herself this time," noted Strong, as Chu disappeared through the kitchen door, "It's too bad your father couldn't stay and enjoy it," he added as an aside to Faith and K.C..

"Yeah, but it meant there was more for us!" quipped K.C. Faith didn't react at all and seemed to be deep in her own thoughts.

"Well, Robert," said Grandma Mary, "I'm sure if he knew I was coming he would have thought up some excuse to leave, anyway. We always seem to get on each others nerves."

"That's not true, Mother. It's just that his belief is so strong he can't quite understand your more eclectic interpretation of God's word. I must say it challenges me sometimes."

While she considered herself a Christian, Mary Strong had long held the belief that all religions shared the same fundamental basis. She saw the world in greys while her son-in-law saw only black and white.

"Well, I guess I'll never understand how anybody can be so sure..." she replied.

"Dad says you'd know if God ever talked to you," interjected K.C., "He says God's voice makes you sure."

"Yes, well, I'm sure that helps," answered Grandma Mary doubtfully, "I guess we'll never know."

"Well Faith does. Right, Sis?"

Faith looked at her brother aghast.

"K.C.!" she burst out, "It's not the same thing!"

"What's this?" asked Robert Strong with real interest, "Faith, is this true?"

Faith stood up, quickly grabbing up some dirty dishes that remained on the table. Her face and ears were flushed.

"It's private," she said tersely, "I just don't want to talk about it - please Uncle!"

Without waiting for a response Faith turned and almost ran to the kitchen. She found Chu placing items into the dishwasher, oblivious to the angst that had been generated only a few feet away. He could see she was upset as he held out his arms to receive the dishes from her.

"Are you alright?" he asked instinctively, while putting the dishes on the counter, only to have the distraught girl throw herself into his arms. She hugged on tight, sobbing. He didn't know what to do, so held her gently, trying to provide some comfort.

"It's just so hard sometimes. I don't know if I can do it."

"What's so hard, Faith?" he asked as she pressed herself closer to him. "Please tell me if there's anything I can do."

She raised her face to him and he could see the anguish in her eyes. It drew him in like a magnet. She raised herself up closer to him, so close he could smell her hot breath. Her lips parted slightly as she inched closer.

"Faith, please," he pleaded as she pulled herself towards him yet again. She was beautiful and vulnerable but he knew it wasn't right. He took a small step back and nearly fell over doing so. It was right then that Doris Strong came through the kitchen door.

She could see at once what was going on but showed nothing of the kind. With a grace that Chu appreciated in the extreme, she moved toward her niece holding out her arms.

"You poor girl," she said sympathetically, as Faith obediently shifted to her aunt's embrace, "I had no idea you were so upset. Derrik, could you please take the cake and ice cream out? The children and K.C. can't wait any longer."

Derrik made a quick and grateful retreat from the kitchen, now his turn to be red-faced.

As the door swung closed, Doris held her niece by the shoulders, looked directly into her eyes and asked, "What on earth was that all about, Faith? What are you trying to do to that young man?"

"I don't know, Aunty Doris. I guess I'm just confused."

"Confused?"

"Oh, I don't know, I just don't know..." Faith responded as she buried her head into her aunt's shoulder, crying.

Doris Strong didn't say anything, but she wondered. She'd never known Faith to be confused about anything in her life.

8 - Loose Ends

Sherman Gale sped down the highway wearing night vision goggles. His lights were off to minimize the chance of being seen. He was dressed in military fatigues because it made him feel more like he was on a mission, operating under orders. For him, it was like going to the office. He felt a wave of relief as he finally reached the point where he could leave the highway and make his way the twenty miles up the rugged gravel road to the meeting place they had arranged.

Gale was not happy. He had been looking forward to talking with Strong, eating the excellent meal he knew Nancy would produce and seeing his children with their cousins. But it couldn't be helped. The call had come and it had to be dealt with. It was the one loose end that could be his undoing and he alone could wrap it up.

Fernandez had called, saying it had to be tonight. 'Tonight or never' were his exact words.

"Fernandez was always like that," Gale thought to himself. "Always on his terms or not at all."

But they went way back, since Nam, and he was one of the best - so Gale had used him, yet again.

"For the last time," Gale promised himself, "Tonight, will be the last time."

———

As Gale's truck came to an abrupt halt just outside the blazing mine entrance, he sensed something was wrong. He tore off his night vision goggles and turned the headlights on. There was the van as expected, sticking part way into the opening, driver's side door ajar.

He got out and waited for his vision to adjust. Through squinting eyes he could just make out the silhouette of a lone figure exiting the tunnel and hurrying towards him. This wasn't part of The Plan. Gale waited by the truck and was quickly joined by a wild eyed Fernandez.

"Bolton's dead! One of the Russians had a gun, for fuck's sake!"

"What? Didn't you make sure they were clean?"

"Of course we did, but the guy must have been a pro. Bolton was just gassing the first guy when the shithole let him have it point blank. Lucky I was ready with the M-16 or it might have been a different story!"

"But you're sure all three are dead? No mistakes this time?"

"No, no mistakes Colonel. They're all dead. You want to check for yourself?"

"Yeah, I do. Let's see what kind of mess you made."

They walked together past the van and into the yawning hole that half consumed it. The main cavern was further in than Gale remembered. As they approached the inner chamber it was Fernandez who broke the silence.

"You know, it wasn't my fault that FBI agent turned out to be fucking Spiderman. We thought we supplied those nuts with more than enough ordinance to get the job done."

"Well, it worked out all right in the end. Amazing coverage, and we're playing up that idiot's heroics. Gained more than four points in the polls since then. At least as much as I projected for Strong if he were the grieving widower."

Gale could smell the carnage before they reached the spot where it had taken place. When they got there Fernandez didn't have to explain what happened, Gale could see for himself. Blood was spattered everywhere. The three scientists lay dead in the middle of the floor. Bolton was slouched awkwardly over by a control panel.

"Did you have to blow his head off?" Gale asked pointing at one of the scientist's bodies.

"That was the guy who smoked Bolton. Him and me have worked together a long time, Colonel. I was really pissed off - I still am."

"I can appreciate that, Fernandez, but it makes identifying the guy a little tough, don't you think?"

Fernandez turned to face Sherman Gale, smiling widely at the Colonel's jest. He was still smiling as the first and then second bullet from Gale's pistol crashed through his forehead. Fernandez was dead before he hit the ground.

—

It had taken some time, but Gale had finished the job to his satisfaction.

He had driven the van into the tunnel and then sealed it shut for good with some C5 explosive he had brought with him. Nobody would be disturbing this grave any time soon.

As he drove away he said a silent prayer to the Lord to ask forgiveness. But this was war, and in war there had to be some casualties. He turned on the radio to help block out his doubts, but in the back of his mind the scientist with the gun nagged away at him. It just didn't figure. Each one of the Russian germ warfare experts had been checked out thoroughly before he brought them into the country. They'd been in isolation and cut off from the outside world for the entire three months since then. It was a mystery and would probably remain that way. And that's what bothered Sherman Gale the most. He hated mysteries.

9 - Down to Earth

"How many talk shows have you been on in the last week? Four? Maybe five? Helping this crazy fundamentalist son of a bitch get himself elected!"

Jenkins was red faced and shouting, already more than twenty minutes into his rant. Chu was sitting across the table from his ASAC with Hinks by his side. He could tell without looking that Hinks was enjoying every minute of the tongue lashing being administered. It was only when Jenkins shifted attention to him that Hinks started to squirm.

"And you thought this was OK? That the Bureau would like to see one of its agents performing tricks like a monkey with the fucking presidential candidate he's supposed to be protecting? What the hell were you thinking, Hinks? Were you thinking at all?"

Jenkins wasn't waiting for either man to respond. He had to blow off steam because a lot had built up as a result of the intense pressure being put on him.

"Do you realize I got pulled off my one damn week of vacation to come back and deal with this? My wife and fucking kids are still over in Hawaii waiting for me! Charlotte won't even answer my calls. HQ is crawling up the SAC's back, and he's kicking my ass hard! Jesus guys, why the hell did you go and do this to me?"

Jenkins sat exasperated, head in hands, deflated as a balloon that's spilt all its air.

"Sir, I really didn't think going on those shows would cause any trouble. I was there anyway and they all seemed to think it was a great idea. I guess I just got caught up with all the attention."

"And Hinks thought this was OK?"

"To be fair to Agent Hinks, sir, I never discussed it with him. In fact, I've hardly seen him in the last week."

Hinks looked pleased that some of the heat was being deflected from him. What Chu said was true. Unless they could help it, Chu and Hinks stayed clear of each other.

"Great. I have two agents down here who won't deal with each other. One is acting like he's a household pet and the other is doing God knows what!"

Hinks' aloof countenance noticeably shifted to rancour. Chu could tell because Hinks got his 'I smell something bad', pinched nose look on his face before responding.

"I've been working extensively with Tony Wheeler and with the Secret Service. I thought our job was to protect the Strongs and provide a visible FBI presence. With respect, I think we've been doing that, sir,"

"Well then, you won't mind answering the emails and calls I'm getting from just about everybody, including the Secretary of State and the Director of the FBI, asking me what the hell is going on!"

Hinks had no response to Jenkin's sarcasm other than to drop his eyes to the table and look sullen. Chu couldn't help but try again.

"Sir, I've been trying my best to make the Bureau look good. Letterman said I was the best thing to come out of the FBI in years..."

"Oh, yeah, I saw that one. Right after that statement, he made some quip about it beating J. Edgar Hoover coming out of the closet. Really classy, Chu. Everybody was so fucking impressed."

"Hey, I didn't ask for this assignment, remember? I was ordered to do it. If I'm fucking it up so badly why not remove me?"

"You don't think I've tried? Hell, I tried to stop it before they sent you down. I warned them that you cause nothing but problems."

"But I did save Mrs. Strong. You can't tell me you think that was a mistake, can you?"

Chu was starting to get pissed off. He hated to agree with Hinks but he thought they had done their job – at least he knew he had.

"Listen, you puke, don't use that tone with me – understand? If it were up to me, you'd be on your way to Irkutsk and I'd keep you there forever. However, for whatever reason, the 'powers that be' want you to stay. But they want you to stay in the background and be as inconspicuous as possible. Got it?"

"Yes, sir, no more talk shows."

"And you, Hinks, I need you to report to me by phone at least twice a day. I want to be directly involved in any decisions made regarding Mr. Chu here. Which means, Mr. Chu, that you are actually going to have to talk to Hinks every day. Is that asking too fucking much?"

Jenkins took their silence as indicating acquiescence, so continued on.

"Now, we gotta make this clear to everybody. I've asked for a meeting with the other agencies involved so we can establish a new protocol for sharing information. And I'm going to let them know exactly what you are and aren't allowed to do, Mr. Chu. Any issues with that?"

He looked at Chu in a way that suggested he had better not have any issues. Chu wanted to respond but decided the best thing to do right at that moment was just keep his mouth shut.

———

Chu was getting impatient. They were waiting for Tony Wheeler to begin the meeting, but he'd been hung up with some last minute details to do with Robert Strong's upcoming interview with Caroline Shapiro. Chu looked at his watch for the fifth time in the last five minutes and saw there was just over an hour before they had to leave. O'Reilly was there from the Secret Service with one of his people, as was the mystery woman from the CIA. When Wheeler came in, he was clearly agitated.

"Well, there's no way we can avoid using the main entrance. All the alternatives are just too hard to secure."

They were in Los Angeles, and what Wheeler was referring to was the TV studio where the interview with Shapiro was to take place.

"I don't know why he's doing it, anyway," he continued, "Neither of the other candidates will do an interview with her. She's just such a bitch."

Chu had always admired Shapiro's work. She refused to tell the people she brought onto her show what she was going to ask them, and she never shied away from the really difficult questions. She asked whatever questions she thought the public had a right to hear an answer to.

"I suppose I'll be travelling with the Strongs in the limo as usual?" asked Chu, ignoring Wheeler's last comment.

"Yes, as usual, Mr. Chu," answered Wheeler before adding, almost petulantly, "They wouldn't have it any other way."

Jenkins looked perturbed. He had called this meeting and he meant to get his agenda on the table front and centre.

"Look, I know you're all busy with this stuff," he began, "but we have to get some ground rules straight."

Having got their attention, the participants waited to hear what Jenkins was going to say.

"The Bureau will continue to make Mr. Chu available, but I have been directed to say that he cannot make any more public appearances with Reverend Strong, or any of the Strong family, for that matter. We acknowledge the valuable service that Agent Chu is providing, but feel it will be undermined if he gets too involved. There can be no exception to this."

Jenkins paused and looked around the table seeing if there were any objections or questions.

"That is going to put a bit of a damper on things, Jenkins," noted Wheeler, "Shapiro was hoping to get five minutes with our little hero."

"Well, that's not going to happen. I have been authorized to pull Mr. Chu if I have to."

"Anything else, Jenkins?" asked an annoyed Wheeler, "Don't get me wrong. I like the fact that Agent Chu stays in the background, or better yet, that you guys pull him, but the Reverend will certainly have another opinion on the matter."

"I appreciate that, but try to see it from our vantage point. We can't have a federal employee seen to be helping any of the candidates."

"We've been wondering about that ourselves," said O'Reilly, breaking into the conversation, "Our policies on the matter are very strict."

"Yeah, well so are ours. It's just somehow they seem to have gotten a little less defined in the past few weeks," Jenkins responded.

"What do you mean?"

"Well, we're on tricky ground here. If we interfere too much, the President will be accused of meddling by using Federal agencies to his advantage. If we don't do enough, he looks like he's not in control. All the brass are getting mixed messages too. It's no secret that Strong's campaign has been a royal pain in the ass to both 'official' party candidates. And let's face it. Sherman Gale and the Federal government aren't exactly 'buddy buddy'."

The unnamed raven-haired woman cracked a very slight smile and wrote something neatly in the small notebook she had placed in front of her. She gave them a slight nod indicating they should continue, when she realized they were all looking at her.

"Anything you'd like to add, Dr. Kunitz?" asked O'Reilly, locking eyes with her.

The woman, though asked a direct question, just stared at him without answering.

"Okay, I guess that means no," said the Secret Service man, raising his eyebrows and not trying to conceal his exasperation at all.

"So like I was saying," continued Jenkins, "we're doing a fine balancing act here, but I think the more we cooperate, the better off we'll all be."

"We'll try and do our part, Jenkins," Wheeler said flatly, "Just as long as you realize we'd rather be doing this on our own."

"Yeah, well that goes for us too, Mr. Wheeler," O'Reilly broke in, "But you know what they say, don't you?" asked the big man, with a wry smile.

"What's that?" responded Wheeler almost reluctantly.

"Well, to quote a famous song, 'You can't always get what you want'."

They all shared in a short laugh. Everyone, that is, except Dr. Audrey Kunitz. She had her head down, and was writing frantically.

"That was the Rolling Stones I was quoting Dr. Kunitz," O'Reilly said facetiously, "for the record of course," he added with feigned seriousness.

Kunitz seemed as if she didn't hear him and went back to staring impassively straight ahead.

———

The meeting broke up a few minutes later. The only thing that was agreed to by all was that Chu needed to be kept on a shorter leash and out of media view.

O'Reilly had a moment to touch base with the disheartened FBI agent on his way back to the Strong's room.

"Well, you got quite a ride from everybody. Not exactly what you were expecting I'll bet."

"No, it wasn't. I thought things were going really great. Shows you how much I know."

"For what it's worth, I think you're doing fine. Saving Mrs. Strong was certainly the right thing to do and I'm pretty certain nobody else could have pulled that off."

"You'd think I set it up, the way they're acting."

"Well, there are lots of things at play here. Wheeler wants to be the 'go to' guy for Strong, so you threaten him. Jenkins is scared of getting his ass kicked again, so he's kicking yours. Hinks hates your guts no matter what you do."

"And you, how about you? What does my being here do to you?"

"Hey, I told you up front that I didn't really want you here. I'm like Wheeler and would rather be running this thing on my own – as usual. Jenkins wasn't kidding in the meeting when he said things were confused. I've been involved in four campaigns and I've never seen anything like it. Nobody knows how to handle Reverend Strong's bid for the Presidency. Of course it would be a lot different if Sherman Gale wasn't so intricately involved."

"And what about that woman from the CIA - Dr. Kunitz?"

"Yeah, that's her name. What an asshole. I'm not even sure she can talk!"

They both laughed and Chu shook his head with disbelief that O'Reilly would share that thought with him.

"Yeah, she is something else, isn't she? But she's pretty nice looking," said Chu.

"Oh, so you like strong, dark and silent types?"

"No, it's not that. It's just that she seems to know a lot more than she lets on. I'm trying to figure out why she's here."

"Me too, Mr. Chu, me too. Let me know if you find anything out about her and I'll do the same for you, okay?"

"It's a deal Mr. O'Reilly," said Chu as they reached the room, "And now, if you'll excuse me, I've got to accompany the good reverend into the proverbial lion's den."

10 - It's My Dime

Chu stood beside Doris Strong as they watched and waited for the interview to begin. In less than one minute her husband was going to do something no presidential candidate had done in the past twenty years – face an aggressive interviewer with no control over what would be discussed or how far it would go. Strong looked his usual relaxed self as they fussed with his makeup and had him do sound checks. His wife looked relaxed as well but the force with which she was clutching Chu's arm told him a different story.

Shapiro almost seemed to be ignoring her guest as she perused a raft of papers that a staffer had handed her almost five minutes earlier. She looked younger to Chu than she did on television, with softer features and a more feminine air. But when the call came indicating they had ten seconds before going live, the harder, chiseled face he had become accustomed to appeared before his eyes.

"Hello, *America*," Shapiro began with the usual catch phrase she employed at the opening of her broadcasts. She paused and let the studio audience's applause subside before introducing her guest. "My name is Caroline Shapiro and you're watching *It's My Dime*. Today we are truly honoured to welcome Independent candidate Reverend Robert Strong to our show. First off, Reverend Strong, I would like to congratulate you for coming here today. You must know that our invitations to the other candidates to come say hello and have a little chat with me have been declined. How do you explain that?"

"Well, Ms. Shapiro, I don't know if I can explain it. I have found that the campaign trail is so hectic, it's hard to fit in everything you want. Maybe they just don't have the time."

"Always the gentleman. But come now, Reverend, do you really think that's the reason?"

"Like I said, I really don't know. Why do *you* think they won't come?"

A member of the audience screamed out something about them being chicken. Shapiro heard this and picked up the theme immediately.

"Someone out there thinks it's because they're afraid."

"Well, I don't know about that. While I don't know either of them very well, I doubt it's because they're afraid. I would guess it's because they both have, how can I put it, 'no fly zones' that they wouldn't want to have to deal with in an uncontrolled environment like this."

"Yeah, I think you nailed it, which begs the question – why are you here?"

"Well, Ms. Shapiro, you have a large audience and I'm trying to get a message across to as many people as will listen. I want people to see that our campaign has nothing to hide."

"Before we go on here, can we please drop the Ms. Shapiro tag? Sounds like you're talking to my mother."

"Certainly, if you will call me Robert."

"It's a deal, Robert. But getting back to my question, why did you really decide to come on the show?"

"Sorry, Caroline, I did think I answered that already, but let me try again. I guess it's no secret that we're running behind the Democratic incumbent. If things don't change, it doesn't look like we'll succeed in making it to the Oval Office. Simply put, I need as many votes as I can get, and your show puts us in front of folks who normally wouldn't give us the time of day. Does that answer it a little more to your satisfaction?"

"Yes, it does, but it raises a point I did want to discuss with you. As you admitted, you're running behind right now. Does that concern you?"

"From what I remember about the last polls I saw, and I'd like to point out that they're changing every day, we're running a solid second. That's a lot better than in 2016 when we were a distant third. Of course, I'd like to see us in a stronger position, and our campaign is striving hard to achieve that."

"Alright, does that striving include the negative campaign commercials that aired earlier this week?"

"I'm glad you brought that up, Caroline. First, I'd like to go on record as saying I was very disappointed with the one ad that attacked the President and his family situation. As soon as it came to my attention, I had it pulled. Second, if you look at our ads, they pale in comparison to my opponents' commercials attacking us. My family, my faith and my patriotism have all been maligned and misrepresented by both the Republicans and Democrats. While I admit that some of our ads do warrant classification as 'negative campaigning', they are based on facts and not fiction, like many of the commercials that have been aired against us."

"So, Robert, you're bitter about the attack ads that have been used against you?"

"Look, Caroline, I try to be a good Christian and turn the other cheek, but when they deal with my family and religion I must admit it is very difficult."

"Many of the ads running right now question your experience, or rather lack of experience, in the political arena. Now this is based on fact and not fiction. How do you respond to that?"

"This is a matter that we have had to deal with many times. I'm sure you'll recall the last debate where we had a tag team effort going on between the Republican and Democratic candidates as they slammed my lack of experience. I admit I have no experience in Washington. No experience accepting donations from special interest groups, lobbyists and even foreign governments. No experience exploiting interns, supporting partisan bills or blocking progressive legislation. No experience prostituting myself to corporate America, big banks and big money..."

"Okay, okay Robert. We get the picture. But could you climb off your soapbox for a second and address this very real concern that your inexperience might put the United States at even more of a disadvantage than we currently find ourselves in on the world stage?"

Strong paused a moment, a look of concern on his face, apparently deciding how to tackle the challenge Shapiro had laid down.

"Sorry, Caroline, I guess I did get a little carried away with my own rhetoric, but I've had to deal with this question over and over in the past few years and I fear I grow weary at answering it. I suppose this is why the other candidates don't want to come on your show."

Strong paused again, actually mugging at the camera. The response had the desired effect, as Shapiro and the audience erupted in laughter.

"But seriously," Strong continued before the laughter died away, "I feel that what America needs now is more of a patriot than a politician. George Washington didn't have much experience in politics but he seemed to do just fine. I don't believe that leadership can only be learned by sitting in a state or national legislature. I do believe all of these professional politicians are overrated. And if I can climb back onto my soapbox for just a minute, I'd like to assure all Americans that in our country's darkest hours I will not falter. When all others see hope as lost, my belief will see me to the light. Praise Jesus!"

"So now you've turned your soapbox into a pulpit," Shapiro said, turning to look straight at the camera and playing it up with a weird face. Laughter broke out anew. "But since we're there already, how can you, as a devote and born-again Christian, represent the interests of all Americans? Didn't we go through separation of church and state hundreds of years ago? Didn't the Founding Fathers specifically and intentionally leave reference to religion *out* of the Constitution?"

For the first time during the interview, Strong looked uncomfortable. The rapid-fire questions had him struggling to make a response.

"But before you deal with those issues, we have to take a commercial break to hear from our sponsors. Now make sure you stay with us when we come back. You're not going to want to miss how my special guest Reverend Robert Strong is going to respond."

As the red light on the camera went off, someone shouted, 'Two minutes!' from offstage. Shapiro jumped from her chair and moved quickly towards her dressing room, a harried assistant carrying a clip board following closely in tow.

Strong remained seated, trying desperately to collect his thoughts. He glanced over to where his wife was standing, just off stage behind the curtains. He couldn't help smiling at the worried look on her face. She noticed him looking towards her and smiled back, adding a weak 'thumbs up'.

Tabloids and talk show hosts had poked fun at and questioned the Strongs' relationship heavily in the past year. It just looked too perfect – and ever so convenient. But Chu had seen it for himself and he could see it now – they were still truly in love.

Weak as it was, his wife's attempt at encouragement rallied Strong. By the time Caroline Shapiro had plopped back into her chair, just in the nick of time, he had renewed his resolve and his confident look. The camera came on and Shapiro immediately launched into her opening.

"In case you're just joining us I have the great privilege to be interviewing Reverend Robert Strong, Independent candidate for the President of the United States. For those of you coming back after our first round - I mean, of course, segment," she paused and waited for the laughter to die down, "just let me refresh you with where we were. If I recall, it was 1. How do you, a evangelical Christian, represent all Americans? 2. The question of the separation of Church and State, and 3. Founding Fathers – did they get it wrong?"

Strong smiled and even chuckled along with the audience, waiting patiently for quiet so he could respond. He had to admire the way Shapiro worked. She was a true professional.

"Alright, first off, Number One: How can I represent the interests of all Americans, because I'm a Christian? Well to begin, I have always preached and practiced religious tolerance. Just because I'm a Christian doesn't mean I don't support freedom of religion. My wife and I have worked with agencies all over the world, some based on a religious order, some not. I think to suggest that a Christian cannot represent the interests of other faiths, and here I mean not inhibiting the practice of their religion, is absurd.

"Now I also want to point out a fact here that is, of course, overlooked by the media and public in general. Although we talk about a cultural mosaic in America - and certainly we're not going to suggest that is wrong - when Americans are asked the question of what religion they practice, almost eighty percent of them identify themselves as Christian. Now, that's a fact. And where I come from, eighty percent is a mighty big majority. And I can only hope that each and every one of them will vote for me."

Strong paused a gave Shapiro a big smile. She hadn't expected this kind of energy from Strong and was noticeably taken aback. Sporadic clapping around the audience looked for company, and before it could die out, Strong began talking again, dealing with the second question.

"Now the notion of the separation of Church and State is well known to me and I'm sure to many people in your audience. Just because we want to put a reference to God and Christ in the Constitution doesn't mean we want to create a theocracy. Or, put more plainly, we don't want the church running the government. What it does mean is we want to recognize the reality that the vast majority of Americans at the time of the penning of the Constitution were Christians and that today that situation still exists. And *we* believe it should stay like that into the future. We also believe as we go into the future there is a very real threat that other nations and religions, not as enlightened as us, may undermine the Christian foundation that has made America great. We want to maintain the core belief of Americans in Jesus, and recognize this belief that has helped to make these United States strong."

"Time out, Robert. Time out," the hostess motioned, creating a T with her hands, "So what I hear you saying is that the Founding Fathers got it wrong, and now, more than two hundred years later, we should radically change it?"

"The wording we're proposing was actually in the penultimate draft of the Constitution. There was a great deal of debate then and shortly afterward about excluding the specific reference to God and Christ in the document."

"Debate that was undertaken and settled," retorted Shapiro, "I think I'll stick with their decision and trust they got it right."

"Well, Caroline, you asked me if I thought the Founding Fathers got it wrong and I want to tell you and your audience that I really don't think they did. They got it right – for their time. When the Constitution was written there was a lot of infighting within Christian sects and none of them wanted to see the establishment of a National religion or the super-ordinance of one of them over the others. That, and the inclusion of some very erudite idealists in the group, led to the omission of the words we're hoping to reinsert.

"But the Founding Fathers were very clever and they *did* get it right, because they realized the Constitution had to change over time and built provision in it for amendment. Since it was signed off in 1791, the Constitution of the United States of America has been amended twenty-seven times. There have been several attempts to add a reference to Christianity as an amendment – the last one as recently as the 1950's.

"And, Caroline, you have to realize that in 1791 there were no Islamic nations in the world like there are today, there was no Zionist Israel, no atheistic China. Did you know that today Christianity is discouraged or outlawed throughout Asia and Africa? In some countries, finding Jesus in your heart is punishable by death. In Europe, once a bastion of Christianity, churches everywhere are being converted into mosques or being torn down. While we preach religious tolerance and freedom, and will accept no less, we are firm that America needs to show the world that it is a place where Christians can grow and prosper. A place they will always belong. *Our* chosen land, as it were."

Shapiro's eyes were open wide in wonder.

"Wow, you're good, Robert. But let's move on from this history lesson. What do you think of gays?"

"What do you mean, what do I think of them?"

"You know, are they going to burn in hell? Should they be allowed in the military? Stuff like that."

"First off, I don't think they're going to burn in hell just because they're gay. We have lots of homosexual members in churches across America and I've personally worked with some very spiritually committed gay people in my own community. The whole question of sexual orientation is a very difficult one to prescribe and I believe it is the private business of individuals. As I've said over and over, we believe in equal civil rights for all."

"What about gay marriage?"

"Well, on gay marriage we take a bit of a hard line. Civil union is one thing, and our platform supports that, but we believe that marriage in a church before God is a holy bond between a man and a woman, the main purpose of which is to bear children. It may be corny and old fashioned, but that's that."

"Abortion."

"Do we have to?"

"I'm afraid it goes with the territory, Robert."

"Okay, here goes. It's one of those things that gets down to a 'yes' or a 'no' and those are always so difficult because there are so many mitigating circumstances."

"I think this is the first waffling we've heard from you!"

"No, please, hear me out. Like I said, it is difficult, but I have to go with 'no'. My belief is that life starts at conception, so there's no way around the need to protect that life. I know that this position is going to affect many people's assessment of me and the campaign, but I do want to be clear – and not waffle like you say so many others do in answering the same question."

"What about a woman's right to choose?"

"And, as always, the counter argument about the rights of the unborn. Like I said, these 'yes' or 'no' questions can't be settled to everyone's satisfaction. Sometimes consensus just isn't possible. Unfortunate, but true."

"Robert, I have just a few more questions for you and then we'll let you get back to the campaign trail. But before that, let's take a quick break and we'll see you on the other side."

The red light went out, the two minute warning was given, but this time Caroline Shapiro remained in her seat and stared at Strong hard.

"Do you really believe that – right at the time of conception?" she asked.

"I'm not sure when it happens or how it works, but it just seems to me that even if there's a chance a soul is there we have to protect it."

She looked hurt, like the words pierced her insides. And he knew instantly. He just felt it.

"God is forgiving, Caroline. Infinitely there, and infinitely forgiving."

She opened her eyes wide to keep the tears from flowing. Noticing it, Strong handed her a tissue from the box that sat beside them, as they waited in silence for the red light to come back on.

"Hello. I'm talking with Reverend Robert Strong, Independent presidential candidate, in case you've just tuned in. Robert, I'd like to shift gears now and talk about your association with Sherman Gale and the Coalition of Christians movement. How did you come to know Colonel Gale?"

"As a lot of folks know, Sherman married my late sister Patricia Anne. We became close over the years, and after her death Sherman convinced me that we needed to go to the White House if we really wanted to make a difference."

"I've heard him in interviews saying he promised your sister that he'd make you the first Christian President of the United States."

"Well, Brother Sherman does like a flair for the dramatic. I must admit, I feel my sister's presence every day and know that it would fulfill a dream she had, to make America a true Christian nation."

"So how big an influence would Colonel Gale have on you and your Presidency, assuming you win?"

"Of course, I would plan to have Sherman as part of my executive staff. In what exact capacity I'm not sure, but Secretary of Defense would of course be one of the logical choices."

"So you don't think you'll be overly influenced by him and his agenda to bolster the military?"

"Brother Sherman is my main supporter and strategic adviser, but I don't think it's fair to say he has an agenda. First and foremost, he has taken Christ into his heart and puts his faith before any personal ambitions he might have. He is a true patriot and a great American."

"So the veiled warnings from the government that he poses a danger to our country?"

"Consider the source, Caroline. Just consider the source."

"So, you're saying that the warnings are politically motivated?"

"The timing would suggest that, wouldn't it?"

"I must say, people, that what Robert's saying is proven to a degree by the fact that our request to have FBI Agent Chu appear on the program was turned down. The reason we were given, Robert, was security, but I have it on good authority that it was the White House getting their shirt in a knot about a federal agent helping to get you publicity."

"Well, it wouldn't surprise me at all, Caroline. We've had nothing but harassment from the government since we began the campaign, although I do want to thank the Secret Service and FBI Agent Chu for the excellent work they've done for us. I'll forever be in the debt of Mr. Chu and I must say, he's become like one of the family."

"Well, we'll close off today with the video clip of Agent Chu saving your wife from the bomber, but before we go there I'd like to thank you so much for being here today. It took real courage to come out here unprepared, and I applaud you for it. Now, you other two candidates, I know you're watching. Don't be such chickens. Come and have a chat with me, Caroline Shapiro, on *It's My Dime*. And now, here comes the exciting part..."

Strong looked relieved when the camera light went out. After saying his goodbyes to Shapiro and the show's crew he made his way off stage and to a huge hug from his wife.

Chu looked at Robert Strong with his wife and was filled with admiration for the man. Even though he couldn't agree with everything that Strong stood for, he couldn't help thinking to himself that he really would make a good President.

11 - Morning Constitutional

The alarm jarred him from a deep sleep. He hated the noisy things, usually finding them unnecessary, but to get up at this ungodly hour, he needed all the help he could get.

Chu thought about his grandfather as he sat bolt upright in bed. During his teenage years, the old man had continually pressed him into a regime of morning exercises or, as he used to call it, the 'morning constitutional'. He had to smile at the thought of his grandpa trying to pronounce the English phrase in his thick Japanese accent. Truly worthy of inclusion on a TV sitcom.

Like it or not, getting the basic level of exercise meant getting up well before five. That was the only part of the day he could call his own – otherwise he was with the Strongs, swept up by their schedule, which was unbelievably frantic. Breakfast was in the Strong's suite at 6:30 sharp. Sometimes ten people would show up to eat. The morning meal was used as a way for the campaign team to touch base before the day got going, and was not to be missed. At seven there was the security meeting with Wheeler, O'Reilly and the rest. Chu used this meeting to connect with Hinks, who was always there, living up to the agreement he made with Jenkins. If he didn't show, Chu knew Hinks would immediately inform his superiors. By eight he was in the limo with the Strongs most mornings, beginning a day that would last at least fifteen hours.

But now, this was the time that was his, between when he begrudgingly gave into the alarm and got up, until six thirty and breakfast with Nancy's pancakes. He had to admit to himself that he did look forward to those luscious, ever-present pancakes. He didn't look forward to the run because he hated running in the morning. Especially in the early morning when his body just wanted to sleep. Getting up and working out was one thing, but running was a whole other matter.

Today they were in Portland, near the river, so he had already picked out a promising route using a map. It was still dark when he began in the fog and drizzle. He plodded along slowly at first, hearing only the sound of his own feet hitting the pavement. It produced a kind of hypnotic effect for him and soon his mind wandered as his body came alive.

Suddenly he was aware of another jogger's footsteps behind him. The sound was getting closer as he listened, letting him know that the person was gaining on him. Chu picked up his pace, automatically assuming one that would distance himself from the other guy. He figured it was about time that he picked up the pace anyway.

Instead of hearing the footsteps fade away, the sound of feet hitting the ground behind him got louder and closer. Chu picked up the pace again, not nearly full speed, but enough to dust off most runners. He couldn't help getting in these little races, mainly a product of his own imagination, and had done this dozens of times. Somehow he just didn't like being passed by anyone. To his surprise the footsteps of the other runner kept pace. Not gaining, but if they were falling back it was only ever so slightly. This went on for almost five minutes, the other jogger seeming to just hang on. Then, with a sudden burst of energy the footsteps increased their pace, quickly closing the gap that separated them. Chu almost laughed out loud when he took off at competition speed. A speed he could run at for almost half an hour before having to change pace. He'd never done it this early in the morning and somehow it didn't come with the feeling of exhilaration that he usually got when running flat out. From behind him he heard the other runner give up, almost coming to a halt.

"Agent Chu, wait! Please wait," a small, exhausted voice came from behind, "Please."

He stopped in his tracks and turned to see a woman, almost doubled over clutching her sides. As she slowly moved towards him trying to catch her breath, he could see it was the silent CIA woman, Dr. Kunitz.

"Dr. Kunitz?" Chu asked knowing the answer but still sounding unsure.

"Yes, it's me," she confirmed, still out of breath and barely able to choke her words out. She held up her index finger, signaling for him to wait while she caught her breath. After a minute or two she was able to talk again, though still with heavy breathing.

"Say, you don't kid around, do you? I'm considered a pretty good runner but I feel like I'm going to barf up a lung right now."

Chu was surprised by several things. The first was that Kunitz had followed him, obviously with the idea of talking to him; the second was that she spoke so normally, he'd expected she would use more formal language, maybe even have a British accent; and the third, that her voice was so small and shrill it was almost comical.

She looked up at him, waiting for a reply as his surprise waned and words came back into his mind.

"Yeah, uh, sorry. I guess I was trying to dust you off. I didn't realize it was you."

"I've been wanting to talk with you alone for a couple of days but the schedule you're on just doesn't make it possible. So I thought I'd catch you during your morning jog. I hope you don't mind."

"Not at all. But why do you want to talk with me? And why in secret?"

Without answering she motioned for them to continue running, which he did. Only after they had gone a few feet did she continue to talk.

"Hope you don't mind going this speed."

"It'll be fine. So what's up?"

"I've been watching you since you came on board, and I'm going to make a leap of faith here and hope you can be trusted."

"Okay. Me, trusted, as opposed to...?"

"Everybody. I haven't been able to trust anybody for quite a while. We've been compromised."

"The CIA?"

"No, everybody. The CIA, the Secret Service, the FBI..."

"Hold on, you're saying the Bureau is compromised?"

"Probably the worst," she said with real disdain.

"Look, I'm having a hard time believing this. And if you're right, why should I trust you? You could be part of the problem, if there really is one."

"I don't blame you for being cynical. I know I would be. Some squeaky-voiced little bitch coming to you with a story that's hard to swallow."

Chu had to smile. At least she knew how weird her voice sounded and how others on the team perceived her. She noticed him smiling, taking it as a good sign, and went on.

"But I'm telling the truth, and I'm going to give you a couple of pieces of information that I hope will prove it to you."

Chu said nothing in response and waited for her to continue as they ran.

"Well, first, let me ask you a question. I know you don't like Agent Hinks, but do you trust him?"

The question took Chu by surprise. He hated the guy and had already expressed his own doubts about Hinks to Jenkins. He struggled, figuring out how much he should let this woman know.

"That's a very interesting question, Dr. Kunitz. I'm not sure how I should answer it."

"If you want this conversation to go on, I would suggest you answer it honestly, Mr. Chu."

Chu decided to make his own leap of faith and tell her the truth. Even if she wasn't on the up and up, he couldn't see how letting her know his opinion about Hinks would damage anything.

"No, I don't trust him. But all I have to support that is gut feeling. Nothing tangible."

"What would you say if I told you we have very good intelligence that Hinks was involved in the death of your Agent Petersen?"

Chu stopped running and turned to look at her, horrified.

"But they were friends...Hinks was so upset."

"Let's keep running Mr. Chu, in case someone is following us."

Chu started his feet moving again with difficulty. He was having a hard time assimilating this new information. He'd thought a lot of bad stuff about Hinks but this was over the top.

"We have eye witness reports placing Hinks with Petersen just minutes before he went missing. You know, you're not the only agency with a presence at The Ranch. We've been watching its operation pretty closely for more than five years."

She paused, waiting for him to mull over her words before adding corroborating information.

"Hinks was in the Marines and served as a Lieutenant in a Special Ops unit commanded by, you guessed it, Colonel Sherman Gale. We have also confirmed that he is a born-again Christian, although it is not on record at the FBI.

"Agent Chu, I know for a fact that Sherman Gale is bad news and is planning something big. Something very bad. A few days ago I was given a message to translate, sent by one of the Russian scientists Gale smuggled in. Since then I've been gathering intelligence on a name mentioned in the transmission, the name of Fernandez. And I think I've come up with something. But the problem is, I don't know where I can take it. I'm not sure who to trust. The security of our country is at stake – maybe even the security of the entire world. I have to leave this morning to see if I can confirm what I think and if I do confirm it, I'm going to need help. I was hoping I could at least count on some from you."

They were getting close to the end of their run. They could see the lights of the hotel looming up out of the fog a few blocks away.

"But why me? Why do you trust me, and why should I trust you?"

"In this game, Mr. Chu, it's really more a matter of who you think is lying to you least – not who you trust. Anyway, you think about it and I'll be in touch somehow in the next couple of days. Look for me."

And with that she abruptly swung off the the right and up a different street, leaving Chu to jog on his own. His mind was numb. Thinking hard at this time of morning was even worse than exercising hard.

———

The pancakes at breakfast looked the same as they always did, but somehow they didn't taste as good. Chu was severely disturbed by what Kunitz had told him. He usually kept pretty quiet during the meal, but today he could only be described as withdrawn. Doris noticed his morose demeanor and made it her business to find out why.

"Derrik, you seem unusually quiet today. Is there anything wrong?"

He hesitated before answering, manufacturing a response in his mind.

"I just think I'm getting a little tired. I'm not used to keeping the kind of schedule that you are. I don't know how you do it."

At least that much was true. He marveled at the way both of them kept it up, day after day.

"But I see you're pretty down. Do you think getting up so early to go for a run every day has something to do with it?"

"It might, I'm not sure. This morning's jog was extra tough for sure."

Again, not a lie but not the truth either. He hated not being able to confide in Strong's wife, and suspected she could tell he wasn't telling her everything.

She looked at him as if she wanted to know more, to push to find out why he was so down. But she decided to respect his privacy and let it be. She didn't want to make it harder on him than it already was. Both she and her husband were becoming quite attached to Chu and he had come to admire and respect them in turn. No matter what he'd heard during the morning run, he found it hard to believe the Strongs could be involved in something that threatened the country and he hoped with all his heart that it wasn't true.

———

Going into the morning briefing was one of the hardest things Chu had ever had to do. They were all there waiting, everyone except Dr. Kunitz. Chu noticed immediately that she was missing. Hinks nodded to him as he took the seat to his right. They had actually been getting along tolerably well over the past week. To think the man sitting beside was involved in the murder of a fellow agent made Chu sick. But what if Kunitz wasn't telling the truth? Wasn't it the kind of thing you'd make someone believe if you wanted to cause trouble? Chu wasn't sure who to trust anymore. He wasn't even sure if he was working for the good guys.

The meeting started slowly. Wheeler began by laying out the week's schedule, which included a two day strategy session on Sherman Gale's super yacht, Victory. When Wheeler said the name, everyone made noises like the name meant something to them. Unknown to Chu was that Gale's ship was one of the largest and most lavishly outfitted private yachts in the world.

Chu wasn't listening very hard. All he could think about was Hinks sitting beside him. One moment he was sure the guy was guilty, the next he wasn't sure at all. Chu wondered if it was just his intense dislike of Hinks that made it easy to believe what Kunitz had told him. Or was it really true? All he did know, was that he couldn't show anything. He was caught in a wait-and-see game. The kind of game he had always hated. The kind of game that he almost always lost.

Suddenly he was aware that Wheeler was addressing him.

"Agent Chu, did you hear me? I was just saying that the session aboard Victory will be a closed affair, so you'll be free for a couple of days to do whatever you want – or whatever it is you do when you're not babysitting."

"Pardon me, I'm sorry, Wheeler. What was that again?" Chu stammered. While he'd groused about having no time of his own, the thought of not being around to ensure the Strongs were safe, very much disturbed him. He wondered at himself. Was it for them or himself that he was concerned? He'd felt pretty much like one of their family since he'd met them almost three weeks ago, and to be cut out now seemed weird.

"Well, we've been informed that no federal agent, including yourself, is to accompany the Strongs aboard Victory. It's anchored off the Grand Caymans right now, so outside of US jurisdiction anyway."

"Just wait a minute, Wheeler," piped in O'Reilly, "You're telling me that Gale won't even let the Secret Service provide security on board? I'm going to have to run this up the ladder."

"Well, do what you have to do, Mr. O'Reilly. But I have my orders. I don't always agree with them, but I sure as hell follow them - to a tee."

"I understand, Wheeler. It's just taken me by surprise, that's all. I didn't mean anything personal, but I am going to have to check this out. I've never run into anything like this before. Everything about this assignment is different to my experience on other campaigns."

Next O'Reilly gave his update, but seemed distracted and distant. Chu could tell he just wanted to get out of the meeting and touch base with his brass regarding the Victory situation.

The meeting went on until quarter to eight. Chu dreaded its breakup because it meant he would have to deal with Hinks one on one, briefing him on what had happened in the past twenty-four hours. Doing it without showing his disdain, or worse, was going to be almost impossible. But he knew that to give something away to Hinks at this point was the stupidest thing he could do, that the best thing was to watch and wait.

"So anything of interest happen in the last day?" Hinks asked, almost bored.

"No, not especially. There was another protest going into yesterday evening's event that got pretty ugly. The Strongs discussed the death threat from the far-right religious group that Wheeler mentioned this morning. Jenkins might be interested in knowing that neither of the Strongs mentioned the strategy session aboard Gale's yacht. Something tells me they didn't know about it. At least as of last night."

"That *is* kind of interesting," remarked Hinks, not seeming to be interested at all, "But I'm not reporting to Jenkins anymore. Forbes has taken over for him."

"Forbes has been promoted to A/SAC? What the hell happened to Jenkins?"

"Seems he was the victim of a hit-and-run. They thought he might not make it at first but he's over the worst now. Be out of commission for at least a few months with a badly broken leg and a fractured skull. At least he'll have some quality time with that little family he's always going on about."

Hinks was pleased and couldn't hide it, even though he tried. Alicia Forbes and he had been partners in the past and they always supported each other when they could. Chu took one look at Hink's smug face and couldn't help himself. He knew he shouldn't but it just came out.

"Speaking of little families, how's Petersen's wife and kids doing?"

"Petersen's family? How should I know?"

"Well, I thought you guys worked together and were friends."

"We worked together but I wouldn't say we were friends. Besides, why do you care all of a sudden? I thought you and Petersen shared a mutual dislike for each other."

Chu struggled to find a valid reason for his concern. Hinks watched him closely as the wheels spun round in Chu's head.

"Oh, I don't know. I guess I still feel bad about the crack a while ago about Petersen not getting out. Anderson still hasn't forgiven me."

"Well, I suggest you just try and forget about it. I have. In this business there's going to be some risk. You could have been killed the other day yourself. It comes with what we do for a living."

"Yeah, I guess you're right Hinks. Thanks."

And with that Chu got up from the table, leaving Hinks to sit by himself. Chu could see the pinched look back on Hink's face and felt like an idiot. Why had he gone there? Why couldn't he just play it cool? He hoped he hadn't done too much damage.

As he exited the room, shoulders drooped, he was met by O'Reilly waiting just outside the door.

"Say, Chu, we need to talk."

"Sorry, O'Reilly, but the limo leaves..."

O'Reilly held up his large hand to stop Chu's words.

"I'm aware of that, but this is important. Really important."

"Okay. Where do you want to go?"

"Let's take a quick stroll around the block. You'll be back in ten minutes, tops."

The two men made their way in silence to the lobby and out the front entrance of the hotel. Chu could just tell O'Reilly was upset. It seemed to him that today, everyone was on edge.

They got outside and had walked about two hundred feet when O'Reilly almost exploded.

"What the fuck is going on? I thought you were a straight up guy – a guy I could trust. I've leveled with you since the beginning and now you fucking stab me in the back! I thought we had an understanding..."

"Hey, wait right there. What are you going on about?"

"Oh, please, don't give me that shit. You were seen coming back from your morning jog with a woman that fits Audrey Kunitz's description. Then she takes off without a word. I have no idea what the fuck is going on. And we agreed to share any information we got on her – or don't you remember? I have fucking had it with her and you and Wheeler and all the others! I used to know what my job was, but now I don't have a clue!"

Chu didn't know what to do. O'Reilly was right to be pissed off. They had made an agreement. But who was he to trust? He'd already made one big mistake this morning and he didn't want to make another. He looked O'Reilly in the eyes and could see the real frustration there. A guy trying to do his job, playing on the up and up and getting nothing except being jerked around. Chu swallowed hard and made up his mind to tell him almost everything he knew, which admittedly wasn't much.

"Okay O'Reilly, I hear what you're saying, but the main thing Kunitz did tell me was not to trust anybody. She told me that all of our agencies have been compromised – hers, mine, yours and God knows what else. I don't know if she's telling the truth or just trying to muddy the waters. She also told me something that the Bureau is already aware of, that Sherman Gale is about to try and do something, something really bad, to influence the election. She said it was not just a threat to the US but to the whole world."

"The Secret Service compromised," repeated O'Reilly, trying to wrap his head around it.

"Yeah, and all the others as well. At least that's what she said."

"Anything else?"

"Only that she was going to try and corroborate some information she'd just received and that she would be in touch with me again in the next few days."

"You know, that woman has been here for almost two weeks and she hasn't said more than three words at a time to me. Why the hell did she go to you?"

"I don't know O'Reilly, except that if she is a double agent she knows what an idiot I am and that I'd likely pass the bad information along."

O'Reilly's dark countenance lifted a little and he almost smiled.

"Well, of course it's true, you are an idiot."

"Thanks."

"But seriously, I know these are just words, but you can trust me Chu – and I sure hope I can trust you. For what it's worth, I think that bitch Kunitz is right. I think Gale and his gang have people everywhere and it's really starting to disrupt the chain of command. I told you and the others last week that I'm getting mixed messages all over the place. When I reported in just now that we were being excluded from accompanying the Strongs aboard Victory, my boss didn't think it was worthwhile to escalate the issue. He just took the information and thanked me very much. No rancor, no indignation, nothing."

"Did you hear Jenkins was hit by a car and is out of commission? He's lucky he's not dead."

O'Reilly looked surprised.

"And his replacement?"

"One Alicia Forbes. Not one of my biggest fans."

"Man, that's too bad. Jenkins was a little jumpy but he seemed pretty level."

"I think so, too, but who knows."

"Yeah, its very fucking confusing."

"And scary, Mr. O'Reilly. Very scary."

12 - Victory

She floated like a gleaming white island, towering up from the surrounding turquoise-blue waters. Her name, written boldly in 24 karat gold, was splashed conspicuously across the stern in ten foot high letters - VICTORY. Seven stories high and more than five hundred feet long, she boasted luxury accommodation for fifty, not including sleeping quarters for the crew of twenty-five.

Victory was a one-of-a-kind floating castle. A jewel of modern technology, complete with two submarines, eight tenders, anti missile-launchers, bulletproof glass, armor plating and a laser defense system that, when deployed, detected and disabled all recording devices within a radius of half a mile. She'd cost Sherman Gale more than two billion dollars, and when delivered in late 2014 was easily the best equipped, best defended privately owned vessel in the world.

Her beauty and unparalleled elegance belied the fact of how hard the ship had been to build. Many disappointments and setbacks were encountered during the ship's design and construction, but the worst was the failure to equip her with a nuclear power plant. Gale had thought it was a done deal - after a great deal of hard work and a special deal with the US Navy - but a last minute veto by the White House had ruined it. The result of the veto meant that work on Victory halted in the German shipyard for six months while his team of naval architects and engineers madly redesigned the engine room and drive mechanisms. In the end, he had been forced to pay a premium price for a boat that didn't perform anywhere close to original design specifications.

A nuclear-powered Victory could have gone years without needing to refuel. Instead she had ended up a true fuel hog, particularly when operating near her top speed of forty knots.

The impact of the decision on his ship's cruising range was by far the most upsetting of the compromises Gale had been forced to make. It meant he couldn't stay out at sea for months or even years at a time if he wanted or needed to.

Building Victory had represented more to Gale than a lavish token of his enormous wealth and power. It was meant as a safe haven for him, his family and his friends. A place they could escape to if necessary. In a very real sense, Gale constructed Victory to be his Arc.

Now Victory could never be used for the purpose he had intended, ending up more albatross than Arc.

Sub-optimal is how he had put it, and sub-optimal was something Gale didn't accept. It still made him furious when he thought about it.

But it didn't matter any more. He had more important things on his mind than to worry about the past. Things were coming to a head with the election looming. All that mattered to him now was the next few days. Days that he knew would change the course of the election, the destiny of his country and the future of the entire world. The moment of action he had been anticipating for so long had finally arrived. It was now or never. The realization of God's will. Nothing in the world was more important to Sherman Gale than that.

It was late. Gale knelt in earnest prayer at the alter in the small family chapel adjacent to his quarters. Beads of sweat poured from his brow. He wasn't praying for his plan's success because he now believed it was assured. He was praying because of what he had done, and what he would have to do, to make it a reality.

There were only a few rough edges left in The Plan. Foreign dignitaries, media moguls, politicians, lobbyists, military men and others who had come and gone all day by launch, helicopter and even submarine, were all very much on board. Gale had used their own greed and ambition to manipulate them like lumps of unshaped clay. Of course, they didn't know much, only enough to make them useful.

Gale's Executive Board, a group of seven hyper-rich and influential men from all over the nation, had reached an accord on power sharing earlier that afternoon. They knew more about the real plan than the others, but even they could not fathom what was about to transpire. Even in ignorance they would help the plan unfold, each doing his part, until it was too late to change course.

Overall, he was very satisfied. The meetings had all gone smoothly. All except the one involving his presidential candidate. It was clear that Robert Strong wasn't with the program. That he was hellbent on doing and saying what he thought was right, not in doing and saying the right thing. Gale knew he needed Strong to play his part. And he knew now he would probably be forced to give Strong the right kind of incentive to make him do it.

That is why he prayed as he waited for Strong to join him, imploring Jesus to show him mercy, begging God to give him a sign that would allow him to change the path he felt ordained to follow.

When a light knock at the door came, no such sign had been given. An unsteady and trembling Gale rose from his knees and slowly turned to face his brother-in-law who opened and walked in the door.

"Brother Sherman, are you alright?" Strong asked, quickly moving toward Gale to offer assistance. He noticed at once that Gale was dressed in battle fatigues.

"Of course, of course, I'm fine. Just woozy from standing up too quickly," Gale responded, shooing Strong away.

"But you look sick and you're sweating…"

"I've been pleading with God, down on my hands and knees praying for guidance."

"Guidance for what, brother? I thought you got everything settled today."

"Guidance on how to make you understand how important it is for you to do everything I ask of you."

"If you mean giving the speech you showed me today, no, I won't do that."

"But it's the only way. You must trust me on this. God's will demands it!"

Gale looked at his brother-in-law with fury in his eyes. It frightened Strong to see Gale so desperate.

"I read the entire text and I just can't see how it can help us right now. If I give that speech we'll lose support. I'm certain of it."

"Didn't you hear the analysis today, Robert? We're at least eight points behind, with seven days until the election. If something doesn't change dramatically, we're going to lose for sure."

"So how would reading a fire-and-brimstone speech help us? It'll just drive our marginal voters away. That speech belongs in a church along with holy rollers speaking in tongues. We'd be crucified in the press, and I don't use that term lightly."

Gale wanted to shout out the real plan to him. Show him once and for all why the speech mattered. Why it was critical that he give it exactly as scribed. He wanted to scream at his candidate that he was a fool to doubt the will of God. But he knew he couldn't, because Strong would never agree. He hadn't been touched by the hand of God. He had no idea of the true power of the Holy Spirit.

"Do you think I don't know that? Let the harlots of the press do their worst. They'll be made to eat their words. We'll lose if we do it by the book. Don't you realize that we'll lose doing it your way? Things are in motion that you can't understand – that you don't want to know about. We need to touch this election with the very hand of God."

"But it's there already Sherman. It's what the people choose, right or wrong. I'm willing to accept defeat, if that is what the American people want to deliver to us. I'll keep fighting to the bitter end. You know that I want this as much as anybody. But there's only so much we can do. Only so much control *you* can exert. We must trust that God reaches into every Christian's heart and shows them the right thing to do."

"You talk about God, but what about Satan? Satan can confuse and lead men astray. Every day the masses are inundated with mindless television that promotes fear and moral corruption. It makes people fear death, instead of welcoming it and being certain they'll be with Jesus, waiting for the day of reckoning to come. It's gone too far and we have to stop it now! Don't forget, God has spoken to me. Told me what I must do. God has spoken to Faith too! The Holy Spirit has talked through my flesh and blood, and told me the time is now. Who are you to doubt?"

"I've never doubted your intentions, Sherman. But what's the hurry? We're succeeding in showing people we can be a real alternative. A better alternative. There's nothing stopping us from running again. Next time..."

"Next time? Next time! Weren't you listening to me, you fool?" Gale hissed at the startled Strong while jabbing his index finger repeatedly into the candidate's chest to emphasize his words, "I said God has told us *now*, and I'm going to do *everything* in my power – *everything*, you understand, to *make it happen!*"

His words, met with silence, allowed Gale to continue in a calmer tone.

"You'd be nothing without me – my money, my strategies, my vision. Even with all that, I wouldn't expect that you'd do my bidding if it were against your principles. But we're talking here about the *will of God*."

"But the will of God as manifest through the rule of law, Sherman, surely to goodness."

"The rule of law? The law that allows abortionists, murderers and rapists to go free and fosters the attack of basic Christian values? The law is part of the problem, Robert, and it all has to change!"

"You're making it sound more like the overthrow of the government than a democratic election, something we've always said was the furthest thing from our agenda."

"The agenda, as you put it, is being set by God, not by you or me, or any one else for that matter. So please, just read the speech in New York Thursday night. The broadcast is being picked up by all the major networks, so the audience is going to be huge."

"No. I'm sorry, Brother Sherman, I can't. Doing it would be going against what I believe God is. Please know, I do respect you and realize that you've put me in a place that I could only have dreamed about without you. I haven't talked to God but

I know I have felt His divine presence many times. Some of those times I have shared with you. You knew what kind of man I was when you first approached me about running for the presidency. I can't go against what I truly believe in my heart."

"You speak of your heart and yet you are breaking mine," Gale replied, his voice faltering. He paused, trying to regain his composure before continuing in a businesslike manner.

"As I said, you will give the speech and you will do it well."

"What didn't you - " began Strong, only to be cut off immediately.

"I suppose your family's doing fine?" said Gale in a loud but uninterested way.

"What, why do you - "

"Your children. Your mother's staying with them isn't she?"

"They're fine, as far as I know, Sherman, thank you. But getting back to the speech..."

"Oh, I am talking about the speech, Brother Robert. It's all about the speech."

"I'm sorry, I'm not really following you," Strong said, confused.

"We've had numerous threats against you and your family, as you know. It would be a shame if one of them should succeed. But of course, there's all of the security we have in place. One lapse of diligence and who knows what could happen."

"Are you threatening me, Sherman?"

"No, I'm threatening your family. I can't afford to lose you. *You* are part of *The Plan*."

Robert Strong was stunned and at a loss for words. Gale waited for a response, but getting none continued.

"So please, do the speech - here's another copy - and everything will be fine."

"How can you do this, Sherman? What could justify threatening to hurt Marcus and Angela?"

"We wouldn't hurt them. Just allow some fanatic or other to do what they want to do anyway. It's pretty easy, really."

Strong was horrified, and looked at Gale with pure terror in his eyes. He didn't recognize this man. Gale was acting and speaking in a way he had never seen before. He wondered if this was Gale as he really was, and if all the times they had interacted in the past had simply been an act.

"What would Patricia Anne think? What would she say about what you're doing?" implored Strong emotionally.

"Patricia Anne!" Gale exploded as he leaped at Strong and seized him roughly by the shoulders. "I told you not to mention her, didn't I?" he screamed, shaking his wife's brother wildly before throwing him to the ground. Strong hit the ground hard. He got up slowly on his hands and knees and tried to shake it off. Gale reached down, grabbed Strong by the collar, and pulled the dazed candidate straight up onto his feet, and his face to within inches of his own.

"Even in my old and crumbled state, I could break your neck with my bare hands if I wanted to – just keep that in mind if you ever bring up my late wife's memory against me again. Don't you realize this was her dream? To see the big brother she adored as President of the United States? I'm doing this for her under orders from my God. Don't you see? Haven't I made it clear? I don't have any choice."

The two men looked directly into each others eyes. Strong could see that Gale was beyond reason but still clinging to enough sanity to care about justifying his actions. Gale could see that his candidate was frightened enough to deliver the speech and save his family from harm.

"Now get out of here," Gale said gruffly, releasing Strong with a push, causing him to stumble backwards and almost fall. Gale watched impassively as a limping Strong made his way out of the chapel. A few seconds after he was gone Gale turned, went back to the alter and knelt down to pray anew.

———

Sherman Gale was still praying when he heard a knock at the chapel door once again. This time it was a hard rap and was not followed by the opening of the unlocked door. A perturbed Gale got up slowly, went over to the door and answered it. It was his Chief of Security, Steve Thomas, and he looked both anxious and apologetic at the same time.

"What the hell, Steve? It's way after midnight. Couldn't this wait 'til morning?"

"Yes, Colonel. I know, sir. I am sorry, but I thought you'd better know. We've got a situation."

"What do you mean, situation? Just come out with it, man. Stop being so damn cryptic!"

"You want to talk here, sir?"

"It's as soundproof as any other room on the boat. Just lock the door and tell me what's got you all worked up."

Steve Thomas did what he was told and locked the door as quickly as he could, then went to sit down.

"Just tell me standing up, if you don't mind."

"Yes, sir. Of course, sir. It's just that CIA girl, the one who's pretending to be one of O'Reilly's team."

"Dr. Kunitz?"

"Yes, sir, that's her. Well, she's been snooping around Dallas asking questions about Bolton and explosives. Seems she knows quite a bit. We got a copy of her report from an operative we have in her office. She's linked Bolton to a man named Fernandez. They made sure it didn't go anywhere, but there's supposed to be enough in it to cause us a lot of grief."

"Do you have a copy?" asked Gale holding out his hand expectantly.

Thomas smiled and handed him the three page report he held. Thomas was pleased with himself for remembering to bring a copy. He shuddered to think of what the reaction would have been if he hadn't. Gale read the report quickly at first, and then a second time more slowly.

"Have you read this?"

"No, sir. I didn't have time. I wanted to bring it straight to you, to find out what you wanted me to do."

"Do? Liquidate her, of course. She poses a severe threat to us. I'm surprised you even asked. In fact, I have a question. Why isn't she dead already?"

"Well, one of our people tried."

"Tried?"

"Yes, sir. But she killed our man and got away."

"Then you'd better try a lot harder because she could bring us all down, harder and quicker than you know."

"Yes, sir, Colonel. We'll get right on it as soon as we can locate her."

"What? You don't know where she is? She hasn't contacted her office?"

"No, sir, she's disappeared. Seems she figured out there's a breach in her division and gone underground."

"Then I suggest you start digging hard right now. She has to be eliminated immediately."

13 - Corroboration

Chu stood with O'Reilly in Miami Airport. They'd just finished watching Wheeler and several of his security people escort the Strongs onto the private helicopter that awaited them. Chu was feeling like a fish out of water. O'Reilly still couldn't help feeling bitter about being excluded.

"Man, it really pisses me off," he mumbled, trying to keep his loud voice down, "This is just wrong. It's not the way it's supposed to be."

"I just hope nothing bad happens to them. At least they'll be safe once on Gale's yacht."

"I'm not sure that anyone's safe when they're that close to the Colonel. He's one twisted puppy from what I've heard."

"He can be very charming. My mom thinks he's the nicest man."

"Your mom has talked to Sherman Gale?"

"Oh, yeah. He's phoned her a couple of times. Now that's something that pisses *me* off."

"It would frighten the hell out of me, that's all I can say."

Chu hadn't really thought about it. It probably was dangerous to have his mother and grandfather involved in any way. He'd only thought about it as Gale pushing into his private business.

"I'm such a ass sometimes. All I was thinking about was how Gale's dealing with her was an affront to me. I never thought about it from the point of view you just gave me."

"Sorry."

"No, I'm glad you made me think. I can be a really stupid sometimes."

"So it doesn't piss you off to be cut out? Left off the guest list?" said O'Reilly, changing the subject.

"It just feels weird not going. But what's weirder is how much at home I feel with them. They just seem like nice people. Honest people, with good intention."

"Yeah, I know what you mean. I haven't dealt with them much, but when I have it's all been good.

"I just don't believe they know what Gale's up to. I think they're totally unaware that they're part of some horrible scheme."

"Hope you're right Chu, hope you're right. But you never know. People can seem one way and then turn out to be something entirely different."

Chu nodded in agreement but he was sure in his heart that Robert Strong wasn't involved. After a few seconds of contemplation, it was Chu's turn to change the subject.

"So, where are you going for the next couple of days? Staying around here?"

"No, been summoned back to Washington for a fucking briefing. My flight's in an hour. I'm betting they didn't like the tone of my last report."

"The Bureau never likes my reports, either," lamented Chu, "I've got in so much shit over paperwork."

"I guess you and me are just a couple of fuck ups!"

"Yeah, got that right. Misfits to the end!"

"So what about you? What are you going to do with 'Mom and Dad' away?"

Chu looked at O'Reilly and shook his head, chuckling at the ribbing.

"Well, I've been directed to stay close because they might need me. When Wheeler told me that, he looked very unhappy. They've booked me a room in downtown Miami. It's supposed to have a killer view."

"Fuck me, that sounds a hell of lot better than what I'm going to do."

They both laughed and shook hands.

As they parted, O'Reilly looked at Chu intently and said, "Let me know if anything turns up or you need some help. You got the number?"

Chu nodded in the affirmative. He hoped O'Reilly was honest, that he was one of the good guys. He liked him, and he needed *somebody* he could trust.

———

After leaving O'Reilly, Chu walked out of the airport and got in line to wait for a cab. It was sticky hot and his suit made him feel claustrophobic. He couldn't wait to get to the hotel and change into something that suited the climate better. He was looking forward to relaxing.

The line moved quickly as taxi after taxi arrived, loaded up quickly and sped away. In less than five minutes Chu was stepping into his cab when a woman came in behind him, forcing him to move over. He was startled and just about to protest when the woman spoke first.

"Share a cab downtown?"

The squeaky, high voice was unmistakeable. He recognized it at once as belonging to Dr. Kunitz. She sat down beside him and pulled the door shut. She looked completely different, and he wouldn't have recognized her if it wasn't for the voice. She was blond, had large dark glasses on and appeared to be at least forty pounds heavier than when he had last seen her. She put her head back and sighed, sounding exhausted.

"Dr. Kunitz, what the hell is going on?"

"Can't go into details here. Where do they have you staying?"

"The Marriot. It's supposed to have a great view. You want to try and get a place there?"

"No, things are a little more serious than that, Mr. Chu. I'll get out before you and find a place to stay. I need to sleep…been up for almost two days."

She held her hand up to her forehead and he could see it was swollen. She'd done a good job covering it up, but you could still see bruising if you looked carefully.

"Are you okay? That looks like a nasty bump."

"I'm fine."

"Take your glasses off and let me see your eyes."

"No."

"Then I can't know for sure if you're fine."

"So, looking in my eyes will tell you everything, huh?" she said taking her sunglasses off and looking directly at him, attempting to hold a steady gaze.

"Oh yeah. You're corked. You have a pretty good concussion. I'm surprised you're still able to get around."

"You can tell all that just by looking at my eyes?" she asked, putting her glasses back on.

"Yeah, I'm kind of an expert. I've seen a lot of people knocked out, trust me."

The cab drove steadily toward downtown Miami and its towering, oceanfront buildings. Kunitz put her head back and sighed again, louder this time.

"Hey, nothing personal, doc, but why come to me? Shouldn't you be reporting in or something?"

Chu waited but got no response.

"Hey, I asked what gives? Hey, Dr. Kunitz. Hey!" he reached for her arm and jostled her but she was out cold and slumped sideways.

"Shit!" Chu swore as he pulled her into a more or less upright position. "Hey, buddy. Can you drop us near some budget hotels?"

"I thought you was going to the Marriott. It's a mile up the road."

"Change of plans. Tell you what, you take my bags up there and drop them off with the concierge. I'll be along soon, after I help my friend here."

"Looks like she had one too many."

"Yeah, I guess so."

"Here's as good a place as any. You'll find lots of cheap hotels and motels around here," the taxi driver said as he pulled over.

"Great, how much will it be to the Marriott?"

"About twenty bucks."

"Here's thirty. Tell them the name is Chu and I'll be checking in soon. I have a reservation."

"Sure thing, mister. And thanks."

Chu nodded to the driver as he pulled Kunitz from the taxi and carried her onto the sidewalk. He was glad she was carrying only a purse. She was light in spite of her bulky appearance. He could feel the body padding underneath her clothes as he carried her. He wondered why she felt the need to go undercover.

He did his best to make sure he wasn't being followed but he couldn't be sure. It was hard to be inconspicuous carrying a limp body. People stared as he moved as quickly as he could away from the main drag. He crossed the street and doubled back to a motel he noticed about two blocks from where they had been dropped off.

In the lobby he explained to the clerk that his comatose wife had a few too many drinks on the plane ride down from New York, something that apparently did not seem to surprise him in the least. Chu registered the room in the names of Mr. & Mrs. Suzuki using cash from a wad he found in her purse. He paid the two hundred dollars for two nights in advance but had to put down another five hundred as a security deposit in lieu of a credit card imprint. Once inside the room he wasn't sure what to do. He laid her gently on the bed and stood back, trying to figure it out. At first he thought he should contact somebody, but then he realized he needed to talk with her before he did anything. Who knows what she had found out and what kind of danger she was in.

He decided the very least he had to do was get her into bed. He started by taking off the wig she was wearing, and was strangely relieved to find her long raven hair still intact beneath. The rest of his job wasn't so easy. She was so incapacitated she could offer no help, a true deadweight. Getting her outer clothing off was hard enough, but getting her out of the padded suit was another thing all together. After half an hour of struggle, he managed to extract her from the suit and got her down to her underwear. Next he propped up her head with a pillow and covered her up with blankets, tucking them in tight so she couldn't fall out. He checked her eyes by lifting her lids and thought she'd likely stay out for some time yet. Chu was feeling uncertain. He didn't want to leave her like this, but also realized not checking into the Marriott very soon might arouse suspicion. After another twenty minutes of waiting and worrying, he checked her one last time and then slipped out the door.

———

When he reached the Marriott he was sweating profusely. He had run most of the way from the motel down a side street parallel to the main road. After collecting his bags he crossed the lobby and made his way towards the check-in counter. Before he got there he was intercepted by two men who had obviously been waiting for him.

"Mr. Chu?" said the smaller of the two.

"Yes, that's me. How can I help you?"

"More like the other way around. Colonel Gale wanted to make sure you were comfortable, sir. We got a little concerned when you took so long to arrive. Thought you might have got lost."

"No, I just decided to do some sightseeing. It really is a beautiful city. I wasn't expecting that."

"Looks like you were really working at it," the man said, referring to the nearly drenched suit that clung to Chu's body.

"Guess I'm not used to the heat. It'll be nice to change into something a lot cooler and hit the beach."

"Yeah, well, the water's cooled off a bit but it should be okay. Lots of titty to watch, if you know what I mean." The big man with him laughed and nodded eagerly in agreement. "If you need anything, or would like to go anywhere, just give us a call," he continued, handing Chu a business card, "My name is Mike and this here is Angelo."

Chu looked down at the card, recognizing the logo of Gale Security at once.

"Hey, thanks guys, I really appreciate it. Do I need to get a ride to the beach or can I walk?"

Both men laughed at the question. Mike was still sniggering as he answered.

"When you get up to your room just look out your window and you'll see. Miami Beach is across the water. You need to take the causeway."

"Crap, I thought I was going to be on the beach. Well, if you'll excuse me, I'll just check in."

"Yeah, of course, no problem. I'm sure we'll be seeing each other again," Mike said, smiling. Angelo smiled, too, but there was something about the way he did it that gave Chu the creeps.

———

Chu got into his room and quickly had a shower. Afterward he felt much more refreshed as he stood out on the balcony with nothing on but a pair of shorts. The room they had booked him was on the thirtieth floor and had unobstructed views of the city, Miami Beach and the ocean beyond. Watercraft of all types and sizes made their way up or down the various channels that surrounded the city. It was truly beautiful.

He wished he could just take it easy and enjoy it, but the vision of poor Kunitz lying comatose in the cheap motel bed kept flashing back to his mind. One thing he knew was that it was bad practice to leave somebody with a concussion alone for too long. He quickly threw on a shirt, grabbed a pair of sunglasses and dug his sandals out. Before he left, he counted the cash he had taken from the purse. There was more than eight thousand left. Why did she have so much?

As expected, Angelo was watching for him as he got out of the elevator and stepped into the lobby. He waved at Chu congenially as he walked towards him.

"Goin' to the beach?"

"Not today, it's getting a bit late. Maybe tomorrow, though. I'd like to take in a few rays and watch the girls."

Angelo smiled lasciviously, "South end is where the best T&A is. Some of the broads go bareback."

"Thanks for the tip. Are you staying here? "

"Looks like it," answered the big man, "Want to get a few brews later?"

"Sounds good. Is Mike coming back?"

"I'm not sure. He said he had something to check out."

"Alright, I think I'll snoop around downtown for a couple of hours and see what kind of trouble I can get into. See you later then, Angelo."

"You bet, Mr. Chu. Remember, just give us a shout if you need anything. We'll be close by."

"Yeah, I got the card, thanks," Chu said as he departed, even though he'd left the card and his cell phone in the room. Chu knew he was going to be tailed but it didn't bother him. He'd seen the city. It was so full of people that any fool could lose a tail without even trying – and he was no fool.

———

Chu opened the door to the motel room, struggling with the grocery bags he was carrying. He'd stopped to get a variety of supplies to make Kunitz more comfortable. He was shocked to see she wasn't in the bed. He panicked for a second until he realized she was in the bathroom. He put the bags down, went over to the door and knocked gently. Getting no answer he knocked again and tried to open the door. It wasn't locked but something was holding it closed. He pushed harder only to find that Kunitz had fallen to the ground and was blocking the door with her body. It was hard but he finally pushed the door ajar enough to get in. He could see that she'd been sitting on the toilet when she collapsed, her panties still down around her ankles. He pulled them up as best he could and half carried, half dragged her back to bed.

She was trying to talk to him but it made no sense. Something about Russians and Fernandez but for the most part it was sheer babbling. He covered her up and went to fetch some water. He was glad he'd picked up some straws, as it made it possible for her to drink without spilling it all over the place.

"You are in a mess, aren't you, my squeaky-voiced little friend?" Chu said out loud, more to himself than to her, as she sucked up the water he offered. He was surprised when she answered.

"That's mean. My voice isn't squeaky," she protested weakly.

"No, of course not. I'm sorry. I think your voice is one of your best features."

She couldn't help smiling, but grimaced as the movement hurt her head.

"Here, I brought some aspirin. Thought it might help."

"Thanks," she replied as he popped two pills into her mouth before giving her another sip of water.

"I brought some soup for you too. And a little bread, if you feel up to it. The room has a kitchenette, so I can heat it up."

"This is so embarrassing. I got up to go pee and next thing I knew I was lying on the floor."

"Looks like you took one hell of a hit to the head. No wonder you're feeling wonky. What happened?"

Instead of answering she closed her eyes and drifted back into unconsciousness. It was another hour before she stirred again, opening her eyes with a start, and then only because he'd put a cold face cloth on her bruised forehead.

"It's okay. Just me trying to get the swelling down. Are you able to speak?"

She nodded instead of answering and he took it as a good sign.

"Look, Dr. Kunitz, I've got to get back soon. Gale's people have got me under pretty close watch, and I'd say by this time they're starting to wonder where I disappeared to. I've got a little food I'd like you to try, then I've got to take off."

"My name is Audrey."

"And mine is Derrik, pleased to meet you."

She smiled and accepted a few spoonfuls of the soup he had made for her. She even managed to get down a few small pieces of bread he'd added. She had a delicate mouth that reminded him of a little bird. She looked so helpless and cute, he couldn't help enjoying what he was doing.

"That tastes good, Derrik. But I'm so sleepy I just can't keep my eyes open."

"That's alright. I'll get back here tonight and maybe you'll feel like talking then. Until then, you just sleep and try to feel better. Do you need to use the bathroom while I'm still here?"

"I think I'll be fine," she said defensively.

"Well, I'm going to leave this pot by the bed. Some tissue too. Use it, instead of trying to get up."

The look on her face at his suggestion made him laugh out loud.

"Just use the pot if you have to. It's a little late to get embarrassed."

"Yes, I guess it is. I'm glad I was right to trust you, Derrik."

"How do you know you were right?"

"Because if I wasn't, I'd already be dead."

And with that, she closed her eyes and drifted back to sleep.

———

Mike and Angelo were waiting for him just inside the lobby when he got back. He had visited some stores on his return journey and was carrying several large bags.

"Hey, Mr. Chu. Looks like you were shopping."

"Yeah, I found some real bargains. Say, you guys still got time for a drink and a bite to eat?"

"That'd be nice Mr. Chu. The dining room here is top notch and the terrace lounge has a dynamite view."

"Sounds good to me. I'll just go change and meet you guys in fifteen minutes."

"Alright, see you on the terrace. You want we should order you something?"

"Yeah, that would be fantastic. How about a Corona with lime?"

"You got it, and I don't know if you realize it, but everything is on the Colonel. He told us to pick up the tab for anything you want. Anything," he repeated, giving Chu a knowing wink.

"Man, this just gets better and better," Chu said, smiling widely. But he didn't believe it and neither did Mike.

———

Dinner was great. He even had a pretty good time talking it up with the boys. They'd had two or three drinks for every one he had, but Chu was the one who acted tipsy when they parted company just before ten o'clock.

"Man, I'm not used to drinking like that," he said, feigning wobbly knees as he stood up to leave.

"It takes a lot of practice," responded Angelo, draining the last of the red wine in his glass.

"You should know," jibed Mike and they all laughed.

"See you tomorrow, gentlemen," he said, taking his leave.

"Manana, Mr. Chu. Manana."

And from what Chu could tell, they were going to stay there and drink some more on the tab.

———

He was very careful leaving the hotel. He put a 'Do Not Disturb' sign on the door, engaged the security lock and headed for the balcony. He looked around, unsure as to the best way to proceed, until he noticed he was only a couple of stories from the roof. He decided the best way out was to go up.

Once on the roof it had been easy. He jimmied open one of the rooftop access doors and made his way quickly down the stairs a few floors before finding a service elevator. By this time he had put on a pilfered hotel uniform, so he blended in perfectly. A large laundry bag concealed the clothes and other items he had bought for her. A few blocks away from the hotel, he stashed the uniform in an alley before running back to the motel, using a different route than he had used the last time. He was relieved to find her still in bed when he opened the door. She was sleeping and hadn't stirred since he left. He got an extra pillow and blanket out from the cupboard and made himself as comfortable as possible on the old couch. He lay awake thinking longingly about the luxurious bed he had left back at his hotel. And he waited for Audrey to wake up.

———

Steve Thomas was aboard Victory but was still directing operations to find Audrey Kunitz. She had last been seen heading to the Dallas airport followed by one of their agents, who was later found dead in the airport parking garage. Her rented car was there but she hadn't returned it. There was no record of one Dr. Kunitz on any flight out of Dallas. And none of her known aliases had been used or any credit card issued to her. It was as if she had disappeared.

He was still pouring over reports late into the night when a call came in. It was an operative based in Dallas who worked in records administration for the CIA.

"So, you think you finally found something?"

"Oh, yes. This is worth something, I tell you," a triumphant woman's voice crowed.

"Just how much?"

"Fifty grand, easy."

"Depends what it is."

"How about the name Dr. Kunitz is probably traveling under?"

Thomas got excited, feeling his stomach jump. But he didn't want to sound too eager.

"How sure are you?"

"Not one hundred percent," a suddenly dejected voice admitted, "but I think I got it. If I do, is it worth fifty grand?"

"If it turns out to be right, I think it could be worth something like that."

"Oh, well then. Do we have a deal?"

"When I have the name, yes. We have a deal."

"Stanley. Margaret Stanley. It was her mother's name. I brought up her record and on file was a picture of her mother. They look almost exactly the same except the mother is heavier set and blonde. And here's the thing. Her mother died less than a year ago of cancer so she'd still have a valid passport. I'm sure I've nailed it – Margaret Stanley is the name you want to check out."

"We'll be in touch," he replied without emotion.

"But when will I…"

But he had already hung up and was sending the name to another Dallas operative who worked at the airport.

———

Chu sat bolt upright at the sound of someone screaming. It was Audrey. He jumped off the couch in one great leap ready to face anything. There was nothing but Audrey screaming and fighting against something only she could see. He rushed to the bed and grasped her by the shoulders.

"Audrey, you're fine. Just fine. It's just a dream. Audrey, wake up for Christ's sake!"

She came to suddenly and grabbed onto him as if her life depended on it. She sobbed uncontrollably and buried her head into his chest. He couldn't do anything but hold her and wait until it subsided. He was starting to wonder if she would ever stop when he felt her grip relax and her breath become slower and more even. It was almost four. He had to start to think about getting back. Another five minutes and she was able to talk.

"I'm sorry, Derrik. I was just having a nightmare about killing that man. It was awful. Have you ever had to kill someone?"

Chu had felt like it plenty of times but he'd never actually had to do it. He'd always wondered how it would feel. Wondered if he could actually do it.

"No, no I haven't. What happened?"

"I thought I hadn't been followed but I was wrong. I was making a run for it, something I was prepared to do if I confirmed what I thought was true."

"Which was..."

"Which was a lot. But the main thing was that the CIA has people in it who are directly loyal to Gale. They're everywhere — it's impossible to know. My boss turned out to be one."

"Go on."

"I wrote a report that showed links between Gale and Fernandez. We already know Fernandez had a lot to do with three Russian germ warfare experts. And the thing I found out in Dallas was that Bolton, an associate known to work with Fernandez, supplied the explosive used in the attack on Doris Strong."

"What? That doesn't make sense. Gale wanted Doris dead?"

"It would appear that way. I guess it turned out better than he'd hoped when you played hero."

"I never would have thought..."

"Don't be surprised, Derrik. These people are pure evil. They say they're working for God but it couldn't be further from the truth."

"So, anyway. You found out all this stuff and put it in a report..."

"Yes. And it went nowhere. When I checked the routing I could see that Henderson, my boss, had erased it. No record of it. So I knew. That's when I decided to get out fast. I took off for the airport where I left my disguise kit. But I was jumped almost as soon as I got out of my rental car in the garage. I didn't see it coming. There was nobody around and he smashed my head with a tire iron. I had my gun ready in my pocket. He grabbed me and was going to hit me again when I pressed the gun into his chest and shot him twice. It was like being in a dream. He slumped like a sack of potatoes, but the sound he made, I still hear it. A kind of gurgling like in a horror movie. I pushed him under the car and went into the airport, got changed and came here to find you."

"Where'd all the cash come from?"

"I had it with the kit I left at the airport. I knew if I had to run, I'd need quite a bit."

"Look," said Chu trying to think straight, "I think you have to get out of here. I'm hot and I know they're onto me. I can just feel it. I don't think they know what's going on, or they'd be way more aggressive. But it's only a matter of time."

"But I don't have anything to wear. Where would I go?"

"The real question is do you feel up to it? Maybe you should try getting up and see how you feel. I brought you some clothes and other things I thought you might need. I was in a hurry so it's probably going to be pretty bad."

She moved slowly but surely out of bed and started looking through the laundry bag of stuff he had brought. She started trying things on. Chu turned his back while she did this and got some food ready.

"I've left my gun and holster for you. I noticed you were unarmed."

"I dumped my gun at the Dallas airport."

"Yeah, I guessed that. Anyway, I want you to take it just in case."

"What are you going to do?"

"I'll get another one soon enough. It's not what I do, anyway."

"Prefer the hand-to-hand killing?"

She dressed as they talked and in just a few minutes Audrey was fully clothed with her hair in an elegant braid. She sat down, looking much healthier than she had just a few hours before. He gave her a large bowl of soup and some bread and cheese. She ate with enthusiasm which Chu knew from experience was a good sign.

"Man, let me think. Who can we trust?" he asked.

"I don't know if I trust anybody anymore. Henderson must have set me up. Henderson! I wonder if he knew they were going to kill me?"

"Look, it doesn't do any good trying to figure out why these people are nuts. They just are. I'm sure a lot of them are doing it for money. I'm always surprised at what people do for money. Anyway, how about we meet in New York on Friday? I know I'm going to be there with the Strongs. He's giving a big speech."

"Where in New York? It's a big place."

"Yeah, well, how about Columbus Circle between three and four in the afternoon? Wear a red hat."

"A red hat?"

"Yup, a red hat. Columbus Circle between three and four on Friday. If I don't show up, try again Saturday."

"Why wouldn't you show up?"

"Lots of reasons. The point is I won't be able to contact you. I don't think we can trust cell phones."

"What am I going to do when I get to New York?"

"You're going to wait for Friday."

"So what are we going to do there? I mean, how are you going to fix things?"

"I'm not sure right now. I was thinking of giving O'Reilly a call."

"That jerk? He's a real piece."

"Yeah, but I think he's honest. I really believe it."

"You and your gut feel. I don't know. The Secret Service!"

"We need some help. I'd like to think I can get the Strongs to do something but I'm just not sure. I can't believe it, but maybe they know what's really going on. Can you think of anybody?"

She shook her head indicating that she could not.

She finished her food and was looking for more, finally deciding on an orange which she began peeling.

"Like I said, I think you have to get out of here, and I have to get back to the hotel. How about I get you to the bus station?"

"The bus?"

"Yup. They take cash and you don't need ID. Oh, that reminds me, I put the money back in your purse."

"You think that's the best way? Bus to New York City?"

"Hey, it's some people's way of life. And trust me, in spite of the bad rap it's got in the past few years, it is the safest way to travel."

"Okay, let's go," she said standing up confidently, "Say, how do I look? I think you've found the new me. What do you think?" she asked as she folded up her hair and donned the blonde wig once more.

He paused, unsure how to answer. She looked good. In fact, she looked great.

"You're ravishing," he mugged, "I think I'll start a new career as a stylist."

"Well, I'm taking a few of the clothes you bought with me and some of this yummy food. You really do have good taste. But I knew that already by watching your running videos."

"Give me everything you're not taking including your old clothes. We shouldn't leave anything behind," he said, pretending to ignore the last comment. But he couldn't help feeling flattered.

"You watched those?" he asked incredulously, unable to let it go.

"Who didn't? And I really liked them. I mean, I thought they were more than just running."

"Thanks. That means a lot to me. But let's get going. Daylight is coming fast and I have to be back in my crypt before dawn."

They slipped out the back entrance and were early enough for her to get on the 5:30 bus north to Charlotte.

14 - Paradise Lost

Steve Thomas was working through the night trying to figure out where Kunitz could be. When they searched for the name Margaret Stanley against airline manifests, they got a hit right away. Margaret Stanley had booked a flight to Miami at 11:05. A security camera recording showed her arriving in Miami but there was nothing to indicate where she went from there. The security chief took the information to Gale, who studied it carefully before announcing his verdict.

"Think about it, man. If she's gone to Miami, it's probably to contact our good friend Mr. Chu. Ask those idiots of yours who are supposedly watching him what's been going on. Have they noticed anything? I'd bet my breakfast if they'd kept proper tabs on him we'd have found Kunitz already. Tell them to start talking to airport cabbies. And get them to ask around at all the budget places near downtown. Find out who paid for their room using cash. As for Mr. Chu, he's clearly not being kept busy enough. Tomorrow let's throw him a curve ball to keep him on his toes. Let me tell you what I have in mind."

——

Chu had been asleep for only an hour when there was a loud knock on the door. Right on schedule, he thought to himself as he tumbled out of bed and peered through the door's peep hole. There was Angelo looking all rumpled, like he'd sat in the lounge all night – which he probably had. He banged again, only harder this time.

Chu opened the door, looking bleary eyed and seriously sleep deprived.

"What the hell do you want? It's only 7:30 for fuck sake."

"Sorry, Mr. Chu, but I got orders to check on you. And I got a message, too."

"What's the message?"

"Get your ass downstairs as quick as possible because Steve Thomas is here to have breakfast with you. Do you know who he is?" Angelo added, almost in awe.

"I've had the pleasure, Angelo. Now if you'll excuse me, I have to get ready."

"You don't mind if I wait out here, do you Mr. Chu? I got nuthin' else to do."

"Do you want to wait in here, Angelo?"

"No, sir. I don't want to take away none of your privacy."

"As you wish. I'll be about ten minutes."

"Quicker would be better."

"I'll go as fast as I possibly can. How's that?"

"I couldn't ask for anything better than that, Mr. Chu, now could I?"

Chu closed the door and jumped into the shower. The quickest he'd had in a long time. As he dried himself off he was thinking about Audrey and their time together. Coming back to his hotel had gone smoother than he thought it might. He'd dumped the extra stuff, picked up the uniform, slipped into the service elevator, gone to the roof and climbed back into his room by 6:15. A piece of cake.

He wondered how Audrey was doing on the bus heading north as he brushed his teeth. He hoped her head didn't hurt too much. As he pulled on some clothes, he thought about her voice and smiled. When he remembered Steve Thomas waiting for him downstairs, his concern for Audrey evaporated. He wondered if they'd caught on to him yet and now, for the first time in quite a while, he became concerned for his own well-being.

———

They entered the hotel's half empty dining room exactly fifteen minutes from the first knock at Chu's door. Angelo escorted him to a table where Steve Thomas sat, looking uncomfortable and impatient. Thomas was dressed in the naval version of the Gale Security uniform, a uniform that had become increasingly familiar to Americans all over the country in the past few years. It was gleaming white, with gold braids and buttons, commanding respect and authority. Chu could see the head waitress scramble to help his fidgeting breakfast companion get whatever he wanted, although she had no idea what that might be. She bossed several people into action just for something to do, but it did not help Chu get to his seat any faster. And that was truly what Thomas desired. She came rushing over to take their order the second Chu sat down.

"I'll have bacon and eggs, eggs sunny side up, and brown toast, no jam. And you Mr. Chu?"

"Oh," he answered a little taken back and glancing ineffectively at the menu, "Um, that sounds good. Same as Mr. Thomas but I'll have an extra egg and side of bacon."

"Yes, sir. Right away. Coffee or orange juice while you wait?"

"Both for me, and make it a large orange juice, please." answered Chu quickly.

"And just water for me."

"Yes, sir. Right away."

The woman scurried away like she was on a mission. Now that she could do something she was happy and bounced along with purpose.

"It makes me laugh the way people act when I wear this uniform."

"It's pretty impressive and a little intimidating."

"Intimidating, Mr. Chu?"

"Some people respond like that to authority. They'll do anything to stay in favour."

"But not you."

"No, not me."

"By the way, you referred to me as Mr. Thomas just now. I prefer being addressed as Major Thomas."

"A Major in what branch of the Forces?"

"Gale Security, of course. We have our rank structure."

"With Colonel the highest you can go and there's only one of them, right? So Major is pretty darn good," Chu mocked.

The security chief smiled dryly but inwardly was seething. He hoped this whole thing would go as he had planned.

"Truth hurts, don't it?" continued Chu, on a roll.

Thomas ignored him and took a drink of water from the glass the eager waitress had brought him. After a few moments of thought he decided to let it go and broached a new topic.

"Are you at all curious about why I'm down here? Why we're meeting like this?"

"I'm not sure what you mean, curious about what?"

"Why I should come to Miami and want to have breakfast with you?"

"Let me tell you, since the first time I met with Mr. Gale, he's done nothing but surprise me. I'm a little beyond surprises right now. So why not just come out and tell me why you're here? We'll save a little time and be able to enjoy our breakfasts."

"Colonel Gale, not mister!" burst out Thomas with more passion than he meant to show.

The waitress, who was just about to deliver their food, actually recoiled back as the words were spat out. She waited until Thomas motioned for her to continue and even then moved with caution. He waited for her to leave before continuing, trying to keep his voice low.

"Forever the wise guy, aren't you, Mr. Chu? The first thing I need this morning are answers to some questions. First off, why in Hades have you been running all over town?"

"I don't know what you mean."

"Mike said you did a lot of shopping, were gone for hours. They weren't sure where or why."

"Yeah, a bit yesterday afternoon."

"You didn't meet anybody you knew?"

"No."

"You sure?"

"Of course I am. Why ask?"

"Dr. Audrey Kunitz. We're looking for her. You've met her, I understand."

"She was in a couple of meetings I attended. We never spoke to each other. In fact, I don't think she ever said a word to anyone."

"Well, we've confirmed that she flew into Miami airport yesterday. Colonel Gale thought she might have tried to get in touch with you."

"I don't know why she would."

"Yeah, that's what I said."

"But if she does, contact me, I mean, while I'm here in Miami, I'll be sure and let you know," Chu said earnestly.

"That's not going to be for very long, Mr. Chu. The Colonel wants you to join him and the Strongs aboard Victory. He's decided to take it up to New York. Already started steaming up there by now. We'll take a chopper and meet up with them at sea."

"Now?"

"No, after breakfast."

"That's what I mean. I'm being asked to go now? I don't get to go to the beach?"

"No, I'm sorry, Mr. Chu, but I guess your vacation is over. And to make it very clear, Colonel Gale isn't asking you. It's an order."

A voice in Chu's head screamed out, begging to give response. He struggled to keep it under control. He heard his grandfather's voice deep inside, telling him that sometimes it was just better to relax, to give in. To take your advantage by remaining calm.

Thomas sat looking at Chu with interest, as he took a bite of egg. He could see that Chu had stopped eating. He was hoping Chu would try something. He had six men ready to intervene, all equipped with stun guns. He needed to make sure they didn't kill Chu, but there would be no recriminations if he taught this famous, cocksure agent a little lesson in humility. Chu looked around and could count at least four heavies poised for action. He determined there were probably more he couldn't see. To the surprise of Thomas, Chu cut a piece of bacon in half, put an egg on top on it and scooped the lot into his mouth.

"So, Mr. Chu, you'll be coming with us then?"

Chu had taken another large mouthful so held up his hand to request a moment before responding. He was still smacking his lips with satisfaction when he spoke.

"Seems I don't have a choice, and to be honest, I can hardly wait to see this tub. I hear she's a beauty."

"Very well. When we're finished, you can collect your bags and we'll go. Angelo and a couple of his associates will help you. I'm sure you understand."

"Oh, I do understand. In fact, I get the impression you'd like me to start something."

"Only so I could finish it," he laughed.

"Yeah, thought so. Well, looks like I'm done here," Chu said, looking down at his empty plates almost sadly, "Should I just get up and start walking?"

"I wouldn't advise that."

"What do you want me to do then?"

"Why don't you just sit there and think about ordering something else, if you'd like. Or have some more coffee."

"So wait, now I'm confused. I thought you were in a hurry."

"No, no hurry at all. I'd be delighted to watch you eat while I tell you what you're really going to be doing for the next two days."

"I'm sorry, you have definitely lost me."

"You just went through a kind of test. To see if you'd do as you're ordered."

"And how'd I do?"

"Not great marks - a bare pass, really. But that's all that counts in the end."

———

Chu was sitting in his room getting ready to go to the beach. He still couldn't believe it. Instead of taking a day away from him in Miami, Thomas informed him he'd be staying for an extra one. The Strongs were on their way to New York on board Victory just as Thomas had first told him. The real change in the itinerary was that Faith and K.C. were to spend two days in Miami and that Chu was to provide them security, in the same way he had done it for the Strongs. Angelo, Mike and several others were assigned the duty as well.

Angelo and Mike were waiting for him right now down in the lobby. They made a funny looking pair standing there. Angelo, a giant of a man, heavyset and slow moving, and Mike, a small, thin character who bounced rather than walked. The plan was to pick up Faith and K.C. at the airport just before noon, and after lunch take them to the beach.

As Chu sat there, he wondered to himself why Thomas had lied to him. He also wondered why Gale wanted him to babysit. The only thing he could think was that it helped them in their quest to locate Audrey Kunitz in some way, but he wasn't sure how. In fact, Chu's agreement to depart Miami so quickly told Thomas one of two things. Chu knew nothing about where she was, or he knew and had already helped her escape. Thomas made it his mission to find out which was true.

In the meantime, Chu had to be managed until after Strong's big speech in New York. In Gale's mind, the best way to do that was to send him two distractions that were sure to keep him fully occupied.

———

When Angelo saw Chu step out of the elevator, his face lit up.

"Hey, Mr. Chu, we're over here," he called, waving. Mike looked at his partner as if he were a moron and rolled his eyes.

"Thanks for waiting for me," Chu said as he joined the pair. It was hard to tell, but Chu was being facetious. The subtlety escaped Angelo completely but wasn't lost on Mike.

"No problem, Mr. Chu. Imagine us all working together! Mike and me, working with the FBI!"

"If we're going to be working together, how about you drop the Mr. Chu thing and start calling me Derrik."

"Yeah, sure, Derrik. That'd be great."

"Maybe if you're both over this lovey-dovey thing, we can get on the road. Traffic's going to get bad in a few minutes, so we gotta go now," Mike broke in, forcing out a laugh when he was finished.

"Lovey-dovey! Mike, sometimes you kill me," Angelo responded, shaking his head and adding, "Get that, Derrik – lovey-dovey! Where's he come up with stuff like that?"

———

Mike was driving and Angelo was riding shotgun. Chu sat in the back of the limo by himself watching as the airport terminal loomed larger and larger. Chu recognized the place immediately as they rolled up to terminal that served private aircraft. It seemed like it had been a week since he had seen the Strongs off. In fact he'd been in Miami just twenty-four hours.

After a brief chat with an airport curbside security officer, Mike pulled the stretch Town Car over to the curb in front of the arrivals area. Mike turned to Chu with a look of expectation. Chu remained seated and said nothing.

"Mr. Chu, I mean Derrik, would you be so kind as to go with Angelo to meet the Gales? Neither of us know them, see."

"Sure thing. I'll go with Angelo."

Chu could tell that Angelo was excited. The big man's pace quickened and he held himself taller as they walked into the terminal building.

"It's an honour to be guarding Colonel Gale's kids. Praise God!"

"Let me ask you something, Angelo. Is everybody who works for Gale Security a Christian?"

"Well, yeah. You have to be baptized and believe in Jesus and all that."

"Mike, too?"

"Of course. Mike is very religious. Not like me. I was always religious, part of my upbringing. But Mike, he found Jesus the way the Colonel did. He believes powerful now."

"They'll be exiting from those doors, so if we just wait here we can't miss them."

"Okay, Derrik. So, you know these kids?"

"I've met them once or twice," Chu admitted.

"So, what're they like?"

"They're nice. At least they seem so. He's about as big as you, Angelo. And she's just pretty much perfect."

As he was describing them to Angelo, the doors opened and the brother and sister appeared. They were in animated conversation and didn't notice Angelo or Chu standing there. He was dressed in a track suit with sneakers. She had on a pretty pink and white dress with red high heels. A Gale Security member in fatigues loosely escorted them, their luggage attended to by a porter.

K.C. was bigger than Chu remembered. And Faith was even more captivating. She finally looked around the arrivals area and saw Chu standing there. Her face broke into a wide smile and she rushed over like she was seeing a long lost relative. K.C. and the others followed her lead.

"Hello, Faith," Chu managed to get out before the girl ran into his arms and gave him a familiar hug. Angelo stood back, looking surprised and impressed.

"Oh, Agent Chu, it's so good to see you," she said breaking away, "I'm glad Daddy listened to us for a change."

"Yeah, we didn't think he'd go for it. But here we are!" boomed K.C., grabbing Chu with one large hand by the shoulder, the other titan thrust out for him to take. Chu shook K.C.'s hand in wonderment. He had no idea why they were putting such stake in him.

"Good to see you K.C. I can't think why you guys would want to hang around with me, but it's given me some more time in Miami, so thank you," he said truthfully.

They all stood around smiling and generally feeling happy, until Chu noticed Angelo looking expectant.

"Oh, K.C. and Faith, this is Angelo. He and his partner Mike are going to be driving us around."

Angelo beamed, as first K.C. then Faith shook his hand.

"Well, we're on our way back, so I'll take leave," the Gale Security man announced generally. The group all but ignored him as they made their way to where Mike and the car were waiting.

———

They were on the beach in front of the hotel they would be staying at for the next two nights. Chu and his charges were in bathing suits. The siblings had insisted he join them on the beach, which meant the suit he'd bought would come in handy. Mike and Angelo were still in their dress suits, but had taken off their ties and abandoned their shoes.

When they arrived at the hotel, Chu's bags had already been moved from the Marriott. Chu was sure that careful study of his luggage had been made, and was glad he had bought some clothes for himself when shopping the day before. Otherwise, it would have been a dead giveaway.

They had cordoned off a special area of the beach for them – something that didn't seem strange to either Faith or K.C., but did to him. A small crowd of people gathered to gawk and try to determine who these obviously famous people were.

When it was time to swim, Faith removed the cover up she was wearing to reveal the bathing suit beneath. K.C. was the first to react with a gasp. Although it was a one piece, it was extremely revealing.

"Sister Faith," he stammered, "I'm not sure our father would approve of all that - that skin showing."

"The woman said that this was the style this year, K.C.," Faith responded, taken aback, "I mean, it shows way less than a lot of girls we've seen today."

This was true but not many of the girls had a figure like Faith. She looked both innocent and sexy at the same time. The suit wouldn't fit one in a thousand like it fit her.

"Tell me, Agent Chu, does this look terrible?" she said turning to Chu and modeling the suit for him.

"No, Faith. Uh, it looks good, very good. I think that's what K.C. means."

Faith started to flush. First her neck went red, then it spread to her face.

"I mean," Chu continued as words spilled out, "I mean what if somebody gets a picture of you and it makes its way into a tabloid? It could be embarrassing for your father."

Faith grabbed her cover up, threw it on in a panic and then rushed from the beach towards the hotel. Nobody else moved, seemingly paralysed by not knowing what to do, so Chu pursued her.

"Faith, please! Please come back."

She stopped, her shoulders hunching as if she were crying. He reached where she was standing and put a hand gently on her shoulder. She turned and looked up at him, tears streaming down her face.

"Don't let it ruin our fun. Come back. We can still go swimming."

"I can't! You say I'm going to end up in some girly magazine if I wear this suit!"

"Not a girly magazine," Chu laughed, "I was just using a 'what if.' I know it's not fair because of how you look and who you are. But it could be worse."

"How?" she asked through pouted lips, her eyes swollen with tears, nose running freely. Chu thought she looked adorable, as he handed her the towel he was holding.

"You could look like me."

Faith laughed as though she couldn't help it, burying her face in the towel while drying her tears.

"That would be terrible," she said, coyly peaking out from behind the towel.

Now it was Chu's turn to laugh. This girl was something else.

"You can still swim, if you want. Use my tee shirt as a cover up in the water. Probably safer for your skin anyway."

"You'd let me use it?"

"Of course."

He put his arm around her in as brotherly a way as he could, and led her back to K.C. and the others. They had been watching to see what the outcome would be. Angelo raised his eyebrows when Chu brought her back. Mike looked bemused. K.C. was delighted.

"Can we *please* get into the water now?" he asked impatiently.

They all laughed at that, including K.C., although he wasn't sure why.

———

They had a great time on the beach. Childhood in the Gale household had seldom seen such fun. The surf was up, so Chu got Angelo to rent them body boards. They spent the afternoon riding waves and being tossed up on the beach, laughing and sputtering at the same time. Being with Faith and K.C. on the beach made Chu feel like a teenager again. It wasn't all that long ago he had been K.C.'s age. Trying to figure out what to do after high school. Everybody having an opinion of what was best. Ignoring what he thought was best.

K.C. was a great football player but terrible at school. It had cost him playing first string even at the high school level. He just couldn't learn the plays. He gave one hundred and ten percent effort, but it wasn't enough. To be an elite athlete at the college level meant at least being able to get passing grades. For K.C., it was impossible.

What K.C. lacked in brains, he made up for with his personality. Riding the waves with him, Chu found that K.C. was one of the nicest kids he had met. He loved football, Jesus and his family, unwaveringly. Chu noticed that he particularly doted on his younger sister, though she frequently treated him with disdain. Chu was beginning to see that Faith Gale was truly an anomaly. Intelligent beyond her years but so naive in the strangest ways. One minute coy and vulnerable, the next, petulant and vindictive. She wore a purity ring signifying her chasteness but was one of the sexiest girls Chu had ever seen. Even when she was wearing Chu's oversized tee shirt in the water, she attracted attention. Her movements, gestures and curves suggested by the shirt clinging to her body, had heads turning all over the beach.

The three of them had dinner together in the hotel's dining room though they were not quite alone. Mike and Angelo dined at a separate table close by. Faith and K.C. were surprised to find out that Chu didn't drink. When pressed, he admitted he had at one point in college but found it too debilitating, so had sworn off the stuff. They were both impressed.

"Did you ever do drugs?" Faith asked in hushed tones, "I mean when you were in college?"

"I did smoke quite a bit of pot. Nothing else, though, because I was too afraid of what it might contain."

"Did it make you go weird? That's what some guys on the football team told me. They told me I should never do it because I was weird enough already."

Faith made a face at K.C., but Chu smiled at his lack of decorum.

"No, it's a real kick at first, but then you get used to it — just like everything. Made me a little paranoid and a lot anti-social. My mom's convinced that it kept me from getting to law school. I don't know, maybe she's right."

"Our father warned us that he'd tan our hides raw if we drank or took drugs. And that he'd shoot anybody who gave them to us. You're lucky he isn't your daddy," mused K.C.

"You can say that again. I think your father would pretty much have given me the boot before I reached sixteen!"

They all laughed at that one, Faith and K.C. nodding in agreement, and ordered some dessert.

———

It was almost ten when they finally finished dinner. Mike and Angelo protested when the three of them got up to leave, as they still needed to polish off the remains of their third bottle of wine. Chu suggested they meet in the lobby in fifteen minutes, as both brother and sister wanted to take a short walk around the hotel grounds before calling it a night.

As they exited the restaurant Chu surveyed the lobby and could see nothing untoward. However, as they made their way to the outside doors, that changed. Chu spotted a group of four burly men coming in from outside. They were loud and had obviously been drinking. They didn't look like agents or hit men but Chu had grown a healthy respect for the impetuousness of drunks, finding the best thing to do was avoid them. But K.C., slightly ahead and intent on getting outside into the fresh air, plodded along on a collision course.

The four drunks walked side by side, almost shouting back and forth to each other, seemingly in their own world. K.C. tried to get out of their way at the last second but one of the men caught him with his shoulder as he went by, sending K.C. sprawling.

"Hey, Tiny, watch the fuck where you're going," the man who had hit K.C. snarled.

K.C. sat on the ground nursing his shoulder and looking like he had hurt feelings.

"Hey, you watch out, mister!" Faith screamed pointing at the man, "You're the one who's out of line."

The men laughed at the girl who stood before them trembling with anger. Chu knew where this was going and he wanted to stop it fast.

"A simple misunderstanding. Come on, Faith, it's not worth it. Here, K.C., let me help you up."

Chu reached down to help K.C. up, only to have a strong hand stop him.

"I want that moron to apologize to my friend for getting in his way."

Chu froze. This situation was not unfolding well.

"Okay, enough is enough. We're sorry. Now if you'll please, let us get going."

"How about you two go but leave us the girl. That seems fair, huh fellas?" piped in another of the men.

"Hey, baby. Man, what a rack on her," added a third.

That was enough for Chu but he forced himself to issue one last warning.

"Please, get out of our way before there is trouble."

"Trouble?" the biggest of the men burst out, "Trouble for you, maybe! If you think some little Chink is going to stop us, you're -"

The man didn't get a chance to finish his threat. Faith's leg had shot out with a well-placed kick to his groin. He crumpled to the ground on his knees, then collapsed in a heap. The buddies, taken by surprise, sprang into action as quickly as their deadened nerves would allow, but it was no contest. Chu went at them spinning, kicking and punching, and in only a few seconds all three were vanquished. Chu looked up to see Mike and Angelo running towards them, guns drawn.

The front desk had called 911 and the police were on their way. People were being kept away but they couldn't be stopped from taking pictures using cameras and cell phones.

Chu was mad. The entire incident was avoidable. Now there would be plenty of explaining to do and all he wanted to do was get to bed and sleep. He walked over to the man Faith had knackered, still lying on the ground, and grabbed his face hard.

"Let me tell you something, Shirley," he began, talking through clenched teeth, "First thing, I'm more Japanese than Chinese so the more appropriate term for you to have used was Jap, not Chink. Got that?"

The man nodded affirmatively because Chu had such a tight grip on his face he couldn't talk.

"And the other thing is that you've just assaulted Sherman Gale's children. When he finds out, it's going to be interesting to see how he reacts. Let's just put it this way, I wouldn't want to be in your shoes right now."

———

"I just don't see why you're mad at me!" Faith complained as they rode up the elevator to the special floor that had been secured for their use. K.C. had gone up earlier with Mike when the police realized he wasn't a particularly reliable witness.

"I'm not mad, Faith. I'm just saying that kicking that guy escalated things. That's how come we spent the last two hours dealing with police and fighting off television reporters."

It was agreed to by all involved that no charges would be laid. The four drunks were eager to please, now that they knew who they were dealing with, and had apologized profusely. They were filled with concern that there would be recriminations. One of them was openly crying.

When it had become known that Sherman Gale's children were involved in a public brawl, the media from all over Miami had converged on the hotel. When they found out that the super FBI man was part of the story too, a frenzy erupted. Satellites were beaming images worldwide, caught accidentally by enthralled vacationers, celebrities for a minute while the video clip they had taken flashed across the screen.

Chu and Faith rode in silence to their floor. The door opened and they got out. Two Gale Security agents checked them out, confirming their identity. As they walked down the corridor to their rooms Faith stopped and turned to face Chu.

"Those guys started it. They walked into K.C. And then when he called you a, a..." She sputtered, unable to bring herself to use the word.

"A Chink? He called me a Chink. So what?"

"It doesn't bother you?"

"Not really. For one thing, I'm only one quarter Chinese. And if people want to call me something because of the way I look, that's just their ignorance."

"Well, I suppose kicking him in the privates was wrong. Turn the other cheek, right?"

"For what it's worth, I do appreciate it. I mean, you standing up to that guy like you did. It took a lot of guts."

She stood looking up at him, and a smile returned to her face. She looked so pleased at this faint praise, he just had to continue.

"I have to tell you that I was glad you gave me the opportunity to take out those guys who made cracks about you. How they treated you made my blood boil."

"Really?" she said, standing on her toes, "It made you mad because they were rude to me?"

"Of course! You don't deserve that any more than I deserve to be called a Chink. You can't help the way you look."

"How's that?" she said, lowering her voice and inching closer to him.

"Well, you know, like, really good. I - I mean, very appealing," he stammered, moving back a little but not as far as he should have.

"You think I'm very appealing?" she said, leaning even closer still.

It was as if she was a magnet. As she got closer, the urge to close the gap between them grew stronger and stronger. He wanted to kiss her. Every fibre of his body screamed for him to crush his lips against hers. Instead he pushed himself away and took out his key card and opened the door to his room. He knew that kissing Faith right now would be the worst thing he could do for her. He knew that he was too old for her, that she was just a kid with a crush. That he would be taking advantage of a virtual child. And yet, it seemed so perfect, so meant to be.

So irresistible.

She followed him in and drew closer to him once again. Chu had never in his life experienced such inner struggle. With him it was usually black or white, with hardly any shades of grey. Now everything was grey. To want something so badly and yet not being able to embrace it. It was painful.

Then suddenly it happened. He reached for her. She came willingly. Their mouths locked together spinning his head like a top. Mouths opened and tongues probed trying to get closer. Melding together as one. At that moment, Faith's cell phone started playing God Bless America.

"Oh, that's Daddy!" Faith exclaimed, pushing away from him and grabbing at her purse.

At first she just listened, then she smiled and finally, she spoke.

"Well, he's right here, Daddy, if you want to talk to him."

She handed the phone with flair to Chu, who took it reluctantly.

"Hello, Colonel," he said, purposefully addressing Gale with his military title in the hope of pleasing him. All Chu could hear on the other end was laughing. It took Sherman Gale a few moments before he could contain himself enough to speak.

"First off, get to someplace you can talk in privacy."

"It's alright sir, we're in private now."

"Oh, Mr. Chu, you never cease to amaze me. I suppose you thought I was going to be angry. It couldn't be further from the truth! Well done, Mr. Chu, that's what I wanted to tell you. Great press! Great news coverage! We were running a little short today and then you brought us this."

"It was really Faith who you should thank. She got it going."

"Quite a girl, isn't she?"

"Yes, sir, she really is," Chu answered, looking at the expectant Faith standing right next to him.

"And it's your duty to protect her, correct?"

"Yes, sir. I take that seriously."

"I know, Mr. Chu. You have her best interests at heart, don't you?"

"Absolutely."

"That's good, Mr. Chu. Thank you. Now if you could pass me back to that little firecracker of mine..."

Chu complied and listened while father and daughter talked. She was still such a little girl, as was made obvious by hearing her side of the conversation. At last she signed off, put the phone back in her purse and stood looking at him.

"He's really pleased with me. Well, I guess with us. So it all worked out for the best, isn't that great? And you were worried!"

"Yeah, I was expecting a lot worse," he said, smiling weakly.

Faith looked around the room, unsure of what to say or do next.

"I could stay for a while," she offered demurely, moving towards him.

Chu recalled the words he had exchanged with her father just seconds before and took a step back.

"Well, you know Faith, it's getting late and I've been up a long time. I really should call it a night."

She looked disappointed. Like she'd been rejected.

"Oh, fine then. That's fine. I just thought, you know, whatever..."

In a sudden hurry, she turned and headed for the door. With a hand on the doorknob she looked back to address him. Her voice was calm and detached.

"Oh, by the way, Daddy wants you to teach K.C. some of your self defence moves tomorrow. He's arranged a gym."

"Guess no beach tomorrow, then?"

"Guess not. Just a one day thing," she said with resignation before opening the door quickly and rushing out.

He wanted to call after her. He could see she was upset. He wanted to make it better. To tell her that he couldn't take his eyes off her when she was around. That all he could think about right now was her. That she would be the last thing he thought about before he went to sleep that night and the first thing he thought about when he woke up next morning. That he burned to hold her, smell her, taste her...

But it wouldn't be right. He couldn't give into his desire when she was so young and at such a disadvantage. Maybe at a future time there would be hope, slim as it may be. When she was older. When she wasn't in his care.

Maybe then...

———

In spite of being exhausted, Chu couldn't sleep. He tossed and turned in his bed thinking about Faith. Wondering if he had done the right thing. He ran the last few minutes of the evening over and over in his head, choosing different words and watching the different imagined outcomes. He liked the scenario where she stayed, such sweet bliss, although the vision was so sweet it was tortuous to think it wasn't real.

Hell, he knew he had done the right thing - it just felt so horribly wrong.

It was a feeling that Robert Strong could identify with. He too, was having trouble sleeping that night, as Gale's behemoth Victory steamed ever closer to New York City. To him, the lavish ship had come to represent his floating prison. A ghost ship whose destination was the very gates of Hell.

Gale had cancelled all engagements Strong had been booked to attend both before and after the New York speech. Further, he had disconnected Victory from the outside world, meaning no messages or calls could go in or out. It was clear that Gale wanted to keep his candidate under wraps and in his complete control during the final days of the campaign.

Strong now faced the prospect of a new day with a heavy heart. He hadn't told anybody what had happened when he and Gale had met in the chapel, not even Doris, who was lying in bed beside him pretending to be asleep. She sensed something was terribly wrong and was waiting for her husband to share his burden.

Strong was still trying to make sense of it – to figure out what to do. But he was at a loss.

The couple had seen Sherman several times since the fateful evening meeting and everything appeared normal. Even more cordial than usual, if that was possible.

"Please, Robert," she finally blurted out in the dark, after yet another of his uncomfortable shifts in the bed, "tell me what's troubling you. It's not like you to be this way."

"I can't tell you. It's too terrible," he moaned.

"You can tell me anything. You know I won't judge you. I leave that to God."

"Oh, Doris," he broke down, "My darling, I fear I have put us in grave danger. We appear to be at the mercy of a madman."

"Whatever do you mean? If you're referring to Sherman, I know he's very driven. But mad?"

Strong sat up and turned on the light.

"Whatever in the world are you doing, dear?"

"I need to show you the speech that Sherman is insisting I give in New York on Thursday. You have to read it."

He handed it to her. She put her glasses on and read it. Twice.

"Well of course you can't do it. Is that what all the fuss is about?"

"Doris, please," he pleaded, but continued sternly, "don't be so flippant. Of course I could handle that! I refused even after he practically begged."

"So what is it then?" she asked, surprised at the tone of his voice.

"If I don't deliver that speech, word for word, Sherman intimated that he would let something terrible happen to the children."

"What? Robert, are you certain?" She took one look at him and continued, "But of course you are. What are we going to do?"

"I've got to give the speech. I have to. Marcus and Angela are more precious to me than my integrity. I have been tricked into taking help from the devil, thinking him to be my salvation. You've warned me for years about Sherman, and now it turns out you were right all along."

"Worse than I ever could have dreamed! I knew he was ambitious, but this means he's a monster. That he's capable of doing almost anything..."

"Yes, and I fear just that - that he'll do anything to get the presidency. Any unspeakable thing. He's as much as said so. And I'm a part of it - a big part."

He cried openly and unashamedly, his wife joining him but doing her best to console. After he was done they prayed and prayed, late into the night.

15 - Self Defence

When Chu woke up the next morning, he surprised himself. It wasn't Faith Gale who was on his mind. Instead it was Audrey. He'd dreamt about her. A very disturbing dream. In it, she was on the bus but her wig kept falling off. Two men sitting behind her seat seemed to recognize who she was. He was about to say something, to warn her to look out, when suddenly one of the men took a gun out from his jacket and aimed it directly at her head. He'd wanted to scream to get her attention but his voice failed him. He heard the click of the trigger and waited for the explosion. That was when he had woken up with a start, unable to go back to sleep, with Audrey foremost in his mind.

Tomorrow was Friday and he still had no idea of how or when he would meet up with the Strongs in New York City. All the earlier schedules had been thrown out when it was decided the Strongs would cruise to New York. That meant he had no clue whether or not meeting Audrey at their prearranged time was going to work. He hated the idea of her sitting there waiting, no idea of what was going on. And it was dangerous to risk being out in the open. They'd be looking for sure - everywhere. Who knows how much they knew already? Lying awake with his restless thoughts Chu had to face up to the fact that he needed help. A backup in case he couldn't make it.

He resolved to trust O'Reilly in spite of Audrey's reservations. Who else was there? O'Reilly was the only one Chu felt good about at all, and he still wasn't one hundred percent sure about him. But he didn't see any other way. The question that plagued him now was how to do it without being found out.

———

Breakfast in the hotel dining room was a sombre affair. They had been segregated from the rest of the guests as a security precaution and ate their meal in a separate, cordoned-off area.

Chu was feeling low because of the dream about Audrey and the fact that Faith refused to join them. He had hoped he might get a chance to talk with Faith before going to the gym - that perhaps he could explain a little better. Tell her why, in spite of his strong feelings, it was impossible. Instead, she took breakfast alone in her room, leaving him feeling half empty, like the plate of food sitting in front of him.

K.C. sat, head in hand, picking unenthusiastically at his six-egg hungry man omelet. He was depressed because his father had chewed him out mercilessly for not standing up to the drunks. It was a complaint K.C. had heard most of his life. He was never tough enough or mean enough for his father. K.C. felt he had let him down once again.

"Took your little sister to put them straight. Cripes son, you're the one who's supposed to protect *her*! Where's your pride?"

Those had been the senior Gale's exact words, according to K.C.. They had agreed to meet Faith in the lobby at nine thirty which, because of their general malaise and lack of conversation, took forever to come.

———

Members of the media camped overnight outside the hotel, waiting, hoping and even praying for something newsworthy to happen. They needed something – almost anything - to get on air or a byline in a tabloid. Like sharks, they smelled fresh blood, and were getting fractious with anticipation of a big feed.

When the limo pulled up, a stampede to the front entrance erupted. Several police officers watched at the ready, as security staff cleared a way for them to get through the throng. When the door of the car opened, it was Angelo who got out. He looked around for a few seconds and smiled. He enjoyed the jangle and prestige. He kept facing the mob, mugging shamelessly as he opened up the passenger door and waited for the famous threesome. Mike waited at the wheel, shaking his head at his partner's antics.

As arranged, K.C. and Chu were waiting in the lobby for Faith to join them. She was running late, only fifteen minutes, but that was abnormal. K.C. kept telling Chu this while they waited - at least ten times. Each time with exactly the same words.

"She's always on time, I just don't understand it. No, siree, it isn't like her at all."

Over and over like a broken record. It really started to get to Chu. When he heard the words, all he could think was that he was to blame. Every time it made him remember, and it made him feel guilty, and he hated that. Chu was sure that Faith was still upset about what happened, or rather what didn't happen, between them. He imagined her, red-faced and bleary-eyed from crying, attempting to muster the courage to face the day.

He could tell that K.C. was going to loop into his spiel again. It was getting too much. Chu was just about to say something to stop him when the elevator door opened. Faith exited in grand fashion, being escorted by two Gale Security agents in full uniform. She strutted out confidently, wearing a designer pant-suit and spike heels with a large wicker hand bag draped over her shoulder. Acknowledging everyone present gracefully and with a radiant smile, she walked like royalty through the lobby. She looked like she could be on the cover of a fashion magazine and she looked at least five years older than seventeen. She ignored Chu and K.C. completely as she passed by. But under her breath, they clearly heard her utter a command.

"Let's get going and get this over with."

They followed as directed, pulled along by the energy vortex Faith was generating. Chu was full of wonder. How could a girl of seventeen, a girl who only yesterday seemed so young, exhibit such poise, grace and authority as she led them through the crowd of screaming, jeering, camera-wielding yahoos? She had turned the media circus into an opportunity to show America, and the world, who she was.

While he hid it as they walked confidently toward the car, inside Chu was a mess. He was embarrassed to think he had ever imagined Faith would be pining over him. And while he would not admit it, not even to himself, the feelings of guilt he experienced earlier had been usurped by bitter disappointment.

———

The gym that Sherman Gale had booked was in the seedy end of downtown Miami. Getting there from the hotel had taken half an hour and entailed crossing the causeway that connected Miami Beach to the city.

Faith hardly uttered a word during the entire trip, even though her brother tried to engage her many times. It was almost pitiful seeing the older boy trying so hard, only to be spurned again and again by his younger sibling. Faith finally reached the end of her patience and lashed out in anger.

"For goodness sake, K.C., will you please just leave me alone! Sometimes you're just too dumb to take a hint."

K.C. responded like a dog that has just been kicked by its master. There was no anger. Just a profound sense of sadness and dejection. Chu sat as far away from the siblings as he could, pretending to be engrossed by the spectacular scenery. He was trying hard to come up with a way of contacting O'Reilly. A way that would avoid using his cell phone, as it was almost certainly being bugged. A pay phone might work, but ever since yesterday morning they'd been watching his every move.

As he tried to think, he found himself sneaking glances at Faith. For whatever reason, she looked even more beautiful to him than ever before. He tried not to think about her, but it proved impossible. He was no closer to a plan or avoiding secret looks when Mike rolled up to their destination.

"Alright everybody," he barked, "You all hop out and I'll go park the car. I want to see this."

"I think you're probably going to be disappointed," said Chu, "It's going to be pretty boring. We're just going to cover some basic stuff."

"We'll see, we'll see," Mike laughed.

Angelo turned to face the back seat with the strange smile Chu had seen before. Something was up, he thought, and he wondered what it could be.

———

Chu was in the ring with K.C. and feeling very frustrated. They'd been working for almost an hour and a half but the young man still couldn't understand even the most basic moves. Faith had brought a book to read but paused to watch the debacle from time to time. Mike and Angelo had lost interest and were having coffee at the snack bar, talking earnestly.

"I don't think I'll ever get it," a depressed K.C. muttered, "Like Faith said, I'm too dumb."

While Chu might have agreed, he spared K.C. confirmation, instead focusing on teaching him some exercises that, with practice, would help. K.C. and Chu were wrapping it up when Mike and Angelo joined them at ringside.

"You guys calling it quits already? We have this place booked for three more hours."

K.C. rolled his eyes. Chu shrugged his shoulders.

"So Angelo and me have been talking. How about doing some boxing with him?"

"Just wait, what are you talking about?" replied Chu. "I'm not much of a boxer."

"Angelo said you wouldn't want to. He's convinced he can kick your ass as long as you don't do that fancy martial arts stuff, but I disagree. "

Angelo said nothing, but there was the weird smile again.

"Faith, you okay with waiting?" Chu called up to her in the stands.

"Whatever," she replied, seemingly uninterested, though putting her book down.

———

When Chu came out from the dressing room, he was surprised to see the bleachers around the ring more than half full. Several people were placing bets with Mike when Chu approached him to find out what was going on. Mike looked happier than Chu had ever seen.

"What the hell is going on Mike?"

"Well, this has got a little bigger than we expected, but word gets around you know."

"No, I don't know. I thought we were just going to do a little sparring."

"Yeah, well. Too late to chicken out now."

"I didn't say anything about chickening out, but what the fuck is happening?"

"Okay, here's the drill. We started yammering about how tough you really were. Angelo said that you was nothing much except for the Kung Fu crap. When Colonel Gale arranged the gym we thought it would be a perfect way to find out."

"So how do you think he's going to react when he finds out about all this?"

"Oh, he's found out. We're recording the bout for him to see later. He's got five grand riding on it."

"On me or Angelo?"

"On Angelo. He's a two to one favourite over you."

"Angelo's the favourite?"

"Yeah, well, he was a ranked heavyweight at one time, you know. Personally, I think he's way too out of shape, but not everybody agrees. I'm betting you're going to win me some nice coin today."

"So, it's a fight, not just sparring?"

"Yep, I'll be in your corner, and Danny, Angelo's old trainer, will be in his."

"How about a referee?"

"We got that covered, Derrik. Don't you worry none."

But Chu was worried. When he looked over at his oversized adversary, Angelo was staring back, with that strange - almost maniacal - smile pasted on his face.

———

The referee called them to the middle of the ring and explained the rules. It didn't take long, although Chu was not completely sure what it meant.

"Three rounds, Olympic rules and keep it clean."

Chu had never been in a real boxing match. He'd goofed around a bit with some friends and watched quite a bit on TV, but this was different. The gloves felt too large to be effective, and the thought of not using his feet was intimidating.

Angelo glowered at him intently as the ref went on to explain the judging system. He wasn't scoring but three ringside judges were. His eyes followed the referee's finger as he pointed to where they were seated. Chu saw that Faith and K.C. were seated just behind. She smiled very slightly in recognition. K.C. gave him a wide grin and a thumbs up. Chu felt his ears grow red.

"So got all that? Now touch gloves and let's get this show on the road."

The now bursting-full gym exploded in a roar as the ref stepped away, leaving the two men facing each other. Angelo was a good seven inches taller than Chu and weighed almost two hundred pounds more. His legs were as thick as Chu's waist and he seemed to fill up the ring. He stood, hands up at the ready, looking at Chu to come at him.

Chu stood, hands at his side, not knowing how to start. The crowd booed and jeered almost at once, their collective thirst for action demanding satisfaction. Mouth guards garbled words, making them almost impossible to understand. They exchanged taunts anyway.

"Come on you pussy!" Angelo screamed, finally breaking through the crowd noise.

"After you, tubby!" Chu bellowed in response as loudly as he could, not sure why he said it but hoping it would make Angelo mad. His grandfather had always taught him that fighting an angry man was to your advantage.

"That how matador defeat bull," he told Chu over and over, "Bull much stronger but no use head. Head wins fight – always."

In fact, the words did infuriate Angelo. He attacked with a series of heavy blows that sent Chu staggering back on the ropes, making him wonder if he had used the right tactic. Chu moved sideways just in the nick of time as a crushing right barely missed its mark. Maybe his grandfather's advise didn't apply to boxing. Maybe the difference in size was more important in this sport than it was in the martial arts.

Chu was surprised at the speed with which his opponent could move. The Angelo he was familiar with was a slow-moving, affable giant. This person was a punching machine. A very large and angry punching machine. The crowd exploded with anticipation. It looked like it was going to be quick. Quick and decisive. Angelo was relentless in his pursuit, and those watching could just feel that one of those big punches being thrown was going to land. And that would be it. Lights out.

Chu tried to remember everything his grandfather had taught him about fighting a much stronger adversary. Once when he was ten, he had fought in a tournament against teenagers more than five years older. He had ended up winning against all odds and made Chu's grandfather prouder of him than he could ever remember before or since. He recalled what his grandfather had said to him over and over during his march to the finals.

"Trick is not be there when they expect. When they expect, you move. Only when you decide, you be there."

People got to their feet, egging Angelo on. He was clearly the favourite. They wanted him to knock out the smart ass Asian. Angelo chased Chu around the ring several times trying to do just that, before he realized that Chu could avoid him all day if he chose to. He was impossible to pin down and Angelo could feel he himself running out of steam. It had been a long time. Angelo let up slightly with about thirty seconds to go in the round. He faked to the left but then lunged to the right, trapping Chu's foot beneath his own. With Chu pinned, Angelo let him have it with a right to the head.

Chu could see it coming but there was nothing he could do. He managed to pull his foot away but not quickly enough. The blow hit him hard, but because he turned at the last second, glanced off the right side of his head. He absorbed as much of the force as he could, but still knew this was a damaging blow. He'd had enough of them over the years. His world suddenly slowed down. The shouting of the crowd disappeared. He knew he had to keep moving.

Angelo could see Chu was hurt. The look in the smaller man's eyes said everything. A vacant kind of stare. There was fifteen seconds left, lots of time to for Angelo to polish him off.

His grandfather was with Chu now, deep inside his head. He was screaming at the top of his lungs, "Make circle with legs. Keep legs moving! Go back. Move legs. Pivot head!"

Angelo stepped back and took a wide swing. Just as he was expecting the connection, the satisfying confluence of hand to head, he swung through air, almost falling over. Chu had ducked down and around, out of harms way. He would survive to round two.

Throughout the break Chu drank water and just tried to come to his senses. Things were coming back into focus now. It had been a while since he was hit that hard. Mike was still screaming at the referee about the foot fault. There was only a few seconds left when Mike asked Chu if he was okay.

"What the fuck do you think? Say, is that legal for him to stomp on my foot?"

"Of course not."

"Any advice?"

"Only that hitting him in the head will get you nowhere. He's never been knocked out. Not enough brains. He may not have been the champ, but nobody ever knocked him out. Go for that big belly. I know it looks big, but I think it's his Achilles tendon."

Chu was a little punch-drunk and started laughing. Achilles tendon.

"What's so funny?" Mike asked, confused.

"Nothing," he replied with a smirk, "Thanks for the tip."

When the bell sounded to begin round two, Chu jumped up still smiling and ran towards the centre of the ring. He remembered another thing his grandfather had taught him.

"Smile when you hurt. Make other guy very worry. They think you crazy."

Angelo had been watching Chu and didn't like what he saw. The guy wasn't acting like he was hurt. He had seen him laughing during the break. And now, at the centre of the ring, there he was with a big smile on his face.

Chu had decided to listen to the old man inside his head and fake it. During all his years in tournaments he'd found his grandfather was right. A great deal of combat sport was how you made your opponent feel. If you showed a sign of weakness it spurred them on. If they thought you were strong, it made them weaker.

Angelo came out of his corner slowly and raised his hands. With a sudden fury that shocked the big man, Chu closed the gap and threw a series of hard blows to Angelo's ample gut. Angelo finally managed to push him away and cover up.

Chu could feel the effect of his punches on Angelo almost immediately. As they moved into the middle of the round, they were back at the cat-and-mouse game with Angelo stalking and Chu running away. But Angelo's blows were getting weaker and easier to block.

Chu went inside for another attack when he saw an opening. It was like hitting the heavy bag but with even greater resistance. Angelo tried to get away and stumbled backwards. It was then that the crowd sensed the momentum was shifting. Chu could feel it, too, and pursued, forgetting about Angelo's right hand.

Too late Chu heard his grandfather yelling at him again – warning him not to over-commit...

"Take slow. Not so crazy!"

But it was too late.

With about twenty seconds to go in the round it hit him. One last desperate blow from the giant, swung with all his might. A crushing right to the head that sent Chu down on one knee. A follow up from Angelo's left put him flat on the canvas.

The fight was over.

The crowd went wild.

———

When Chu came to his senses he realized he was in the back of the limo with his head in somebody's lap. He could smell Faith's perfume and imagined it was her. But when he opened his eyes, he saw it was K.C. who was tending to him.

"Gee, things looked like they were going great – until he socked you with that right."

"I got carried away, I guess," he replied trying to get up. A spiking pain drove through his head.

"Just give it a few more minutes. I've seen lots of guys with their bells rung and they always try to get up too fast."

"Where are we, K.C.?"

"Going back to the hotel. We already dropped Faith at the airport. After we drop you, Mike's taking me back there. Faith and I are flying up to New York tonight."

"What about me?"

"I don't know. I think you're coming up tomorrow sometime. At least I think that's what Faith said."

"Yeah, that's it," chimed in Mike from the front seat, "She said something about the FBI being upset because they couldn't reach you."

"Oh, yeah, I guess I haven't reported in for a couple of days."

"You're lucky you don't work for Gale Security. They get really mad about that kind of thing."

"Hmm, I think I'm going to get another beating when I do make that call. Thanks for the warning. Say, where's Angelo? I thought he'd take the opportunity to gloat."

"They took him to the hospital. Seems you broke three of his ribs. He's going to be out for a while."

"That makes me feel a little better," Chu said, sitting up slowly with K.C.'s help.

"By the way, Angelo told me to tell you, you did good. He was surprised," added Mike.

"That makes two of us," Chu said laughing and holding his head, until he stopped short with a groan because it hurt too much.

"Oh, yeah," K.C. blurted out, suddenly remembering, "and Faith said to say goodbye, Mr. Chu. She thinks you did really good. She was sorry you lost."

"Not as sorry as me," groaned Chu.

"Or me," echoed Mike, "I lost a bundle."

———

When they got back to the hotel, K.C. made sure Chu could walk before they drove away. Chu turned and waved. K.C. was leaning out the back window looking concerned.

"Take care, Mr. Chu. Hope we'll see you in New York," he called, waving.

Chu waved again, smiling the best he could. He didn't even try to call back because he could just tell that it would hurt his head too much. All he wanted to do was sleep but that was going to have to wait. He had too much to do and he knew once he hit the pillow he'd be out for hours.

As he was walking back into the hotel, he was surprised to see a news crew still staking the place out. They intercepted him before he could get inside the doors, effectively blocking his way.

"Excuse me, please," Chu asked politely.

"Yes, of course, Agent Chu, but first, just a couple of questions? Please?"

The reporter was just a kid and looked like he hadn't been home in days. So pitiful, Chu couldn't say no.

"Alright, just a couple."

"Well, first off, what happened to you?"

"I hit a brick wall."

"A brick wall?"

"Yeah, you know I do extreme running. Well, today I hit a brick wall. Now, what's your other question?"

The reporter froze. He looked frantically for his notes.

"Well, uh, is there any truth to the rumour that you and Faith Gale are an item?"

"What? An item? What kind of question is that?"

"There's been talk?"

"By who?"

"I don't know. People."

"Listen kid, here is the kind of question you should be asking - 'What is your advice for young people?' And I'd answer - 'Stay off drugs, don't smoke or drink and stop watching TV.' Now there, that's the kind of thing you ask."

Chu had got closer and closer to the reporter and was waving his finger in his face. That's when he noticed the cell phone sticking out of the pocket of the reporter's pants. Taking the opportunity in front of him, he took the reporter by the shoulders, turned him around and gave him a light push out of his way. At the same time he bumped the reporter's leg with his own and removed the cell phone without him knowing.

"Now, let me through, thank you."

"That was assault!" called one of the crew.

"More like obstruction of a Federal officer, from my point of view," he retorted, walking into the lobby and pocketing the stolen device.

He made his way to the elevators and up to his room. All the security people were gone and it seemed strangely quiet. He got his own cell phone out of the room safe and made his way back downstairs. He checked quickly and could see that the news crew had taken off. Probably on the way to their lawyers' offices.

Chu walked directly out the doors and down to the beach knowing he would be followed in some fashion. He couldn't make the calls from his room, as it was likely bugged.

He sat close to the water, facing out to sea. The location would be difficult for anyone to record, no matter what kind of wiz bang directional microphone was being used. White noise from the waves, a perfect 180 degree front scape that could only be breached if they had a boat out there at the ready, which he doubted.

He would make two calls: one to O'Reilly using the sniveling reporter's phone, and one to his office using his own cell.

He dialled the number O'Reilly had given him. It rang three times before it was picked up.

"Yeah?" the voice at the other end snapped angrily. It was definitely O'Reilly.

"Enjoying Washington, O'Reilly?"

"Who the hell is that? Is that you Chu? Call says it's coming in from a B. Philips."

"Yup, I just stole the phone from him."

"What?"

"Just listen, okay? Kunitz is on the run. She found out some things that will shake everything up. We don't know who to trust."

"Is she with you now?"

"No, she's safe. I have to get up to New York tomorrow to meet with her. Where are you now?"

"I'm still in Washington but flying up to New York tomorrow. There's a meeting of the security team at seven at Trump Towers. Do you know where that is?"

"Oh yeah, right across from Columbus Circle."

"That's right. But haven't they been in touch with you? I know they've been trying. Seems you're in hot water."

"I guess I've had my phone off for a couple of days."

"I noticed. I tried you a few times. When are you getting in?"

"I'm not sure right now. How about you?"

"Think around one."

"JFK?"

"No, LaGuardia."

"You want to meet downtown at two thirty so we can talk?"

"That'd work. Where?"

"Let's try Columbus Circle."

"Alright, see you there. And Chu, thanks for phoning. Things are getting crazier by the minute."

"Tell me about it. See you tomorrow."

"Yeah, tomorrow."

Chu turned off the phone and threw it into the water as far out as he could. Then he picked up his own cell phone and turned it on. There were eighteen messages from Hinks, seven from Forbes, three from O'Reilly and one from his mom.

A sudden wave of nostalgia made him decide to phone home, but all he got was the answering machine.

"Hi, Mom. Just phoning to return your call. I'm fine. The time off in Miami was pretty busy. I'll be in New York tomorrow and will give you a shout then. Love to you and Grandpa." He was going to make the call to the office when he stopped and thought hard. He knew what the reaction was going to be. He'd get it soon enough.

So, this time without turning it off, Chu skipped his phone over the waves. It was with a sense of relief that he watched the still-visible screen fluttering off and on as it sunk to the depths.

Now he could get some much needed sleep.

———

Steve Thomas heard something he hadn't heard before. It was Sherman Gale laughing, out loud and uncontrollably. He waited until it had died down, then knocked on the cabin door.

"Come in, come in," he responded, uncharacteristically inviting.

Thomas opened the door and stepped in to find the Colonel sitting in front of a TV. He was pointing to it and smiling.

"Steve, you just have to see this. I don't care what your business is, or how important it is I know something. Just come sit here and watch this. It's only a few seconds, really."

Thomas sat down as ordered. He was impatient to give Gale the news.

With a smile on his face, the Colonel hit the play button and the television sprang to life. It was a video clip from the fight. It started about midway through the second round. Gale sat on the edge of the sofa, apparently waiting for something to happen. There, in all its glory, was the sudden flurry of body punches thrown by Chu near the end of the round. Gale looked over to see Thomas' reaction and found him sneering. He knew it looked like Chu was going to win. That's what he had thought the first time he saw it.

But then, the unexpected.

As Chu stepped into the pulverizing overhead right, Gale jumped off his seat and into the air pointing at the screen and yelling.

"There, there it is! Isn't that beautiful?"

Thomas had to admit it was. They watched it again a few times before they were done.

Gale was still chuckling to himself quietly when he was finally ready to get down to business.

"Okay Steve, what was so important that it couldn't wait?"

"Well, this is kind of funny, sir. You can't know how much I enjoyed seeing that fight. Particularly in light of the information I have for you."

"Bad news, huh? Well, let's have it."

"Well, we figured out why Chu was so willing to go with us yesterday morning. Audrey Kunitz had already left Miami by that time."

This seemed to surprise Gale, and any vestige of mirth immediately disappeared.

"What did you find out?"

"We finally got a taxi driver to identify Chu. He picked him up at the airport with a woman the driver thought was drunk. Our thinking is that she was injured in her tangle with Johnson."

"You know this as a fact?"

"The guy dropped them off downtown and took Chu's bags to the Marriott. Which we've also confirmed. Chu showed up later that afternoon on foot."

"Did you find the hotel room?"

"Yes, sir. Again Chu was identified as checking in with a woman who was out of it. And you were right, they paid cash for two nights. Only stayed one, though, and never picked up the five hundred dollar deposit."

"How did he do it?"

"Partially us not watching him closely enough and partially because he's really good at what he does. And remember, we didn't know Kunitz was in Miami at the time."

"But don't you see? She must have told him everything she knows. The connection of Fernandez with the assassination attempt and the Russians. That could be very dangerous."

"Should we take Chu out?"

"No, no. Not so hasty, Steve. I have other plans for Mr. Chu." He paused in contemplation before going on, "And when you think about it, who's he going to tell? From what I gather, he doesn't know who to trust. We've got eyes and ears all over the place. And then there's the little matter of proof. No, Major Thomas, he's going to lead us to our little CIA friend. I'd bet anything she's in New York, waiting for him, already."

16 - The Big Apple

Times Square, New York City - one of the busiest places on earth, but strangely, one of the easiest places to hide away. As long as you look fairly normal, mind your own business and pay your bills with cash, you can disappear into the crowd, remaining anonymous.

Clutching a brown paper bag in one hand, containing a coffee and bagel and the morning newspaper in the other, one such anonymous person moved quickly and confidently through the sparsely-peopled sidewalks - a huge contrast from when she had walked there last night when it was swarming with a sea of humanity.

Two young men gave her an approving look as she passed. One of them said something to her in Spanish, spurring her to respond in the language, making them both blush. If asked, they'd have guessed she was in her early twenties. She was short, petite and looked more than a little punk, with short black hair, leather jacket, blue jeans and high top sneakers. The effect was further accentuated by a nose ring, eyebrow stud and dark, post-Goth makeup.

She left Broadway and quickly walked up the block to The Big Apple Hostel where she was staying. She'd stayed there years ago but never forgotten it. So convenient to the bus station, ultra low profile, and they took cash. She had paid for a private room for a week, registering as Lorna Stevenson from Portland, Maine.

"Hey, Lorna," the desk clerk said, acknowledging her as she came into the lobby.

"Oh, hi," she replied, pausing to see if there was a reason to stop.

"Did you find the bagel place?"

"Yeah, thanks. I can hardly wait to try it."

"They're the best. You'll see."

"I'll let you know. And thanks for the directions."

She took the stairs instead of waiting for the elevator. She was taking every opportunity to exercise after spending the better part of two days sitting on a bus. When she got into the room she threw off her jacket, revealing the gun and holster she was wearing. Then she sat down, looking forward to eating her breakfast and reading the paper.

"That's good for about an hour," she said to herself out loud and wondered what she was going to do for the rest of the day. It was only nine thirty in the morning, and Audrey had until three to meet with Chu at Columbus Circle.

———

O'Reilly was waiting for Chu to show up. He checked his watch yet again to see what the time was and found that it was one minute later than when he had checked it the last time, two thirty five. Suddenly from behind him, he heard Chu's voice.

"Don't turn around, just walk away and go into the park. Meet me by the skating rink in half an hour."

"Why not here?"

But there was no reply because he was already gone. When he finally did turn and look, Chu was nowhere to be seen.

Chu circled around the block before returning to Columbus Circle to wait. It was exactly ten to three. He walked around the monument, pretending to be looking at the sights, watching closely for a woman wearing a red hat. On his third turn he almost ran into a tough-looking young woman dressed in a leather jacket.

"Sorry," Chu said without thinking and carried on.

"Well, watch where you're going."

It was unmistakable. It was her voice.

He turned to look at her. It was amazing. He never would have recognized her.

"Are you clean? No tail?" she added in hushed tones.

"Don't think so – but you never know. No red hat?"

"O'Reilly?" she retorted. She'd obviously seen him contacting O'Reilly just a few minutes before. He wondered if anybody else had been watching.

"We need help and we need to talk. Got a place?"

"Yeah, Big Apple Hostel on West 45th. Room 301."

"Can I bring O'Reilly.?"

"If you have to. Gotta go."

"And you watch out where you're going!" said Chu raising his voice before continuing on his way.

It had been more than half an hour since Chu told O'Reilly that he'd meet him at the ice rink. O'Reilly was getting more and more upset with each passing minute. Finally, when the

Secret Service man had concluded there must be a problem, he saw Chu walking toward him.

"Hi, good to see you," Chu said sitting next to him.

"I thought we must have had a crossed wire. What took?"

"Had to meet with her and see if she'd be alright with you coming along."

"If she'd be alright with it? What the fuck?"

"Look, she doesn't know who to trust."

"How can you trust her?"

"I don't know. Except that it's unlikely she would have brained herself. It's kind of hard to fake a concussion."

"She was hurt bad?

"I can't believe she made it here in one piece. I was worried when I put her on the bus but there was nothing else I could do."

"Look, this is bullshit. Either we're in this together or we're not. I'm fucking tired of not knowing what's going on. Gale and his people are working as a team and they're kicking our asses!"

"Shit, O'Reilly, I always thought *I* was impatient!"

"It's not my strong suit, son. It's pee or get off the pot time. Look, I have access to some very influential people. If this thing is what you say it is, they can do something to help if anyone can. They can be trusted, I assure you."

"We need a down-to-earth conversation with Audrey."

"So it's Audrey now, is it?"

"Yeah. I got to know her in Miami."

"Not...?"

"No, nothing like that. She was out of it most of the time, for God's sake. It's just, she's okay, that's all. I mean, I trust her."

"But you don't trust me?"

"I want to. That's what I told her. We need help, it's as simple as that, and I'm betting on you," Chu said pausing, "And the first thing I need help doing is seeing if someone is following me. I have a funny feeling my steps are being dogged and that just won't do."

———

"Our man's off line!" shouted a technician in the small communications room located in the bowels of Victory.

"What do you mean off line?" retorted an agitated Steve Thomas.

"I mean his transmitter just went dead."

"Where?"

"In Central Park. He had Chu in sight walking north from where he met with O'Reilly. He was on the radio reporting in when it went dead."

"Do we have any other operatives in the area?"

"No, he was the only one that managed to stick with Chu from the airport. We have two others on their way to lend assistance. What should we tell them?"

"Tell them to be on the lookout for Chu. What else can we do now?" Thomas said, feeling a sense of panic rising up inside. When he'd been called down urgently to the communications room, he'd known something was up. He'd been convinced the team could do the job but now the entire operation was in jeopardy. Suddenly, and with passion, he pounded his fist on the desk, his frustration reaching the breaking point.

"I don't believe it. We had four of our best on his trail when he hit the city! What happened?"

"He's very elusive, sir, and I guess he was expecting it."

"Well, finding him in the park is going to be like finding a needle in a haystack. But get more people on it, it's our only chance. I don't want to go to the Colonel until we have something or he's going to keelhaul the lot of us! And this time, I wouldn't blame him."

———

After O'Reilly detected and dispatched the guy following Chu, they arranged to make their separate ways to the hostel where Audrey was waiting. Chu arrived first at four thirty as agreed, and went directly upstairs to room 301. When he knocked on the door there was no answer. He waited a few seconds and then rapped again a little harder. The door of room 303, directly across the hall, opened and there stood the little punk girl, aka Audrey Kunitz.

"Didn't you say room 301?"

"Yeah, it's being reno'd right now. Never can be too careful."

He moved inside quickly and she shut the door behind. They were happy to see each other, but unsure how to greet. Shaking hands seemed too formal - a full embrace, too familiar. They settled in the end for something in between.

"We'll have to listen for O'Reilly. He'll be ten minutes behind me."

"Great," she replied, but the look on her face said anything but that.

"Look, I didn't know who else to go to. Say, aren't your eyes green?"

"Bought contacts in Charlotte, along with these little beauties," she said referring to the nose ring and eye brow stud.

"You got piercings that quick?"

"Oh no. I've had the holes for quite a while. Like the tattoos. You're not the only weirdo, you know."

"You have tattoos?"

"You didn't notice? I thought you had a good look at everything I have."

"I tried to be as discreet as I could," he said almost blushing.

"Quite the gentleman, aren't we? Most guys would've taken the opportunity."

He didn't know if that was a put-down or a compliment, so he chose to ignore it and changed the subject.

"Anyway, I'm thinking we level with O'Reilly and see what he says. You still have the gun, don't you?"

"Yeah, of course."

"Well, just keep it handy."

"Right here. So you don't trust him?"

"I do, but as you said, you can never be too careful."

———

They heard the expected knock at 301. Chu could see through the peephole that it was O'Reilly. After a few seconds more of waiting, he opened the door a crack and called to him.

"Here, over here."

O'Reilly spun around and entered the room quickly. When he came face to face with Audrey Kunitz his jaw dropped and he stood there at a loss for words.

"Everything alright, O'Reilly?" Chu asked.

"It's, ah, just that - is that really you, Dr. Kunitz?"

"Yes, it's really me," she answered.

"Oh, yeah, that's the voice."

"Boy, that's annoying," she fumed as Chu and O'Reilly exchanged looks, on the edge of laughter.

"I tried not talking at all so it wouldn't be so noticeable, but that doesn't seem to work, either."

"Don't mind us, it's just you have a very distinctive voice — even though I didn't hear much of it when we worked together," began O'Reilly earnestly, "Thing is, I know you're scared and that Chu here is already in shit for bringing me, but I have to know what you've found out. I really do believe it's a matter of life and death right now. Every second counts."

"Then let's do it," she replied.

"Great! But not here. Chu, I think we should get her to a safe house nearby. We can talk there. It's only a matter of time until they find this place."

"You okay with that Audrey?"

"Like you said, we don't have much of a choice. And I'm kinda tired of this punk look already. Been there, done that, if you know what I mean."

———

The three of them sat around a table in a spacious flat on the upper east side. Audrey was looking more like herself having taken out her hardware, removed the contacts and changed clothes. She got the ball rolling.

"Well, Mr. O'Reilly, you talk about needing information and sharing what we know, but maybe you could start."

"Fair ball, I'll accept that challenge. I'll lay my cards on the table as long as you two agree do the same."

O'Reilly looked back and forth between Kunitz and Chu. Getting nods from both of them he took a deep breath, made himself comfortable in his seat, and continued.

"First thing you need to know is that the Secret Service is supposed to be impartial during an election. A significant conflict of interest can result if the Service starts actively aiding the efforts of one candidate over another. We have to assume the incumbent President acts in the best interests of the country but we also have to acknowledge that as politicians they have their own self-interest as well. It makes it tricky at the best of times.

"This is the first election in a very long time where there have been three strong candidates. In fact, it's the first in almost two hundred years where a main candidate wasn't affiliated with a major political party."

Audrey was patiently listening while Chu was screwing up his face, wondering why O'Reilly was wasting their time on a history lesson.

"There is a reason I'm telling you this, Chu. I'm not just rambling away here."

"Sorry, I was just trying to see the relevance."

"Remember our little chat earlier in the park about patience? Maybe try to find some?"

"Okay, touche. I'll try and stay focused," Chu mumbled, feeling caught out.

Audrey couldn't help smiling at this interchange. The older man was still looking at Chu with raised eyebrows as he went on.

"The point of all that preamble was to impress upon you that we're treading on very thin ice here with little precedent to guide our actions. Anyway, the Secret Service became aware of several issues with Robert Strong's campaign the last time he ran. We passed this information along and, as you know, your agencies and others have been gathering intelligence on Gale ever since.

"The problem is this: we know Strong's campaign is being run by a man who believes he is doing God's work. He is both very powerful and capable. If we make any accusation against Gale or Strong we know they'll scream that we are doing it for political reasons. We're all in the same position. We want to do the right thing but are very wary of crossing over that conflict of interest line. However, if we get something big enough and have solid evidence to prove it...

"Now, here is the difficulty even with that. Because of the fear of being accused of partisanship, many people in federal agencies, including both of yours, are taking a 'hands off' approach. They're bureaucrats, after all, and they worry - what if Strong wins and finds out they were actively working against him during the campaign? Now that's kind of normal at this stage of the cycle, but there's a big difference this time."

He paused looking from one to the other, seeing if they wanted to guess. Not getting a volunteer, he continued.

"There are people who are actively working in Strong's interest this time around. I've run into it, as I know you have. And they're everywhere. So we have lots of people sitting on the fence, not wanting to get involved no matter what information comes to light, and we have people actively working to help Strong get elected. People who are loyal to Gale and his obsession to elect a Christian president.

"As the Republican candidate was demolished in the polls, thanks in large part to some misinformation about her supplied by Gale's people, we started to get very concerned. But then Strong's momentum faded – until the little blip caused by your heroics, Chu. But we now know that if the election were held today it would be no contest. The incumbent would win easily. But here's the problem. Almost every piece of intelligence we've gained in the last month indicates that Gale is up to something. Something he believes will change the outcome of the election — maybe even the course of history. And that's where your information is so important to us.

"I'm going to tell you something now that can't leave this room. I'm a founding member of a group that is loyal to our current President. Not because of his political party, or the fact that he is any more right - but because he represents the rule of law. The law, as established by the people of the United States more than two hundred and fifty years ago.

"That's why we need to know what it is you found out that was so important they tried to kill you," he finished, looking directly at Audrey.

"Can I ask you a couple of questions first, Mr. O'Reilly?"

"Yes, certainly, Audrey. Do you mind if I call you Audrey? And please, call me Roger."

"No, Audrey is fine, thanks, Roger." Chu couldn't help rolling his eyes at this exchange, but she ignored him and carried on, "Well, my first question is, have you told the CIA you've found me?"

"No, not officially, and I don't intend to either. But the group I referred to earlier includes a very senior person in the CIA."

"Good, thanks. And my second question is, what's my status right now?"

"Status. I hadn't thought about it. I guess you're here in protective custody."

"Can I go if I want?"

"I don't think that would be advisable."

"But could I, if I wanted?"

"Being perfectly honest, and I want to assure you that I am, there would be some conditions. Do we need to get into that right now?"

"No, I just wanted to be clear where I stand."

"You notice we haven't taken away your gun, Audrey. We're not trying to hold you against you will."

"I understand. And the gun is actually Derrik's, not mine."

"Whatever. Now can you please tell us what you found out."

"Yes, sure. Well it goes back almost six months now. I was doing research on Sherman Gale and stumbled across a picture of him with another man. It was a startling picture to me. Both men were in combat pants and boots, wearing plain white tee shirts. They were smoking cigars and holding machine guns. Each of them had a foot resting on a dead man like it was a trophy. It reminded me of one of my uncle's hunting pictures. Anyway, I could identify Gale easily enough but I wondered who the other guy was.

"After a lot of work trying to find out, I almost gave up. I could identify the time and place the picture was taken. I had the names and pictures of all the soldiers listed under Colonel Gale's command. But the face of the man in the picture wasn't one of them. Then I got a break: a reference in Facebook from one of the soldiers in Gale's brigade from around that time, about a new guy from Special Operations named Fernandez. He was referred to as a buddy of Gale's from way back.

"Even with that it was difficult. It was as if all trace of him had been erased. When I actually found proof that his records had been tampered with, I tried to dig deeper but didn't have the required access authority – and I have access to almost everything.

"That would have been it. But on a whim I put in his name and picture against the national crime data base just for the hell of it. I got a hit on the picture within minutes. The name he was using was Gomez and it was a mug shot from the Chicago Police Department from 2009. But it was him, the man from the picture. Using the fingerprints on file I asked for a profile and found him again with a 2015 DUI conviction in Arizona under the name of Gomez.

"So I traced Gomez and found his last known address. It was the post box number for Sherman Gale's place in Wyoming."

"The Ranch," said Chu.

"Yup, that's it. Turns out Gomez had a cell phone account in the name of Fernandez that he only used for special calls. I got the records and ran the numbers through our 'contacts of interest' list and found that he was talking regularly with a man we knew was involved in smuggling three Russian scientists into the country."

"Why in hell was none of this information passed along? I'm sure that's new information," interjected an exasperated O'Reilly.

"I tried, but I can only think that my boss kept it and didn't pass on much, if any. My last report I know he got rid of, and then he must have set up that man to try and kill me..."

Audrey started to tear up at the memory but held it together and continued.

"It's still hard for me to believe. But at that time, of course, I had no idea. I contacted the unit working on the Russian scientist brief and was told to keep my nose out of it. They did let me know they thought it was going to be solved pretty quickly as one of the three scientists was a reliable operative the agency had used in the past.

"Well it turned out I did training with one of the team members so we grabbed a coffee to catch up. I took the opportunity to tell her about the connection with Gomez but they were already on to that. Still, she did agree to keep me posted if anything new came up. I didn't tell her about the connection of Fernandez with Gale because it didn't seem relevant.

"Another name that came up when looking at the call log was a man called Bolton. Bolton was a bad boy from way back. Turns out he did a five year stint in the army as an explosives technician. Bolton's cell phone logs registered two calls to a radical Muslim cleric who eventually supplied the explosives used in the attacks against the Strongs. I cross-referenced the radical's name to a watch list supplied to us by Homeland Security.

"That's when I asked to join your team, Roger. But by the time I showed up, the incident had just happened and I got really worried. The fact that none of Gale's people were hurt — by the way, the driver who was critically injured that day was our CIA plant — I knew it couldn't just be a coincidence.

"That was also about the time I was really getting suspicious that my unit was compromised. I decided to get more information about how Bolton was connected to Gomez, aka Fernandez, and how he in turn was connected to Gale.

"Then I got a real surprise. I was contacted and asked to translate a message sent by their Russian scientist operative. It was an SOS just hours after the assassination attempt saying that Gomez was taking them to a secret meeting place. Then all contact with him ended. Also, Bolton and Gomez haven't been seen since. My conjecture is that Gale had them all killed. I didn't put that in the report but it was definitely inferred.

When I realized it had been intercepted and destroyed I decided to make a run for it. That's it."

"Tell him about Hinks," Chu prodded.

"Oh, right. Some time back we found out that Hinks was definitely connected to the disappearance of an undercover agent the FBI had planted at The Ranch. I told Derrik to gain his trust. In fact there are several other people in his office that are connected to Gale."

"That's a mouthful, Audrey. It's no wonder they wanted you silenced. Now if I may ask, how much proof of all this do you have?"

"My report and documentation are on this key – but most of it is circumstantial," she said holding up a memory stick. "I tucked another copy away in case I lost this one," she added, tossing it to O'Reilly, "I'll need to give you the password."

"Alright, Chu, I guess it's your turn."

"I don't think I can add anything to what you've both said. Man, I feel so inadequate sometimes. I've got nothing but opinions, but here goes. Gale's a psycho, the Strongs are dupes, I'm sure of that, and Gale is gong to launch some kind of germ warfare attack before the election. Some sort of jump-start to Armageddon."

"Armageddon? How's that help things?" asked O'Reilly.

"It's not to help things. It's what they're waiting for. For the rapture, the return of the Messiah and the big showdown with evil. He thinks God is making him do this stuff. God has talked to his daughter too. It upset her when her brother mentioned it but I know she believes it to be true. They all do."

"So?"

"I think everybody is looking for a rational reason for what Gale is doing but I don't think there is one. It's based on what he thinks God has ordered him to do and he'll stop at nothing to make sure it gets done. Even if it means destroying everything. Fuck me, they want it to come. The Day of Reckoning."

"That's a frightening thought, Chu." said O' Reilly, sombrely.

"Well, wrap your head around it, because I'm sure it's true."

"And the proof?"

"I have none."

"Ah," responded O'Reilly, "that's the rub isn't it?"

———

Chu was definitely not looking forward to it. Hinks would probably be there with Forbes, and they wouldn't be happy. As the elevator doors closed, O'Reilly looked over at the young FBI agent, sensing his unease.

"Just pretend there's no issue at all. Like nothing's happened. I do it all the time."

"Thanks, it's just I get sucked in so easy. Dealing with Hinks makes me sick."

"Hold your nose to cover the smell, and smile. No matter what, keep smiling."

Chu was doing just that when the doors opened. Two security guards checked them out and then let them pass. The large conference room doors opened and inside they could see that people were already seated. When Chu followed O'Reilly into the meeting the atmosphere in the room immediately changed. Hinks sat up straight and his jaw tightened. Alicia Forbes, who was sitting to his left, scowled, not attempting in the least to hide her displeasure. Wheeler, who sat at the head of the large table in the Chair's seat, stood up and pointed a finger at him.

"Not you," he said firmly, "We don't want you here, Mr. Chu. Not any more."

O'Reilly sat down but Chu remained standing, a forced smile pasted on his face.

"Sorry, is there a problem, Mr. Wheeler?"

"Oh, come now, Mr. Chu. Your own people here have had enough," he said nodding at Hinks and Forbes, "But I'll leave the FBI's business to them. As far as you're concerned here, Mr. Chu, you are done. The Strongs no longer require your services. As a matter of fact, Colonel Gale has ordered that you have no contact with them whatsoever. Seems you're a bad influence."

"I've sure heard that before," joked Chu as best he could, and then asked amiably, "But what is it I'm going to be doing then?"

"I don't know and I don't care. All I do know is that you are no longer on this team, so if you don't mind, please leave."

O'Reilly looked at Chu to see how he'd react. There was a pause of several seconds. Chu still held a smile on his face, as if it didn't matter to him.

"Okay," he finally replied softly and turned to leave the room.

"But don't go too far, Mr. Chu," barked Forbes, "We need to talk."

"Yes, ma'am," he answered looking directly into her contorted face, "I was expecting that. Where do you want me to wait?"

"In the hall. Wait there. I don't think we'll be long," she said more as a question and looking at Wheeler.

"Ten or fifteen minutes," he confirmed.

"You heard him, we'll deal with you then," said Forbes, waving him out of the room with the back of her hand.

Chu, still smiling, took his leave and left.

———

One floor below, Robert Strong was preparing to give his speech. The major networks had already set their cameras up. All that remained were the sound checks. Doris Strong watched her husband getting an additional dusting of powder. Being uncharacteristically nervous, he was sweating heavily and needed his makeup refreshed. He looked over to his wife and gave her a soulful look. Like a man about to face the executioner.

It was more than she could bear. She put a hand up to her mouth and bit down hard to keep the tears from flowing. She wanted to stay, to listen to him give the speech as she always had in the past, but she could not. She needed to leave. She turned and moved quickly to the elevators, accompanied by two security men assigned to her.

"I need to sit down," she told them weakly, "I feel like I'm going to be ill."

After a quick discussion on the radio, a medical room with a cot was identified on the security floor above them.

———

The doors of the elevator opened and Doris Strong and her escorts stepped out. Chu was still waiting in the hall and saw her at once.

"Derrik, Derrik," she shouted waving her arms madly. He moved towards her but was stopped immediately by one of the security men.

"Sorry, sir. Mrs. Strong is feeling sick and needs to lie down."

"But if I could just say hello," Chu replied as the other guard took her down the corridor to another room. Chu could see she was struggling to get free. As she was going through the door, being half dragged, she turned and looked at him. Sad eyes that told him something was wrong, the expression imploring him for help.

"We have orders to keep you away from her," was the reply.

"But surely I can just say hello – we didn't have a chance to say goodbye."

"Sorry, we have our orders."

Chu knew something was wrong - terribly wrong - and he meant to find out what it was.

———

The red lights of the cameras went on. Strong had been dreading this moment and now, here it was. He swallowed hard and raised his eyes to look straight ahead at the millions of Americans who were watching.

"My friends," he began, "tonight I have to talk to you about things I have avoided talking about up until this point in my campaign. Things that I haven't been able to say for fear of losing votes. Things that will not be popular with small pockets of our population whose vested interests lie in maintaining the world the way it is today. But I cannot let this fear guide me any longer. Today I need to say things that need to be said.

"I won't take long, not the full half hour I've been given. I don't need a full half hour to say what I need to say to you. Mine

227

is a simple message and I know it to be the truth. Whatever they say, the truth is always simple.

"Today our great nation is filled with greed, wickedness and sin. Who among us cannot see that we are inundated by evil? Every day we see signs of this all around us. In our entertainment industry with its promotion of sin and debauchery. In our financial institutions rife with scandals, rip-offs and bailouts. In the dogma of our political correctness that preaches acceptance of adultery, divorce, homosexuality and abortion. In our justice system that lets murderers, rapists and terrorists go free. In our political leaders who cheat, lie and tell us what they think we should hear – not the truth.

"The truth is not easy to hear, particularly when it deals with our everlasting souls. But the truth is easy to tell and the cold hard truth is this - unless you bring Jesus into your heart, accept him as your personal saviour, render unto him all of your devotion, you will be thrown into the pits of hell with Satan and the rest of his minions at the time of the great reckoning. A time that is quickly approaching."

Strong paused here and took a drink of water. He looked tired but the delivery was full of energy.

"Come to Jesus and live forever. Cast out the devil or be doomed to eternally suffer in Hell. That is the truth they don't want you to hear. The truth they ignore. The truth I talk about here tonight. Sooner than you know will come of the Day of Reckoning as foretold in Revelation:

'And when he had opened the fourth seal, I heard the voice of the fourth beast say, Come and see. And I looked, and beheld a pale horse: and his name that sat on him was Death, and Hell followed with him. And power was given unto them over

the fourth part of the earth, to kill with sword, and with
hunger, and with death, and with the beasts of the earth.'

"Is it not true that the powers of darkness surround us, our once plentiful nation reduced almost to ruins? Our enemies rejoice at our misfortune. Take advantage of our weakness. Hear the words of God, my friends, hear the words of God and tremble - *to kill with sword, and with hunger, and with death.* These were not just words made up by some hack trying to get the best seller of the day. These are not some lyrics crafted to make a hit song sell. These are the words of God, brothers and sisters, and they say everything about what is next to come.

"I know that most of you, the vast majority of the people I am talking to tonight, are Christians. It is time for you to look into your hearts and choose. Choose between voting for good or evil. Between me standing with Jesus, and the old politicians standing with the money-men and the devil. The way to heaven or the 'good old way'. But I assure you, the 'good old way' represents the path of evil.

"Right now the powers of Satan are rising against me. Against me because I bring you the gospel of Jesus, the word of the Holy Bible. I am persecuted and my followers are slandered. The intellectuals, the media, the banks, the President and all his men - they're all doing whatever they can to discredit what I represent. But know this, I represent the true morals of this once great country – the very soul that made us strong. I believe God has chosen America to be His beacon in the world. You have a choice to support that, to vote for me, or to abandon her to debauchery and avarice.

"People listening to this who are Christians, help me save the soul of this nation. People listening to this who are not

Christians, repent. I repeat, repent. In the Day of Reckoning you must have Jesus in your heart to enter into heaven. I speak the truth that no one else will speak. Bring your soul to Jesus and be free. Follow the true path to righteousness. Together we can make heaven on earth. Together we can defeat the Beast.

"Thank you for listening to me. God bless America and God bless you. In the name of Jesus, amen."

———

They had watched the speech while eating dinner aboard Victory. K.C. and Faith were sombre, but their father exuded energy.

"Well, what did you think? Not truly inspired but good enough?" asked Sherman Gale as he turned off the television and addressed his two children.

"I always find him a bit melodramatic, but today he was better," Faith offered, "Maybe just a little flat."

K.C. was still trying to figure out what his uncle had said.

"What was the Bible quote he read, the one about the pale horse?" K.C. asked.

"Revelation, son. The Book of Revelation from the Bible."

"Oh, yeah. It kind of confused me. I really couldn't understand what the words were trying to say. I sure hope everybody else who was watching got it."

Gale stood looking at his son in disbelief. He'd attended some fine schools, had the best tutors available and yet...

"Well, he did it and that's the important thing. Read the whole text as written and set the stage for the final act. The last one in this long saga. The moment of truth, praise God. The moment when both of you will have your faith tested. Come,

I'll walk you to the dock, children. There's a great deal we need to discuss before you go."

———

"Did you see the speech?" Audrey asked Chu incredulously the moment he and O'Reilly walked into the room. Without waiting for an answer she continued, "Talk about fire and brimstone. I'd say any hope of him winning the election just evaporated. The analysts are going crazy. I just don't get it."

"No, as a matter of fact I missed the entire thing. I was having my ass kicked by a real dominatrix. I've been busted. I'm being sent home to Wyoming tomorrow to face disciplinary action."

"Are you going to go?" asked O'Reilly.

"Not a chance," Chu shot back, "You should have seen the look on poor Doris Strongs face when I saw her. She wanted to talk to me but they wouldn't let her. Something really bad is up and I have to find out what it is."

"Good, that's what I was hoping you'd say. So, is it fair to say that I have two rogue agents at my disposal? Agents I can't direct, of course, because they're doing their own thing?"

"Yeah, I guess so," agreed Audrey, seeing where O'Reilly was going.

"Count me in," added Chu, "But the first thing this rogue wants to do is talk to Doris Strong. I know she and her husband need help and I just won't feel right until I can find out how to do that."

"Okay, but tomorrow, Chu. Let's get at it tomorrow. It's been a long day."

17 - Blonde Bombshell

Faith looked out of the living room window on the darkness that now shrouded Central Park. Even before dawn, the street that separated their brownstone from the vast urban sanctuary was busy with traffic, mainly taxis, shuffling people to their places of work where they would help keep the massive, Godless machine afloat.

Evil, yes. Full of hatred, greed and malice – of course.

And yet, as she watched from the window she saw a young mother in the back of a cab holding a baby. The light caught the mother's face like the Madonna's as she gazed at the baby, her love a testament to all that is good. A short while later, an old man on his morning constitutional stumbled and was helped by a stranger, a young man just standing near, helping for no other purpose than to offer human kindness.

She knew the world was harsh as her father had taught her. It had taken her mother away. It had cursed her with visions and the voice of God inside her head that just wouldn't go away. But it was beautiful. The world was so beautiful. She could see that truth in the bright piece of her heart. The piece her mother had forged with her love before she died. For every act of horror there were millions of acts of kindness and love.

Tears welled up in her eyes. She knew what she had to do. She had read her father's letter over and over.

'Children,

You know what must be done. Remember John 15:10-12,
'If you obey my commands, you will remain in my love, just as
I have obeyed my Father's commands and remain in his love.'

'I know it will be hard and severely test your faith. Know
that God's work is never easy. Find strength in Jesus.

Father'

"K.C.," Faith called, "K.C. are you there? Have you read the letter?"

"I'm coming, sis," he called back from the bathroom. A few moments later he appeared.

"I read the letter and I got sick."

"Is the car ready?" Faith asked him.

"Yeah, I got the keys. But should we?"

"Should we what? You read the letter didn't you? Look, there's no point discussing it. Let's go!"

"No, listen Faith, Dad has always been on my case about standing my ground and this time I'm going to do it. I'm not going and neither are you!"

"Oh, yes I am, K.C.. Now give me the keys! We're late already. He'll be at The Ranch any minute."

"No, Faith. This is wrong! We can't do it."

Faith snatched the keys from K.C.'s hand and ran to go out of the room. She was no match for K.C., however. He caught up quickly, grabbing her around the waist as she started down the stairs.

"Let go of me!" she screamed, kicking and punching, eventually jamming the keys into his shoulder. "Let me go!"

"Hey, that hurts!" he shouted, loosening his grip and grabbing at the keys. Faith went wild but he managed to get them from her and then grab hold of her again.

"I swear I'll kill you K.C., you stupid idiot. Let me go now!" Faith shrieked, near hysteria.

K.C. hung on tight and carried her back into the living room. Unknown to K.C., Faith grabbed a glass paperweight as he hauled her past the desk.

"Now, Faith..." he began but was cut short by the blow to his head. He crashed to the ground taking Faith with him.

In an instant she was up and fumbling with the keys. She could see he was bleeding but didn't have time to see if he was alright. Downstairs she flew, not knowing how long K.C. would be out. She was out the garage door in no time, not stopping to put on shoes or a coat. Her breathing was short and rapid. Her pulse racing wildly. She wasn't used to the car. It was so different to the trucks she'd been learning on. She panicked until she found a spot for the key. The engine roared to life as the car jerked forward and started up the ramp to the street. The garage door opened at the top automatically.

Suddenly a silhouette against the streetlight's glare loomed at the top of the ramp. She realized at once her brother must have come to and made his way out the front door to the street. As she raced up the steep incline, her headlights illuminated a bloody K.C. staggering down towards her, his hands facing out, imploring her to stop. Faith pressed down hard on the gas and watched as her brother first hit the hood and then the windshield with a sickening thud before being tossed high up into the air, up and over the speeding car. Faith never looked back, she drove as hard as she could to where she thought Chu was staying.

———

Chu was rudely awakened. One of the staff had informed him that there was an emergency. That he was to get over to the hotel as soon as possible. As he drove up in the car, O'Reilly met him and provided an escort inside. Chu was confused and non-comittal. He was sure it was going to relate to some more questions about Audrey Kunitz.

"Here he is, Lieutenant. This is Agent Chu."

"Thanks, sir," the police officer said respectfully, "Agent Chu, we have Faith Gale in custody. She's hysterical, sir. Won't talk to anyone but you. She's crunched up in a little ball."

"What?" snapped Chu, suddenly alert and full of interest. "What happened?"

"We don't really know, but we have reports her brother was killed. Hit and run, and by the looks of it, I'd say it was the car that Miss Gale was driving."

"No. No, that can't be," Chu stammered, the words choking out, "K.C. dead? Are you sure?"

The officer told him they were sure and looked sorry that he had to say it. He could see that Chu was stunned. Chu tried to collect himself as the officer took him to the room where they were holding Faith.

When he stepped into the room Faith sat up and looked at him. Her blond mane knotted and dishevelled, her eyes swollen with tears. When she saw him, she started wailing.

"I killed him. I killed him. I killed him..." she repeated over and over grabbing at him.

"What happened Faith? Was it an accident?"

She looked up at him without making a sound and then emitted a mournful cry that welled up from her aching heart. She tried to talk but couldn't. Chu couldn't resist. He reached out with his hand, pushing the matted, wet hair from her face.

"Oh, Faith, my poor girl. My poor, poor girl. Just take your time, breathe deeply. Take all the time you need."

When she finally gained her voice back, she startled him by screaming.

"He tried to stop me. Tried to stop me from coming, so I had to. I had to get away. I had no choice, I had no choice...you see that don't you? I had to..."

"Faith, Faith, please," he said sitting down beside her and putting his arm around her. She nestled against him briefly, then pushed away violently.

"No, no," she yelled, "that feels too good. Too much like comfort. I don't want to feel good. I want to suffer. We all have to suffer..."

He held onto her as she sobbed. His feelings for her flowing out. Much as he did not want to admit it, he was in love with her. Deeply in love. Her pain was his pain, and all he found himself wanting to do was to make it better, somehow. But that just didn't seem possible. Chu felt helpless.

After several minutes she had calmed down enough to speak again but this time it was weak and without any energy.

"I couldn't let him stop me. It's too important."

"Faith, what was K.C. trying to stop you from doing?"

"From coming here. From warning you. Daddy's going to do something awful. There might be time to stop him," she sobbed.

"Stop him from what?"

"Releasing God's wrath."

"How do you know?"

"Because of what he said and because of this. He left it for K.C. and me this morning."

She handed him the letter before breaking down at the mention of K.C.'s name.

By the time he'd finished reading it, Faith had rolled herself up in a ball once more, withdrawn into her own world. She'd delivered her message and now she had to deal with what she had done. Consumed by sadness and remorse, she could do no more. The rest was up to God.

Chu sat with his hand on her back and tried the best he could to comfort her as she cried and cried and cried.

———

The doctors took over, once it was clear that Faith wouldn't be supplying any more information. O'Reilly and the the others, including Forbes and Hinks, had been watching the interview in the room next door on a monitor.

As soon as a drained and heartsick Chu shuffled out of the room, he was pounced on by Forbes.

"Give me that," she commanded, pointing to the letter Faith had entrusted to him.

In a fog, Chu complied and watched as she handed it, proud as a beagle with a ball, to the man standing beside her. If Chu had been watching, he could have seen the man was not impressed. But Chu's eyes were cast down looking at his own feet as he tried to come to grips with the notion that K.C. was gone – that Faith had killed him. Desperately attempting to cut his personal feelings out of the equation, he failed miserably. Forbes, flanked closely by Hinks, seemed oblivious to his struggle.

"Agent Chu is just returning to Wyoming today, sir." she said.

"At this time, Forbes? Does that make sense?"

"Just doing what the SAC there has told me. It's a disciplinary matter."

"Well, I'll give him a call then. Agent Chu, my name is Watson. I'm the Operations SAC here in Manhattan," Karl Watson said, introducing himself, "Look, I can see this has really hit you hard – I'm sorry. "

"What's going to happen to Faith, sir?" Chu asked, full of concern.

"We're taking jurisdiction, so you don't have to worry. She won't end up in jail. Particularly if her story checks out. We've already contacted Washington, so I guess it's their call what happens next. It's pretty scary, if what she says is true. So, don't go anywhere just yet, okay? We still have a pile of work to do here."

"No, sir," replied Chu, looking hard at Forbes and Hinks, who were both frowning, "I wouldn't even think about it."

18 - Last Stand

Sherman Gale's heart was heavy as his private jet touched down on The Ranch's runway.

"Just before sunrise in New York," he thought to himself. Faith and K.C. would have read his letter by now.

Little did he realize that at this very moment his daughter was driving madly across the city on her mission. Unaware that his only son lay dying - shattered, broken and alone on the cold, dark pavement of New York City.

And yet, even in his ignorance, he was full of dread, doubt lurking like a shadow on his soul. In his tortured mind he saw it as the temptation of Satan. A test of his devotion and of his faith in God. Didn't Abraham follow God's edict to kill his own son, even though he knew it to be wrong? Wasn't it the devil's work to dissuade him from what he knew he had to do?

The most daring mission yet. He told himself it was normal to feel some unease. He had tried doing things as his late wife would have done but had been thwarted by Lucifer himself. The path was now clear. God had measured the cost and God had made the decision — issued the orders that had to be followed. Spoken them to both himself and his daughter. He wasn't looking forward to what he had to do — but it was the only way.

He'd be happy once more, if he obeyed. The promise of being with Patricia Anne again. Of being together forever.

As he drove to the lab, he listened to Mozart's Requiem. He drove slowly, trying to enjoy every moment, rolling down the windows even though the early morning air was crisp and bit at him sharply. The pain made him feel alive.

———

When SAC Watson notified Washington of what they had learned from Faith Gale, an emergency meeting, coordinated by Homeland Security was called immediately. People from all over the city rolled, jumped and were pulled out of bed. By seven thirty Washington time, most of the members were accounted for, and the meeting proceeded.

They were informed that the FBI had assembled a team in Cheyenne and were planning to move out within half an hour. Local law enforcement officers would adjunct the team until more Federal agents could arrive. As well, four helicopters were being flown in to supplement the two that were already on hand. The CIA informed members that they were working with the military and National Guards of both Colorado and Wyoming. Discussions were going slowly. Contingencies were being analyzed.

There was debate about what kind of resistance they would encounter if they had to go in. Some felt it would be light, others were not so sure, still others predicted an outcome far worse than Waco.

Finally, the question was asked: who would authorize direct action? After a great deal of discussion it was agreed. The only person who could make this call was the President. It was just too hot a potato for it to be any other way.

———

"What the hell are you telling me? That Sherman Gale is going to unleash a deadly virus because Strong is going to lose the election? Is that it?" the President asked, aghast.

"Yes, sir, that's about it," the Under Secretary nodded, looking at the briefing paper they both had a copy of. Others in the room tried to keep attention from focusing on them.

"And we know this because his daughter told us, confirming suspicions against Gale we've had for some time?"

"Again, yes, sir."

"And why was I never informed? How come this is news to me?"

"Apparently they didn't want to put you in a conflict of interest. But if you ask me, they were just scared Strong might win and then, where would that leave them? Whatever the reason, sir, we got word about this only two hours ago. Flight records show that Gale touched down at The Ranch right around then. The FBI have a team ready to go as soon as they get the word. They're not sure of what kind of fight Gale will put up."

"Oh my God, Peter, this is the worst thing that could happen. We have to go in and try to stop him. We have no choice. If we don't and he does as we fear, it will be too late. Bring me the order and I'll sign it. I just pray to God we're in time."

———

Sherman Gale had been at the lab two hours when his phone rang. He hadn't meant to answer it but checked to see who it was out of habit. It was on the secure channel. A call he had to take. A call that changed everything.

Now an hour after the call, Gale knew they were coming. And he was angry. The security post at the front gate was under heavy fire. A truck load of agents and police had broken through the gates. Though sustaining heavy casualties, they were heading quickly towards the lab.

Gale directed his security people to let one of the trucks pass unheeded, and to his delight found them disappointed. They'd been waiting almost two decades to hand it to the Feds and were hard-pressed to follow orders. But he wanted to deal with these trespassers on his own. He was looking forward to it.

Gale had already ordered the two helicopters that were sent in to be shot down. Nobody was going to fly over his airspace without authorization. And such an unfair advantage. His equalizers, ground-to-air missiles smuggled in from Israel several years before, had proved very effective.

He stood in the foyer of the lab dressed in combat fatigues, complete with full body armour, loading two Marine-issued Glock handguns. Holding a gun in one hand he tucked the other in his pants behind the small of his back. He looked at the helmet with its bullet-proof shield but decided not to put it on. They deserved to see his face. He wanted to look them in the eyes.

With determination he picked up a black leather box on the desk and walked out of the building and into the parking lot. The FBI-marked Suburban was just screeching to a halt when Gale reached his vehicle. He calmly put the black box on the roof and opened the door with his free hand. He still clutched a pistol in the other.

"Don't move!" cried a man jumping out of the truck and pointing a gun at Gale. Several others joined him, some of them bleeding as the result of running the gauntlet at the gate, all with guns or rifles pointed in his direction. They were clearly terrified.

"What's the meaning of this? What right do you have to barge onto my property uninvited? I want to see your search warrant and your identification, you sons of bitches!"

Gale held his gun at his side as he swiftly walked toward the men. He looked threatening. In reaction, one of the police officers twitched, and without meaning to released his trigger. Instantly Gale was hit in the chest and fell back like he had been kicked down hard. The vest saved him from serious harm and before he hit the ground he'd squeezed off several shots, killing one man and seriously wounding another.

Gale rolled behind his truck and screamed at his assailants.

"You chicken shit bastards. Get off my land or I'll kill you all!"

He could hear one of the men moaning as a buddy tried to drag him back out of the line of fire. Gale spun around the back of his truck and took a single head shot that instantly killed the man offering assistance. The groaning of the wounded man continued but nobody tried helping him again.

They were at a standoff.

"Please, Colonel Gale. Surrender, sir. Lay down your weapons and you won't be harmed."

"You think you hold my future in your hands? You think you can dictate to me what will or will not happen?"

Gale suddenly stood up and charged at the men crouching behind their vehicle. It caught them by surprise and cost most of them their lives. Gale came shooting, holding a gun in each hand, blasting everything that moved.

It was a shot from behind that finally stopped him. The man Gale had shot first, Kyle Anderson, Chu's old partner and the man whose buddy had died trying to save him - the man who Gale had overlooked as he rushed forward with a passionate thirst for bloody vengeance - fired in desperation from the ground where he lay. Anderson's bullet hit Gale in the groin where there was a gap in the amour, ripping open a main artery. Gale could feel it at once and knew he was done.

Even so, Gale kept firing as he slumped down, his body's strength failing as his life's blood flowed. More bullets found their mark, tearing into his exposed flesh, opening new wounds, but still he kept firing, until finally he fell in a heap. Caught up with emotion and fear, the survivors kept pumping him with shot after shot, even after he had stopped moving.

The great man, Colonel Sherman Gale, lay oozing blood on the ground of his beloved Ranch, dead.

19 - Recriminations and Retribution

It was late afternoon and dark had begun to spread across a fog encased New York City. Light rain fell steadily, adding to the feeling of gloom that hung in the air.

Audrey watched Chu with concern. He sat, head in hands, elbows on knees.

"Don't worry, Derrik. It sounds like they stopped him in time. Roger will be back in a minute with an update."

Chu didn't respond. In fact he made no sign that he'd heard her speak at all.

"Hey, did you hear what I'm saying? Is my voice so insignificant and small you can't hear it at all?" she joked, expecting him to look up at her with that wonderful smile of his. The smile he normally would have given her.

She was surprised.

"Oh Audrey," he groaned his fingers now massaging his eyes and forehead, "I just feel so...I don't know, guilty I guess."

"Guilty?"

He sat up and looked at her. She could see he was a wreck.

"If I just could have got her to tell me about what was going on in Miami, maybe I could have stopped it then. But I got so caught up in my own feelings. It may have cost K.C. his life."

"How do you mean caught up in your own feelings?"

"Ah, geez Audrey, it's pretty fucking embarrassing..."

"I'm listening and I'm not judging," she said holding out her arms with her hands palms up to demonstrate her willingness the hear him without prejudice.

"Well, I think I've fallen for Faith. No, no that's not true. I *know* I've fallen for her. Through all this mess that's going on, I've managed to totally fuck myself up."

"Oh, I see," responded Audrey taken aback.

She still wanted to help but couldn't stop herself feeling upset with Chu. A schoolgirl!

He was too caught up in his own feelings to notice her reaction and continued talking.

"It breaks my heart to see her suffering and not be able to do anything about it."

"Does she know?"

"Faith?"

"Of course, Faith."

"I'm not sure. Maybe. She was the one pushing things. It was kind of flattering at first, and then a little embarrassing, but then, I don't know, she got to me."

"How much got to you?" Audrey asked, suggestively raising her eyebrows.

"Hey, look. Nothing happened. I just kissed her - once. But man, I sure wanted to do a lot more," he said wistfully.

"You got it bad, Derrik. This could cause a real problem."

"Not if it stays between you and me."

"You're not going to tell Roger?"

"No, but I think he may suspect it already. Please, Audrey, I realize it's crazy. That's why I didn't do anything about it in Miami. I just needed to tell somebody and you're the closest thing I have to a friend. I know that may be sad, but it's true."

"Well, I guess it is a little sad, but it's the same for me, Derrik. We have to stick together, no matter what. Right?"

"Yeah, right," Chu said halfheartedly, lowering his head into his hands once more.

Audrey continued to watch him, more concerned than ever. Chu was oblivious to Audrey or anything else going on around him right now. He was thinking about family. Specifically, how the Gale family had been torn apart. First by disease, then by obsession and now by accident. What would be the next horror that Faith would have to face? And face alone.

He started to think about his family. Things had never been right since he left for college at the age of eighteen. It had been fourteen years since then and he'd only been back half a dozen times. He relied on his sister to do most of the emotional heavy lifting for his mother and grandfather. Her three kids seemed to keep them supplied with ample pictures of birthday parties, school pageants, dance recitals and the occasional babysitting stint. But still...

"I have to go phone my mom," Chu said, standing up suddenly and starting towards the door. The movement was so sudden it frightened poor Audrey.

"Okay. You gotta do what you gotta to do. Me? I'm staying put until Roger comes back. I want to know what the hell is going on. It could be the end of the world, you know."

"Just what I thought," he replied, "time to call home."

———

The phone rang three times before his mother answered. Always the same salutation.

"Hello, Chu residence, Aida Chu speaking."

"Hi, Mom. It's me, Derrik."

"Thank goodness you called! We've been so worried, your Grandpa and me. I tried calling so many times."

"Yeah, well, I lost my phone in Miami. Sorry."

She turned and said something in Japanese to his grandfather.

"What's the TV reporting?" he asked.

"Just about Colonel Gale's son and Faith, his daughter. The speculation is that she'd been drinking. Is that true?"

"No, Mom, it couldn't be further from the truth. Those idiots just like an excuse to trash people. They can't understand what's really going on."

"What is really going on, son?"

"Ah, Mom, I can't tell you, except to say it's a mess."

"But you're trying to make it better?"

"I'm doing as much as I can right now. I'm not sure it's enough."

"I'm sure you are, son. Even when you were a boy you never felt like you were doing enough. Don't be so hard on yourself."

"Anyway Mom, I just wanted to let you know I'm alright and that I love you."

"I love you too, son. Oh, your grandfather wants to say something to you."

"Grandpa?" Chu said in disbelief. His grandpa never used the phone because he was so self-conscious of his heavy Japanese accent, "That'd be great."

"Alright, Derrik, here he is..."

"Hello, Derrik-san," said the voice at the other end of the line, pronouncing the greeting in stereotypical fashion.

Derrik tried speaking a few of the Japanese words he knew in greeting. A sign of respect.

"You still speak Japanese like Korean," his grandfather said, laughing.

"And you're still correcting me, Grandfather," countered Chu.

"Ah yes, is true. Is always true. I just want say I so proud of you."

"You're proud of me?"

"Yes, bring honour to family. You try make United State strong."

"Yes, Grandfather. I try very hard."

"When I come United State after war, I want live place where I be anything I want. Where children be anything they want. Not told what to do like in Japan. Have freedom. You help America keep free, Derrik san. This good work. Like samurai."

"Thanks, Grandfather," Chu said with suddenly melancholy, "And thanks for teaching me. I love you..."

But the old man was gone and Chu's mother was on the line again. They talked for a while longer about his sister and her teaching and the new place being built, and then signed off. Chu made up his mind to go home for a good visit after this whole thing blew over. It had been way too long.

———

When Chu walked back into the room, one look at Audrey's face told him something was wrong. She and O'Reilly were sitting close to the monitor, having just watched a video clip.

"What's up?" Chu asked casually.

"Well, do you want the good news or the bad news?" O'Reilly asked.

"Shit, not one of these, uh, neither?"

O'Reilly looked at Chu and shook his head.

"Yeah, right. Okay, here's what we know that could be considered very good news. Looks like Gale was intercepted at the lab taking a case full of test tubes with him. They retrieved the case and from what they can determine so far, he was working entirely on his own. They've taken away the case for analysis to see what it is. Evidently it was labelled as tissue samples for cancer testing."

"So what happened? Gale's in custody?"

"No, that's what could be considered the bad news. We were just watching the clip taken from the security camera in the parking lot of the lab. It speaks for itself."

O'Reilly took hold of the mouse and hit 'play'.

On screen they watched as the drama unfolded. It was a surprisingly clear picture showing Gale putting the case on the roof, the FBI truck coming to a screeching halt, the exchange of words, the first shot to begin the carnage. When it finished, Chu was dumbstruck. He looked to O'Reilly for answers but all he could do was offer a little more information.

"What's worse is that fighting at The Ranch is still going on. Seems that several of our people have been taken prisoner. Doesn't look like there'll be an end to it any time soon."

"Can we see that clip again, O'Reilly?"

"Sure," he responded, taking the mouse in hand again, "There you go."

Chu watched, transfixed. When it was over he was incredulous.

"Why the fuck did they have to do that? Why did they shoot in the first place? It looks so bad. And then to stand there shooting him after he was dead! Jesus Christ, you wouldn't do that to a rabid dog!"

"It looks terrible," agreed Audrey, "They better hope that video doesn't get out."

"Too late," O'Reilly responded, "It's already been posted on the Web. That's where we got this copy."

"Just wait," Audrey reacted, "how'd that happen? I mean, who posted it? And why?"

"Exactly the questions Washington is asking and the ones folks will be working on through the night. In the morning the press will be looking for answers, and we'd better have some."

Chu was half listening to their conversation. He was worried about how Faith was going to take this. First her brother and now her father. He knew she'd feel responsible for both.

"I wonder if there's any way I can get to see Faith. She must be going through agony right now," Chu said, still looking at the monitor.

O'Reilly gave Audrey a look and crossed his eyes ever so slightly before responding. She almost laughed in spite of the circumstance.

"Well, I'm not sure that would be the best thing to do right now. Besides, she's holed up on Victory and won't see anybody. Seems her dad rigged up some very sophisticated defensive weaponry and there's a kind of force field around the ship."

"What? What do you mean force field?"

"Technically it's known as an Active Defence System using microwaves. We thought only the military had it but it seems we were wrong. I guess if you have enough money you can get anything. The system is simple to understand: the closer you get, the hotter your skin gets, until it burns. Several agents who were sent to interview her again came back almost cooked."

"Oh man," exploded Chu, flinging himself back into his chair. He was upset and didn't try to hide it.

"Listen, Chu, you have to get a grip on yourself. You remember Watson from this morning?"

Chu nodded. "Of course. Seemed like a pretty good guy."

"Yeah, well he is. One of the best. He needs to talk to you again. He's going to be coming over here later."

"Tonight?"

"Looks that way, yeah."

"Do you know about what?"

"Sort of, but I'd rather not say until we're sure."

"I understand," said Chu not really meaning it.

"You too, Audrey. He's definitely going to want to talk to you, as well."

———

Watson had talked to them separately but now Audrey and Chu were reunited. They were waiting in a meeting room and had a chance to catch up.

"So what did he ask you?" questioned Audrey.

"About the whole fucking thing, right back to where I got my ass chased off The Ranch. How about you?"

"Same thing for me. How I began the research, the picture of Gale and Hernandez, Miami..."

"He had a lot of questions about you and Miami, let me tell you."

"Like what?" she asked, suddenly red faced.

"No, we didn't talk about any of that. It's just I got the overall impression he was trying to figure out if you're legit. Wanting to make sure you'd really been hurt, weren't just faking."

"No way. I don't believe it. Now I'm a suspect?" Her tiny voice rose to a crescendo almost making a mockery of anger.

She was about to continue when O'Reilly walked in, followed by Watson.

As he sat down, O'Reilly addressed a seething Audrey Kunitz.

"Now, please, Audrey. We realize that this is confusing. I heard you as we were coming in and please believe me when I say you are not a suspect. We just have to make sure of everything at this point. We have quite a situation on our hands. Watson, you want to take it from here?"

"Yeah, sure. Agent Chu, Dr. Kunitz, from what we can determine so far, the vials Sherman Gale was taking from the lab contained nothing but routine tissue samples. We've started going through the lab itself and turned up nothing so far. Without that substantial proof we have to go back to other evidence and it very much gets down to both of you, and Faith Gale. We can't get to Miss Gale right now, so you're it. And to be honest, other than knowing that three Russian scientists came into the country, and having a couple of pieces of circumstantial evidence you've provided, Dr. Kunitz, we have nothing but hearsay."

"What about the letter Gale left for Faith and K.C.?" asked Chu.

"I read it quite a few times and it admits nothing. Taken with what Faith was telling us in the heat of the moment, it looked a whole lot more concrete than it does now. It appears it was crafted to be misinterpreted. Here, let me read it to you and you'll see:

'Dear Children,
I will be gone when you wake up, on my way to do God's
work, as you know. Praise Jesus.
The next few days will be hard.
God bless you both — my Christian soldiers.
Father'

There, you see, it really proves nothing."

"So, what's that mean?" asked Audrey.

"Well, if something doesn't show up soon, I'd say the press is going to eat the President alive tomorrow morning. By then I have to write up a report for the President justifying why the federal government barged onto private land without a court order and killed a man for doing no more than taking cancer samples to an outside testing centre. Cancer samples from a facility he privately funded to help combat the illness that killed his dear wife. A facility recognized world wide as a leading-edge cancer research lab."

"In other words, the President is fucked." Chu said bluntly.

"Totally discredited two days before the election," agreed Watson, phrasing it a different way. "It seems the best way to succeed in American politics is to discredit your opponent rather than build yourself up. This one might be a knockout."

"The ultimate set up," offered O'Reilly, "Colonel Gale may just have pulled off one of the most elaborate hoaxes in modern history."

———

Chu got up early next morning to check out the news. As he walked into the room he saw that Audrey was already watching.

She nodded to him without speaking as he pulled up a chair and sat beside her. It was as Watson had predicted. Every station was running its own version of the story – breaking news sucking attention from all other concerns. The usual frenzy associated with the election was replaced by a moribund watch across the country by news anchors and reporters. On screen they perched like carrion fowl, squawking periodically and jostling to secure a choice spot from which to feed.

They showed the video clip of Sherman Gale's death once again, this time with the title 'Execution by Federal Agents'. They asked questions of themselves and then provided the answers, even though they didn't have a clue. Just when it all looked hopeless and interest was starting to wane, there came an announcement: Ralph Osborn, Robert Strong's running mate and former Marine General, would speak to the nation at eleven to provide an update.

The news anchor they were watching was so happy to finally be reporting something new it was pathetic. He smiled, knowing it would give them the chance to profile Osborn; speculate as to why Strong himself wasn't going to appear; probe federal officials, asking them if the President would respond. That would keep the audience watching and the ratings high.

Then more breaking news. Unrest at The Ranch was still no closer to resolve, and the White House finally acknowledged that hostages had been taken. Immediately, all attention turned to Wyoming, where inhabitants of The Ranch were reported to be actively resisting.

Just before Osborn was to go live, it was announced that the President had ordered a withdrawal from The Ranch, except for the lab and the area around it. Residents were shown cheering and waving victory signs on television screens across the country.

The nation watched, glued to their TVs, as the story kept getting bigger and bigger.

When Osborn went live, almost half the TVs in the country were tuned in to watch the press conference beaming directly from outside his home in New Jersey.

Osborn was tall and wiry with a full crop of thick white hair. He was a figure that commanded attention. At sixty, he was seen as the perfect running mate for Strong, having served three terms in the Senate after retiring from an illustrious military career. As he stepped forward to the microphone, he looked assertive and serious.

"My fellow Americans, it is with great sadness that I stand before you today. First I am greatly saddened because last night I, like most of you, watched the execution of one of America's greatest patriots, Colonel Sherman Gale, a man whom I was privileged to serve with. A man who dedicated himself to his country his entire adult life. A man who showed many of us that the American dream is still alive. That by working together in Christ, we can prosper.

"I call it an execution because that is what it looked like to me. From start to finish it was an act of unparalleled violence perpetrated by agents of the federal government. Why was this done? What could justify such horrific actions?

"They say they had proof that Brother Sherman was about to unleash a killer virus on the country he loved. A virus that was going to put every person in America at risk. I'm sure you've seen the President's ads where he talks about the veiled threats posed by Reverend Strong and me. Threats he has used to focus the considerable power of federal law enforcement agencies against us from the very beginning of this campaign. I believe he has turned it into a personal vendetta where he will stop at nothing to slur our names and defeat our cause.

"For Sherman Gale's sake, and for devoted Christians everywhere let me assure you, we will not let them intimidate us. We will not stop until victory is ours. Though they come with sword and gun, we will survive. We will survive and win.

"Reverend Strong has chosen to stay out of the public eye for now. Not only is he too devastated by the loss of his strongest supporter, friend and brother-in-law, he is protecting himself and his family. He has reason to worry. Is he next on the hit list the President and his administration have drawn up? If they can get away with this brazen act of terror could they not do it again? Blame someone else? Come up with fabricated evidence to support their evil deeds?

"My fellow Americans, don't vote for this man. He represents all that is wrong with America. Why our great nation is faltering. He stands with evil and must be deposed. Please, while we still have a democracy, please demand that the President step down. Yesterday, a great American was gunned down on his own land for no reason. Tomorrow, it could be you or me or one of our loved ones. Support Reverend Strong for President. Make your vote count.

"Remember, a vote for the President is a vote for Satan.

"Thank you for your time and God Bless America.

"I'll take questions now..."

———

As the day wore on, and they continued to watch, the attacks against the President and his administration mounted in both number and ferocity. Some pundits called for a postponement of the election, while others argued that would play into the President's favour. There were serious demands for the President to resign and run the Vice Presidential candidate in his stead. The pressure grew, fed by the media finding more information and the public's awestruck fascination with the matter.

It was unbelievably great television being dished up to the entire world.

Pollsters madly polled and provided updates every half hour on the burning questions: How had this crisis impacted the popular vote? How many people would vote for the Democrats if the Vice Presidential candidate ran? How far up the ladder did the conspiracy go?

A montage of video clips from the past, showing the President warning Americans about Strong's candidacy and its links to the far right, had just finished playing. It ended with the suggestion of a conspiracy by the incumbent to scuttle his main opponent's campaign. A suggestion that was, minute by minute, becoming easier and easier for the public to believe.

"Wow, I can't believe how bad this looks. I just can't believe it. Fernandez, the Russian scientists, the whole elaborate set up. Me, buying into the whole, fucking thing."

"He had everyone believing it."

"Now look what fucking happened. It turned out just like he planned it. He even duped his own kids."

Audrey didn't respond. She had her own opinions about Faith's story but she didn't want to go there with Chu. It wasn't worth the drama right now.

"You know what I mean. What kind of fucking man would do all that?" Chu appealed to her.

"Obviously a pretty deranged one," she said, sounding annoyed, before adding, " Ah, Derrik?"

"Yes."

"Would you mind dropping all the *fucking* when you're talking to me? It's driving me *fucking* crazy, if you know what I mean."

"Yeah, of course," he said adding with remorse, "I'm sorry Audrey. I didn't mean to offend you. I just do it without thinking when I'm upset."

"Well, it just gets a little tired, you know."

"Yeah, I got it," he replied, standing up, "Think I'll do some exercise."

"Oh, okay. Guess I'll just hang in here a while longer."

"Alright, see you later."

As he left the room she could see that his ears were burning red and she felt terrible. He took things so hard. It was just that he was so stupid sometimes.

She watched alone, feeling even more depressed, kicking herself for being so honest. It was almost always the kiss of death to her friendships. She didn't even know why she'd said it. It's not like he talked like that all the time.

Only minutes after Chu left there was another breaking news bulletin. It was announced that the President would appear live on Caroline Shapiro's show. No script, no preparation - just Caroline and her questions. It was something positive to hang onto. Perhaps the tide might be stemmed a little by this bold action. She hoped so.

———

Audrey was coming down the stairs just as Chu was going up. She'd finished her bath and was dressed in a robe and had a towel on her head. He was in his workout clothes.

"Have a good workout?" she asked in her sweetest voice.

"Not bad, thanks," he replied his eyes cast down, still hurt.

She walked further down the stairs until her head was level with his.

"Derrik, I just want to say sorry about being so bitchy. You can talk any way you want."

"No, I really don't mind. I'd rather you tell me than stew about it. That's way worse."

She gave him a quick hug which he accepted. He noticed that she smelled very good.

"Hey, there was finally some good news," she said as she moved by him, "The President is going on Shapiro's show later tonight."

"Oh, that should be interesting."

"You don't think it could help? If he tells the truth?"

"You'd hope so, but I wouldn't count on it. All he's got is the truth and sometimes that just isn't enough."

———

They'd had a wonderful meal together and found themselves on their own. O'Reilly was still out and wasn't expected home any time soon. The last of the staff had left at six. Audrey had put together a dinner and suggested they leave the TV off until the interview with the President at nine. It was nice not be harangued continually with breaking news.

"That was a wonderful meal Audrey. Where'd you learn to cook like that?"

She took a moment to respond, obviously touched by a memory.

"My mom. She was a great cook. She could have done what I did in half the time and made it taste twice as good."

"Sounds pretty special."

"Yeah, I really miss her."

"I'm sorry."

"What are you sorry for?"

"I don't know. I'm just sorry it hurts so much. I know how it feels. I lost my dad when I was young and it felt like I was going to die."

He got up and collected the dishes off the table.

"Hey, where did you learn to do that?"

"What? Clean up the dishes after a meal? Well, it's only fair. You cooked the dinner so I'll clean up," he said walking into the kitchen.

"Well, I'm impressed. You're mother raised you right, that's for sure," she replied, following him with the remaining items from the table.

Chu was busy putting plates in the dishwasher when he remembered something and laughed out loud.

"What's so funny?" she asked.

"Nothing. Nothing, really."

"Come on."

"Well, this is what I was doing the first time Faith really played up to me. Putting dishes in the dishwasher."

"First time?"

"Uh, yeah," he replied, realizing he had made a mistake bringing it up.

"Sweet kid. Making plays for the hired help in her uncle and aunt's kitchen."

"Look, Audrey, you've got Faith all wrong," he protested, "You don't even know her."

"I don't have to know her, Derrik. She's like lots of girls I know. Manipulative, vindictive, stab-you-in-the-back kind of girls. Her dad's programmed her. You just can't see it."

"No, I've held her, Audrey. I've looked into her eyes and there's something else there. Something so sweet and innocent."

"Oh come on, Derrik. She looks like a Playboy Bunny. That's it, isn't it? You got to the beach and fell in love. And you're so blind you can't see that she used you."

"What? What are you saying?"

"Faith Gale used you. That's what I think, anyway. I think she did exactly what her daddy told her to do. To come to you and spill the beans. He knew how we'd react. He wanted us to kill him - he would have made us do it anyway. K.C. died because he tried to stop Faith all right, but he was probably trying to stop her for the right reason. K.C. was going against what his father told him to do. It was Faith who did her duty, I'm sure of that."

"Audrey, I just can't believe it," he said, looking at her aghast, "And I won't believe it until we have proof."

He denied it, but in his heart he knew it could be true. A girl had once beguiled him before and then let him down hard. He didn't want to think about it. It hurt too much.

"Look, I'm sorry. Oh shit, I'm always saying sorry to you."

Derrik didn't say anything but stood there with his arms hanging down. She wanted to go over and hold him but she knew how that would look. At least she thought she knew how that would look.

In that awkward instant they heard the front door open.

"I better check that," he said, motioning to the door.

"Okay...say, look," she said hurriedly after a slight pause, making him turn to look at her, his eyes so full of sadness, "Oh, it's just, I *am* sorry."

It sounded so lame, but he seemed to appreciate it, if only a little bit.

Chu opened the kitchen door to find O'Reilly standing in the entrance, head down. He hadn't moved since he'd come in.

"Hey, O'Reilly, what's the word?"

O'Reilly raised his head and looked into Chu's eyes and at once he knew it was going to be bad.

"How bad is it?" Chu asked.

"The worst, I think. It kills me to tell you," O'Reilly grimaced.

"Just tell me, please."

"It's your mom and grandpa. There was a gas explosion at their house. Looks like an accident but...they're both dead, Chu. I'm so sorry."

20 - Counter Attack

Caroline Shapiro was sitting in her chair, waiting. She found that she was nervous about doing the interview, and that surprised her. She didn't think she could get nervous anymore. But this interview was different, so much hung in the balance. The whole country was watching. Hell, the whole world was tuning in.

The President's security provisions had been overwhelming. He arrived with what seemed like a small army just as Shapiro and the crew were starting to feel a rising sense of panic. Two minutes exactly until air time, his makeup applied expertly in the limo. He looked cool as a cucumber just like he always did, almost too calm as he moved smoothly to the chair beside her and sat down. Never ruffled, forever patient, diplomatic. He had just come from hammering out the best deal he could with America's creditors who had threatened to dump the remainder of their dollar reserves yet again. Even then he had never faltered or shown any sign of weakness. Still, in spite of the humiliation, he held his head high.

He nodded to her in greeting, she reciprocated and they waited in silence in the last few seconds for the camera to go live. She looked at her notes: he closed his eyes and hummed a tune.

Finally, the countdown to action.

"Hello, *America*. My name is Caroline Shapiro and you're watching *It's My Dime*. Tonight we take the unusual step of interviewing a candidate on the Saturday before the election.

We do this because America is in crisis. Tonight we have with us the President. Sir, it is unfortunate that this crisis I referred to centres around the election and your role in it, but I feel we have to go there first thing."

"Well, Caroline, I can appreciate that and welcome the opportunity to set the record straight. So ask away, I'm all yours."

"When did you first get involved? Is it true that you gave the order to proceed with the action against Colonel Gale?"

"It is true I signed the order. I did that early Friday morning exactly two hours after I was informed that Colonel Gale was going to release a deadly virus."

"Just exactly where was he going to release this virus?"

"That wasn't specified. I was simply told he was retrieving it from the lab on his property."

"And you were satisfied that there was enough evidence to justify the atrocious act of violence we all saw."

"First, let me emphasize that I did not authorize what you saw. That was clearly a mistake - a bad mistake we are still dealing with. What I authorized was the apprehension of a man I was told was going to release a virus that would destroy this entire country, if not the whole world. Secondly, the evidence was overwhelming. Gale was known to have the capacity to make the virus; he had Russian germ warfare scientists brought into this country – scientists we are still trying to locate; his own daughter came to us with the information, begging us to try and stop him; now she won't talk to us about it or the hit-and-run death of her brother. I could go on and on..."

"Your sources were reliable? You trusted them?"

"Yes, implicitly, otherwise I would never have signed the order."

"Mr. President, with respect, it begs the question, how did they get it so perfectly wrong?"

"We're still trying to figure that out, Caroline. But from what we can see, it was an intentional act of deception. Plain and simple - we were fooled."

"So you expect people to believe that Sherman Gale got himself killed on purpose? All to discredit you?"

"We just received results from the autopsy..."

"My bet is that he died as the result of *gunshot wounds*?" quipped Shapiro sarcastically. There were groans and even some sporadic laughing from the audience.

"Yes, Caroline, that was, of course, found to be the cause of death. No, the interesting thing is that Colonel Gale was suffering from advanced prostrate cancer. The doctors estimate he had only a few months left to live at most."

"So the point is that people with cancer commit suicide by FBI?"

"No, that's not the point at all. The point is he didn't have anything to live for. He was out of time and felt he had a mission to fulfil. I am convinced Colonel Gale did this because he mistakenly thought it was what God wanted him to do."

"So your defence is, that you were fooled into action so you could be blamed – maybe even asked to step down?"

"Yes, that's it. We were fooled. But I don't know about being asked to step down."

"Come now, sir. There are plenty of reports that suggest a groundswell within the Democratic Party for you to step down and let Alison Muir run. Several Women's groups have openly suggested this."

"I guess I've been too busy running the country to get involved in any of that. As far as we're concerned, its business as usual. The election should proceed, because there is no conspiracy."

"Are you worried about what this might do for your chances? Two weeks ago you looked like a shoe-in for re-election."

"Of course I'm concerned, but I'm sure once people have heard me tell the truth they'll understand and support me. Our policies are sound and we have slowly pulled America back from the brink of disaster. We need another four years to finish the job."

"Mr. President, a few weeks back I had Reverend Robert Strong on the show. He didn't seem like a crackpot to me. Not the right wing, born again crazy so many of your ads depict him as."

"Look, Carolyn, I want to make this clear, I've met Reverend Strong on many occasions and think he is a well-intentioned man. I don't think for a moment he has the credentials to run the country, though. We focus our ads on the credentials of the man as a politician. You know he's never held an elected office? But I do admit our ads do raise questions about the people behind Strong. People like his running mate Ralph Osborn and the fundamentalist military machine he represents. They are frightening because they truly want to bring on Armageddon. Create the final showdown between good and evil because it's been foretold Christians will triumph. Those aren't the kind of people I think should be trusted with running the government. It is in our interests to keep church and state separate as the Founding Fathers wanted."

"Reverend Strong stated that the Founding Fathers got it right because they allowed for the provision of amending the Constitution."

"Well, I'd be happy to discuss that with him anytime. I think it would be an interesting debate that I'm sure in the end I'd win."

"Well, its a little late for that, isn't it?"

"Unless he's watching. He could call in, couldn't he?"

"Yes he could."

"Robert, if you're there, give us a call and we can chat."

A number was flashed up on screen.

"Well, while we're waiting, let's take a break and hear from our sponsors – who are forking out a lot of dough to bring this to you tonight – so listen up!"

The President's people rushed in as soon as the red light went out. There were a million things left to do and no time to do them. This was an unscheduled event and it was wreaking havoc.

Caroline watched as he dealt with issue after issue, quickly and without ego. She was impressed. When the red light went back on, he jumped in from where they had left off.

"Caroline, it doesn't look like Robert's going to phone in, so do I have time to ask a question? Where *is* Robert Strong? Today we heard from his Vice Presidential candidate, but we haven't really seen anything of him for more than a week. Is he hiding? Is he too upset to deal with things? As President you can't take time out because you're having a bad week. You have to be out there dealing with things, no matter what."

"A valid point, Mr. President, the good reverend has been very elusive of late."

"I'm wondering if they've muzzled him after that speech he made. Now, that was disturbing, if I can refresh your memory. Get Christian or get out of town. What's that all about?"

"Now, sir, I've given you a lot of leeway. Can I get back to asking some final questions of you?"

"Okay, I'm being told I have time for two more. Then I'm sorry, but I really do have to go."

Shapiro quickly raced through her notes. She wanted to make sure she asked the right two questions.

"Yeah, here's one. What would you do differently if you had to do it all over again? And here I'm referring to signing the order for invading Gale's ranch."

"Well, I wouldn't sign it, of course. I would ask for more corroboration – I would check the evidence over."

"So you think you made a mistake."

"Yes, I would say that I did. Does that count as your second question by the way?"

"Oh, right. I hope not, I just couldn't help myself with the follow up. So here's my real second question, what will you do if you lose?"

"I'll make way for Strong and his new administration, of course. But I have faith that won't happen. I am confident people will look at our record over the past four years and vote for us based on that. It's really the right thing to do. And with that, I'm really sorry but I'm going to have to leave you. Thank you for the opportunity to come here and tell the truth. So help me God."

And with that farewell he was gone, surrounded by agents as he walked off stage. As he disappeared Shapiro called to him.

"Thank you, Mr. President." And then, addressing the audience in the studio and at home she added, "I've been chatting with the President of United States on *It's My Dime*. Thank you all for tuning in. Catch my post-election show next week. I have to admit I can hardly wait. And remember, whatever you decide, whoever it is you choose to support – *vote*. Make your voice heard. It's your right *and* your duty."

———

Upstairs, alone in his room, Chu had been through it in his head. He could break down and curl up - deny what had just occurred - or he could stand in spite of the hurt, tall and straight like a true samurai. That's what his grandfather had likened him to and that's what he intended to be. He would not give into the sadness, the overwhelming sadness that threatened to pull him down. It would be too self indulgent while the war was still going on.

For that is how he had formulated it in his own mind – a war against the world Sherman Gale and his minions were working to create. He had come to a decision about what he had to do. Now he just had to figure out how to do it. And for that he knew he was going to need help.

Chu stood up with resolve, looked in the mirror and swore a sacred oath that he would not rest until the fight was over, embracing death without fear. The others had just finished watching the interview when they heard him coming down the stairs. Audrey got up and met him as he walked into the living room.

"Derrik, I know no words are going to help, but please... whatever I can do..."

"Thanks, Audrey. But I think I'm okay," he said, accepting her embrace without emotion.

She was surprised by his apparent aloofness and stood back to assess him.

"You sure you're alright? You look kind of spaced out."

Derrik looked at her and smiled, then shifted his attention to O'Reilly who just shrugged and offered a weak smile in return.

"I can't afford to feel bad right now. That's just what Gale was hoping. I see it now. For some reason he saw me as a nemesis all along. That's why he wanted to keep me close, under his control. The murder of my family was designed to put me out of the game. But I'm not going to let that happen."

"You ready to talk?" asked O'Reilly.

"All night, if need be. Audrey?"

"Oh, I'm in, I already told you that, now, more than ever."

———

They talked about their action plan into the early morning, determining there were only two places where they might have some success. The first was seeing if they could get the Strongs to cooperate. The second was to try and get the truth out of Faith.

Faith was ensconced on Victory, surrounded by defences that were the best modern technology could deliver. O'Reilly and his team would have to deal with trying to reach her. Audrey and Chu were to focus on the Strongs.

Towards this end, Chu now sat reading the paper in a little cafe in Rockefeller Centre. It was full of stories related to the election and the mess surrounding it. Chu wished he had brought along a book. Even though he wasn't much of a reader, he thought anything would be better than the crap in the newspaper.

Chu had been there for almost an hour and was starting to get worried. If she didn't show up in fifteen minutes they had agreed to meet back at the safe house. He wondered if her plan had worked or if he'd have to do it his way. Both Audrey and O'Reilly had scoffed at his idea, but he still thought it could work. The disadvantage to Audrey's plan was that it took longer than the one he'd devised. His could be accomplished in half an hour, but of course was a lot riskier and needed at lot of rope.

When a plump, forties-something, red-haired woman in a trench coat walked into the cafe he was relieved. If he didn't know who it was, he would never have recognized her. She looked around as if unsuccessfully searching for a friend and then left. Ten minutes later, Chu folded up his paper and followed suit.

They met at the car O'Reilly had provided. She'd discarded her disguise and looked her usual self.

As he got in the passenger side, he looked at her expectantly.

"Mission accomplished," she said happily.

"You made contact?"

"Yup, only for a few seconds, but it was enough. She slipped me this note to give you."

Chu was elated and felt like kissing her. The smile on his face made it all worthwhile for her. He'd been almost robotic since the news about his mom and grandfather.

"So it worked, huh?"

"Yeah. O'Reilly found out the meal schedule and just slotted me in. I delivered their lunch and managed to tell Doris I was working with you. She had the note all prepared and just had to slip it to me with the tip. Ten bucks – not too shabby."

"Generous to a fault," he replied, "How did they look?"

"They looked scared, Derrik, that's how they looked. There are two guys outside and another one in the room with them. I can tell you, Doris' face certainly lit up when I mentioned your name. Seems you made a real impression on her."

"And her on me. She's one of the finest people I've ever met."

"So how about reading the note out loud while I drive?"

"Yes, ma'am," agreed Chu, saluting in jest, "Looks like this was written only yesterday...

> 'Dear Derrik,
>
> I don't know if I'll get a chance to get this to you – we have to be so very careful. I'm writing it just in case. I hope and pray there is some way you will be in touch.
>
> Robert was forced to deliver that speech the other night. Sherman threatened to harm the children if he didn't. Now we seem to be under house arrest as well. They say it is for our safety but I've never felt less safe in my life.
>
> Please do what you can to save our children. Only then will Robert and I be free to tell the truth. They are being kept with Grandmother Mary at her place on Long Island. K.C. tried to warn us the other night about what Sherman planned but there was nothing we could do, given they have our babies. I fear we have lost our niece, Faith.
>
> Please, please do what you can. I put all my hope in you, and pray constantly.
>
> God bless.
> Doris'

"So there's the proof," he said without intonation, "You were right."

"I wish I wasn't."

He didn't let it sink in, pushing it away. Compared to the other hurt it seemed minor. Still, deep down he felt he had lost something. Something precious and his chest was heavy.

"You okay?" she asked.

"Yeah, but please stop asking me that. Hey, how are we going to let them know what happens? All their cells will be bugged."

"I gave her a no-trace pager we can contact her with. Did I tell you they're going back to Wyoming later today? She was desperate that we be able to reach her with news. I told her to trust O'Reilly."

"We just have to save those kids. Do you know where we're headed?"

"Just got the coordinates and I'm plugging them in now... there it is. By the way, should we contact O'Reilly and let him know what we're up to?"

"That's a good idea. He's going to be busy later. I'll try him now."

The call went on for longer than Chu thought it would. O'Reilly was not surprised the Strongs' children had been used as bargaining chips. He urged extreme caution trying to rescue them, as Chu had expected he would. O'Reilly updated Chu as well. Information he relayed to Audrey at the end of the call.

"He's off with the Strongs to Wyoming. A team is going to try and bring Faith in for questioning tomorrow. They had to go all the way to the top to get approval of the plan. Even with the approval he says they're still trying to figure out a way to get in. Evidently, the Navy could help, but somehow they're not very cooperative right now."

"Nobody really wants to get involved until it's all over. Until they see who their boss is."

"I think it goes way beyond that. I hope I'm wrong, but I think most of the military is backing the Strong/Osborn ticket."

"I hope you're wrong too," she reflected. Looking to change the subject she continued, "You realize it'll be dark by the time we get there?"

"So much the better. Give us a chance to suss things out. No use barging in there and having either the old woman or the kids get hurt."

"Or one of us."

"It'll just be me on this one Audrey. You did your thing today. Let me do mine tomorrow."

———

They had lost their way several times en route to Hampton Bays in spite of the GPS. He blamed it on Audrey not following instructions the machine gave. Her contention was that the instructions it spat out were hard to understand and ambiguous.

"Alright, Audrey, let's see if I have this straight. When it says turn left and you continue to go straight ahead, it's the machine's fault, not yours?"

"I'm just saying it's not as easy as it sounds," she replied, pursing her small mouth and concentrating on the road.

"Right," he said with disbelief, "at this rate we're going to get there about midnight."

"Look, if you think you can do any better..."

"I couldn't do much worse, could I?"

She had no response but to drive on, even though he had told her that the quickest way to get on track was to turn around and go back to where they had made the wrong turn. They drove in silence for five more minutes before another word was spoken.

"So you think if I turn around we'll get there quicker?" she asked, seeing that they were beginning to run out of paved road.

She could hear him sigh loudly. She didn't look, but she just knew he was shaking his head.

"This is fucking nuts, Audrey. I've had it with this shit. Of course it's quicker if we turn around. The way you're going is the worst, back-assed piece of crap I ever saw."

"Hey, that's the first time you've sworn since I hassled you," she said, laughing, "but I really liked that 'back-assed piece of crap' line. Much more creative."

"I've been trying really hard to watch it," he said, still pissed off and not ready to let go of the fight, "I didn't realize how fucking hard it would be."

She laughed again and this time he joined her.

"Would you like me to take over for a while?" he asked.

"Yeah, that would be great. And when are we going to eat dinner? I haven't had anything since breakfast and I'm starved."

"How about after we get to the place and do a quick drive by? Then we find a place to eat and come up with a plan."

———

Audrey still had more than half the food on her plate, but his was long gone. And she had been the one who had to eat.

Chu was preoccupied drawing up a rough schematic of the place. It was much more isolated than anticipated, making surveillance trickier than he had hoped. He remembered Doris telling him that the classic, waterfront residence they'd just driven by was the Strong's summer home when Robert was growing up. It must have been nice. Chu decided that he would come in via the beach, as it offered excellent cover along the high bank. Coming in by the front meant crossing a great deal of open lawn.

"We can talk as I eat," she said, finding herself munching away in silence as he scribbled, "I may have some ideas about how to get them out, you know."

"What? Sorry, I wasn't listening," Chu replied and abruptly stopped writing to look at her.

"I just said you can talk to me while I eat."

"Oh, great. So what I'm thinking I'll do is go in the back way from the beach. It's just so perfect, I can't believe they picked this place – it'd be a bugger to defend."

"And what do you propose I do?"

"Well, I'd really like to get a couple of wireless web cameras set up tonight at the front of the place. You can monitor them remotely and keep in contact with me. Warn me if you see anything coming my way. I can't see taking them out the beach side, so I think you have to be ready with the car to pick us up at the front. I can't see any other way of coming out."

"So that's your plan? Enter from the beach, get into the house, grab the kids and the old lady and then run out the door to where I'll be waiting."

"That's about it."

"So, how are you going to find them, get them all together, take care of God knows how many bad guys and then make a dash out the front door?"

"So you're saying you think its crap?"

"No, not at all. It's just that perhaps a diversion might make doing some of what you want to do more feasible."

"What kind of diversion?"

"I don't know, maybe something to draw the guards out of the house. If we timed it right we could hit them hard as they came out. We've got a sniper rifle in the trunk and I'm really a pretty good shot."

"You think you could do that?"

"After what these guys have done, sure. And if we're in contact, you could let me know when."

"Yeah, my intention was to be wired to you. We'd have to find a place where you could set up. That's going to be a bitch, from what I saw."

"But doable."

"Worth a try. Now let's figure out the details."

———

While Chu and Audrey were figuring out how they were going to rescue the Strongs' children, the team O'Reilly had assembled was trying to bring Faith Gale in for questioning.

O'Reilly had received numerous updates from the officer in charge of the operation. All of them were bad.

As planned, they started with Level 1 which involved making a formal request for an interview. The request was ignored. Next, Level 2 involved serving a Court Order but that, too, was refused. Both actions were documented by network camera crews and beamed live into people's homes across America. The President had publicly pledged openness and he intended to deliver.

It was then, and only then, that they decided to take the plan to Level 3 and storm the billion dollar floating hideout.

But when they tried they were not successful.

The first wave tried a frontal assault on the ship from the dock. But no matter how much protective gear the team put on they found themselves burned by the microwave defences.

At the same time, an attempt was being made to use scuba divers to get on board, but they found an enormous steel mesh curtain in place all around ship. Within seconds of reaching the barrier, the Captain of Victory had dispatched his own scuba force to defend intrusion.

The final piece of Level 3 was using two helicopters. They had attempted to come in at extremely low altitude and land on the fore and aft decks simultaneously. But when the leading helicopter was blasted out of the sky by one of Victory's anti-aircraft missiles, the second chopper was ordered to stand down.

O'Reilly was frustrated but not surprised. He had recommended a four-level plan but got approval for only three. The fourth would have involved an all-out assault on Victory but the President would not approve it, deeming it too risky.

O'Reilly just hoped Chu and Audrey were fairing better than he was. At least there weren't politics constraining their actions.

—

As he crawled along the beach embankment an hour before dawn Chu found his heart was pounding. He had trained extensively for this kind of action but never had to actually do it. To kill unsuspecting people was not easy for him to contemplate. But he steeled himself for the outcome. When even the slightest degree of hesitation crept into his thinking he made himself remember the senseless murder of his mother and grandfather, the mistreatment of Marcus and little Angela, the heartbreaking ruination of Faith...

He was carrying two knives and a muzzled, semi-automatic Beretta. He had no idea of what he was going to face but he was prepared to use any of them when he had to.

"Hello, do you read?"

"Copy that."

"I'm in position to start moving in. Anything on the cameras?"

"All clear."

"I'm going in. Over and out."

He climbed the bluff to the top and slid onto the grassy plateau above. He kept low, concealed behind a small shed at the corner of the property. All at once he started to get very uncomfortable and he realized his skin was itching. As he moved closer to the house his skin began to feel like it was on fire. He could feel blisters forming on his face.

Chu turned and ran back to the embankment diving into the dense underbrush below. The itching subsided but the blisters came up worse than a bad case of hives.

"Hello, hello," he called on the radio trying not to sound too alarmed.

"Check."

"There's a microwave defence system in place."

"You sure?"

"Oh yeah, very sure," he said looking down at his still blistering hands.

"So now what?"

"I'm going to see how much of the perimeter is covered."

"How can you tell where it begins?"

"Oh, I just got a feeling for it. Over and out."

It took him almost an hour to get around the three acre property. Even the front of the acreage seemed to be protected.

"It really is like a force field around the place," he reported to Audrey.

"It's starting to get light. Do you want to abort?"

"Negative. I say we wait. They have to drop the field sometime. They have to get cars in and out."

"Where are you going to wait?"

"I've found a great place in the hedge at the south-west corner."

"Yeah, I see it."

"Only thing to do is wait for the shield to drop and then I'll slip in. We go with the plan."

"Maybe we should wait to get help?"

"This is election day. If we're going to stop them, it's now or never."

———

Hell. Reverend Robert Strong was in a living Hell. That was the only term he could use to describe it.

His mind burned.

He hadn't slept all night. He had pretended to, so that his wife wouldn't worry, but his tortured mind had offered him no such solace. One after one, they swept over him like waves. Pounding self-accusations that singed the very core of his being. His decision to run for the office of President, putting the lives of his entire family in jeopardy. His vanity, making him foolish enough to believe that he was in control. His ambition, blinding him from seeing truth. The pure evil right in front of him he had so failed to see, that now, only now, seemed so painfully obvious. A darkness he had seen as light.

But a blacker darkness than all the rest loomed over him in the night. A darkness worse for him than loss of his life. The blackest of blacks. The loss of faith. Throughout his life he had always had Jesus with him. Now, for the very first time, he could not find Him in his heart. He prayed and he searched, feeling lost and alone in the face of his betrayal.

Election day dawned for him with none of the excitement and sense of anticipation of four years ago. Last time was fun. Even thrilling. This time, it was a nightmare.

He sat on the edge of the bed, staring blankly at his feet, unable to muster the energy to stand up. Doris Strong watched her husband and her heart bled for him. She knew how badly his noble intentions had been shattered. Understood that his only dream now was that his children be saved from harm.

She wondered every moment if Chu could save them. Clung to a remnant of hope that they would survive. Prayed continually that he could pull off another miracle.

The pager Audrey had given Doris was with her at all times. She had to work hard to resist checking it every five seconds, looking to see if it was flashing green. Green meant that they were safe, that everything was okay.

"No news yet," she stated bravely.

"News?" he asked as if coming out of a daze.

"I meant this," she said, flashing him a glimpse of the pager.

"Oh Doris..." he sighed, "What have I done?"

"You've tried to do your best, Robert Strong. You've worked hard and kept true to your ideals. It wasn't your fault that Sherman turned out to be a monster."

"But you saw. My mother saw. She even tried to warn me. I was blind. I am such a fool," he said burying his head in his hands, "A fool, such a fool."

It was too much for her to take, she loved him so. To see him like this broke her heart. She moved to him, held him closely and prayed for her children.

———

After five hours of waiting, cramped up in the hedge, Chu's muscles had started to seize up. After another five hours they were lead. He tried to flex them without shaking the branches but it was next to impossible.

He checked in with Audrey every hour. She was sitting in the car about five miles up the road. She'd given up trying to get him to quit, resigned to his stubborn determination. He was the one, after all, who was lying in a hedge.

When darkness fell it gave Chu more flexibility to move around, no longer confined exclusively to his evergreen cell. He knew he had to stay ready. At any minute he would have to spring into action. It was a long way to run in the open and he had to do it without being seen. If he wasn't fast enough, he'd be toast.

But five more hours passed and still there was nothing. Nothing but aching muscles.

Polls had closed on the West Coast. Results would be tallied over the next few hours. There was still a possibility that they could impact the outcome, and even if they couldn't he was determined to rescue the children and their grandmother.

Two more hours slipped away. Chu dozed on and off. He woke up with a start. He went to talk to Audrey but found his radio was out of batteries. He had a slight moment of panic until he realized she'd made him bring along some spares. He hadn't accepted them with good grace, as he was convinced the whole operation was going to take no more than an hour. As time stretched out he realized how wrong he had been.

"Come in. Come in," he said into the microphone.

"Hey, I've been trying to reach you," was Audrey's frantic reply, "A big car driving fast just passed me a couple of minutes ago. It was headed your way and at the speed it's going, it'll be there soon."

"Okay. Thanks. I was just replacing the batteries."

"Now aren't you glad I made you take the extras?"

He was about to say something else when he heard the sound of an engine.

"Yeah, very glad. You were right. And here comes the car you were talking about. Right on time. You ready to roll?

"Ten-four."

"Yup, the car slowed down and is waiting."

"Yeah, I can see."

"It's going in. Time to roll. Over and out."

Chu ducked from under the hedge and ran as low to the ground as he could to the furthest corner of the house. Once there, he stopped, trying to conceal himself as best he could. He was glad he had the cover of darkness. He drew his gun and moved slowly around the back of the house. To his delight, he could see that a basement window was slightly ajar. Less than five seconds later he was safely inside, crouched down in what appeared to be the laundry room.

"I'm in," he whispered.

"Looked like there were two men in the car. They both went inside."

He didn't answer, but she didn't expect he would. Once in the house he would use the radio only when necessary.

Chu waited and listened. At first he could hear a television playing in the room down the hall, then loud footsteps from upstairs. He moved out of the laundry room, down the hall to where he heard the TV. It got louder and louder. The TV was on, but it appeared the couch sitting in front of it was empty, until Chu got closer. There, lounging half asleep on the couch, were the children. Chu thought it was strange that they were fully dressed. He moved so they could see him better, holding a finger up to his mouth. Angela almost screamed when she saw him but stifled it. Marcus couldn't help emitting a loud 'What the!' before catching himself.

"Hey, you kids, what's going on down there? That movie almost finished? We gotta go to the studio real soon," boomed a voice coming down the stairwell.

"Nothing. It's over in ten minutes," Marcus yelled back.

"Where's your grandma?" Chu whispered.

"I think in her bedroom. That's where she spends most of her time. It's two floors up," Marcus replied.

Chu nodded gratefully for the information, but realized it wasn't going to make his job any easier.

"Do you know where they're taking you?"

"Maybe to see Mommy and Daddy?" whispered Angela, wide eyed.

Chu doubted that but said instead, "You kids go hide and don't come out until you hear my voice. Understand?"

They both nodded and hurried off. He crouched at the bottom of the stairs and called into Audrey.

"Come in."

"Check."

"Showtime."

"Check."

Audrey had moved into position and was ready. Almost instantly there was a loud explosion from the front yard.

"What the fuck?" shouted a voice from the kitchen.

Another explosion went off, shaking the house.

Chu could hear the front door slam open and several people running out. Then the sure, sharp burst of rifle fire.

"I'm hit! Fuck! And Joey's down!" he heard screamed from outside. It was his cue to move.

He flew up the stairs, gun drawn. He met a man face to face running out of the kitchen and shot him twice before he could react. Chu continued into the kitchen where another man was just reaching for his gun. Chu shot him too.

"Come in. Are you there?" he said to Audrey over the radio set.

"Yeah, I'm here, but I'm kind of busy and could use some help."

"On the way."

He rushed out of the kitchen to the front door. As planned, Audrey had them pinned down. At least two, as far as Chu could tell, were still firing.

"How many of them?"

"I think two are left but I'm pretty sure one's wounded. Both behind the car."

Chu rushed in behind them and dispatched them quickly with a volley of shots. He waved to Audrey who was waiting with the car at the top of the driveway. The windows of the car were shot out but that wouldn't matter once they got away.

"I'll go collect the kids and grandma and try to figure out how to turn the defence system off."

"They all neutralized?" she asked him.

"All clear," he replied confidently.

He ran back into the house and straight upstairs. As he hit the top of the landing he called out.

"Grandma Mary, it's safe. We're here to..."

His words were cut off by a tearing pain ripping through his shoulder. Another man, one he had not counted on being there, got a clear shot off from the bottom of the stairs. Chu fell in a heap, not comprehending what hit him. It was the first and only time he'd been shot.

The man cautiously came up the stairs. He saw that Chu was down and defenceless but wasn't going to take any chances. Chu came to enough to see the man taking aim at him. In his ear he could Audrey screaming at him but it was distant. He couldn't respond. It was like he was in a dream. He hoped the kids and Audrey would be okay and he waited for the sound of the gun.

But instead of a bang, Chu heard a dull thump and saw the man holding the gun fall forward, losing his grip on the weapon.

"You old bitch!" he screamed, turning around and trying to grab the fire poker from a resolute Mary Strong. She had her makeshift weapon clutched with both hands and held on tight. Her captor finally prevailed, wrenching it from her grasp and pushing her down to the floor. Enraged, he raised the poker to smash her but a knife, thrown by Chu, pierced his neck, stopping his swing short.

The old woman watched in horror as the man slumped to the ground choking on his own blood. Chu dragged himself to his feet, picked up his gun and went over to help Mary up.

"Are you okay, Mrs. Strong? We have to get out of here now," he said, apparently unaware that blood was pouring from his shoulder, "The kids are in the basement."

He went to take a step and faltered. With Mary's assistance he made it downstairs.

Luckily, Marcus knew how to disable the microwave defences, allowing Audrey to come in and help. Mary's nurse's training in the war came in handy. Audrey was no slouch at triage, either. Between them, they patched Chu up enough so at least he wouldn't bleed to death on the way to the hospital.

They quickly loaded into one of Mary's cars and sped out of Hampton Bays only half an hour after the shootout had begun.

"I never thought I'd be glad to leave that place," cried traumatized Angela, clinging to her grandmother, "but enough is enough!"

"When can we see Mom and Dad again?" Marcus asked from the other side of his grandma trying to be brave. He wanted to cry but didn't think it would be appropriate.

"Soon, sweetheart, soon," she answered.

"Does your shoulder hurt, Mr. Chu?" asked Angela with empathy. He was curled up on the seat that had been lowered to be more like a bed.

"No, not a bit. Can't even feel it. I'm just glad you're okay. That everybody's okay." He paused thinking hard, the medication Audrey had given him starting to take full effect, "Now we have to phone them, the Strongs and O'Reilly. We have to, let them know, let them..."

"Don't worry. It's already done Derrik." Audrey looked down beside her from the driver seat sounding a bit annoyed. "I contacted them already," but as she said it, she put her hand on his arm tenderly.

"It's alright, honey, he's asleep. Or should I say, passed out?" Mary Strong chuckled.

"Oh, that's good. I was so worried. At least he'll get some rest now."

Mary smiled. The old woman could see it clearly. She could see it in the way Audrey had brushed the hair from his blistered forehead when they were tending to him. How she had held his hand while they were patching him up. She had seen it, even if this young woman didn't quite see it herself. Audrey Kunitz was in love.

21 - People's Choice

"Colonel Gale warned us Strong was soft, but I had no idea. Did you see the coverage from the polling station earlier today, sir? Pitiful - just pitiful. The first time he's been out in public in a week and he absolutely blows it. He looked like he was in a daze."

"People like him. The kids we have in the streets love carrying his posters around. He just looks so approachable and fatherly."

"I suppose you're right. It's irrelevant anyway. We couldn't stop it now if we wanted to - even if there was a problem."

"What kind of problem?"

"I don't know, I just don't trust Strong, sir. He could do anything. The sooner we get rid of him the better."

"Patience, Major, patience. Let's stick to The Plan. As long as we have his family, he's not going to give us any trouble."

"I hope you're right, General Osborn. We're so close right now it would be awful to see it slip away."

"I have faith in The Plan. We just need Strong to deliver the speech and then we won't have to worry about him any more," he said, pausing to think before continuing, "but just to be sure, make sure Major Thomas has things ready - just in case. By the way, did you bring it with you, a draft of the speech?"

"Yes, sir. It's on your desk."

"Excellent. How much time do I have?"

"A good hour."

"Let's hope it doesn't take me that long. I've got a mess of other business to attend to. Who wrote the draft?"

"It was left by the Colonel sir."

"Well then, I'll read it over, but I doubt I'll need to change a thing."

———

Other than being taken out for the obligatory early morning visit to the polling station, the Strongs had been confined to their hotel room, locked up tight. Not even family and friends were able to see them. The reason given was security. Renewed threats against the Strongs had been widely reported in the media. There was no telling what could happen after the suicide bomber episode and the execution of Colonel Gale.

The couple had watched election coverage all day, as there was little else to do in the room other than fret about the children.

Voting irregularities were being reported in many states, particularly in those jurisdictions considered too close to call. Everywhere mobs of young men dressed in the uniform of the Christian militia were shown roaming the streets chanting Strong's name and waving his placards. Reports of intimidation and violence in and around polling stations streamed in from all parts of the country.

They watched together and were filled with despair.

Election coverage was dominating the ratings. Everyone seemed to be watching and waiting to see what happened. The media were apoplectic as they reported story after story with puffed up self-importance and worried looks. True harbingers of death, their voices like the shrill calls of carrion fowl descending on a corpse-strewn battlefield.

———

"The networks are calling for us to have Strong deliver his speech. They're starting to lose viewers. The President and the Republican candidate have both made theirs."

"Has the final call been made? Is it official?"

"Yes, sir. Looks like we'll end up winning the majority of States. The President leads in Electoral College seats but doesn't have anywhere near a majority, as we expected. The Networks have confirmed it."

"Very good, let's get our man to the stadium. Do we still have a full house?"

"Yes, sir. They're ready to go."

"Just think, Major, this is the beginning of a new era. Today, we make history."

———

Minutes before they were to go to the stadium, Strong walked over to his wife and held her by the hands. He didn't have to ask if there had been any word, he just had to look her in the eyes to know that the pager was still dormant.

"My dear love," he began, "when I first met you I loved only God. I never knew I could find such happiness on earth. You have been such a blessing to me. I am sorry I have failed you."

"Please don't say that," she cried, "I would still choose you today. Knowing all that I know."

"You realize Derrik has probably failed? We would have heard something by now. Our only hope is that you go there and beg for mercy. Plead for our children."

"Leave you?" she gasped, "Leave you now?"

"It's the only way I can see. Ask O'Reilly to arrange it. I don't want you there when I read that speech anyway. Have you looked at it?"

"Yes, yes I have. It's frightening."

"So please, go my darling. For the sake of the children. We can only pray they're alright."

———

The crowd went crazy when it was announced that Strong was in the building. The Christian candidate who had stood America on its head. The leading contender to be picked by Congress as the next President of the United States.

As they moved into the great hall, Strong was looking for O'Reilly. He didn't have far to venture, as the Secret Service man was waiting for them at the entrance. The exchange of a few words, the look of surprise, the nod of agreement and it was done.

"My wife's feeling very sick," Strong said to Ralph Osborn, who had joined them on the way to the stage, "She's being accompanied back to the hotel."

Osborn hardly noticed. He was too busy smiling and glad handing well wishers to care. Strong was more or less ignoring the throng around them.

"Very unfortunate. My wife Terri was looking forward to standing with her. She's up on stage already."

Strong had made up his mind back at the hotel. He couldn't read the speech he'd been given. He knew that if he read it it would mean turning his back on God.

As he waited on-stage, hearing his name chanted over and over, listening to the audacious words used to describe him, he felt worthless. All of this was a passion play lacking real substance and feeling. A pageant for the consumption of a spiritually starved American public who so desperately needed a new hero.

The speech he had been given would have fed that need. Satisfied the mass addiction. But that is not what he had decided to tell them. He intended to tell them what they didn't want to hear. This was bigger than him and much more important. Even more important than his family. He intended to tell them the truth no matter what the consequence.

When Strong stepped forward to address the crowd *'Hail to the Chief'* started playing. He was almost knocked over by the response. A sea of people waved, hooted, screamed and cried. They were frantic. Eager to hear him speak. Pronounce that he had won. To tell them that they were all winners.

He held his hands up for quiet for more than ten minutes before they settled down enough for him to speak. As he waited, he felt something moving in his pocket. He reached in and pulled out the pager. It was flashing green.

"Praise God!" he shouted out in earnest for all assembled to hear. The cameras zoomed in for a close up and found tears streaming from his eyes. He fell onto his knees and bowed his head in silent prayer thanking Jesus, who he had once again found in his heart. The crowd waited, moved by his tears and his devotion. More impatient than ever to hear the great man speak.

When he finally stood up, eyes still cast down, he said softly.

"Let us pray.

'Our Father, who art in heaven,
Hallowed be thy Name.
Thy kingdom come.
Thy will be done,
On earth as it is in heaven.
Give us this day our daily bread.
And forgive us our trespasses,
As we forgive those who trespass against us.
And lead us not into temptation,
But deliver us from evil.
For thine is the kingdom,
and the power, and the glory,
for ever and ever.
Amen.'"

He held up the copy of the speech in his hands to show the audience.

"This speech, ladies and gentlemen, this speech was given to me to read. It was written by none other than my late brother-in-law Sherman Gale. You all know the high regard I had for Colonel Gale. In it there are all kinds of references to building a heaven on earth. Of the challenge that lies before all Christians at the End of Days. But I have something else to share with you tonight, something more important that you must know, and that is the truth.

"Sherman Gale was a misguided soul who allowed evil into his heart. Until a few moments ago my children were being used as hostages. Used by a group of men who are conspiring to build your new Jerusalem on a false foundation. We have been betrayed. You need to know this, to understand what..."

The lights in the stadium suddenly blinked off and the microphone went dead. Strong stood there not sure what to do. All was blackness. There was yelling and sounds of panic all around.

A beam of white light broke through the inky dark, illuminating the spot where Robert Strong stood transfixed. He looked up into the light, blinking, straining to see where it was coming from. He held up his hand to shield his eyes. Then he saw it clearly in the light, pointing in awe and disbelief.

"Jesus," he said softly to himself, "Sweet Jesus."

At that precise moment a shot rang out hitting Strong in the head, blowing half of it away. And then it was dark once more.

22 - Message from the Grave

Chu was lying in a hospital bed, wide awake. The pain in his shoulder was killing him. It was seven in the morning and the shift change was in full swing with staff members in briefings with their replacements. The halls were empty.

He didn't know that Audrey had stayed by him all night. Refused to go until she knew he was going to be okay. Even now she was just out grabbing a quick breakfast in the cafeteria - chased out by a well meaning nurse who assured her that he wouldn't just get up and walk away if she left for a short while.

A man walked into his room dressed in a white lab coat. Chu assumed it was a doctor come to do rounds, until he looked up at the man's face. It was Hinks. Even in his injured state Chu sprung up in bed, prepared for anything. Hinks laughed derisively, holding up his hands to show he was unarmed.

"Relax, Chu, I'm not here to hurt you. If I was, you'd be dead by now. Say, do you look deep-fried or what?"

"What the fuck are you doing here?"

"I'm here to invite you to meet with Faith Gale. She needs to see you urgently."

"Faith needs to see me?" he asked, checking to see if he'd heard right.

"Yes, Chu, and urgently – like we have to get going now if you want to see her."

"It's my choice?"

"Oh, yeah, the little Miss wouldn't have it any other way."

Hinks guarded the door while Chu got dressed. He nearly passed out putting his shirt and jacket on. He noticed a bottle of pain killers beside his bed and took it.

"Ready to go?" Hinks asked impatiently.

"Yup, lead the way."

Walking to the car Chu couldn't help but ask, "So I guess you've gone over to work for them full time now? No more pretence?"

"I guess you missed what happened last night. I'll probably end up staying with the Bureau after things settle down. Strong basically won the election but a disgruntled crazy knocked him off during his victory speech."

"What?" demanded Chu grabbing Hinks by the shoulder, "What do you mean 'knocked him off?'"

"I mean some crazy fucker blew his head right off. A member of his own church, too," Hinks replied, pulling himself angrily away from Chu's grasp, "Looks like Ralph Osborn will get the job now."

Chu's heart ached as he walked, overshadowing the pain from his wounded shoulder that made him wince with every step he took.

———

"This is where I leave you," Chu's escort hissed.

Chu didn't respond and just kept on walking down the long dock towards the stern of Victory.

"Until we meet again, *Mr.* Chu," Hinks called after him menacingly.

He didn't see anyone else on the dock as he walked, but he was sure there were plenty of eyes watching him. As he got closer to the ship he could appreciate her enormity. He felt like an insect beneath her. Still, he walked on and still he saw no one. Walking ever nearer to the long boarding ramp going up to the ship half-way down her length.

As he approached the elaborate covered gang-way, he saw her standing at the top. She was coming down to meet him.

His heart was pounding at the sight of her. He didn't want it to. He tried to make his desire for her go away. He wanted to hate her for what she had helped to do. For what she herself had done. And yet, her face. It was so sad.

She came down nearly to the bottom then stopped and stood, slightly above where he stood on the dock. She didn't look at him but addressed the dock generally, like she would have done if she was talking to a group of people.

"It was good of you to come on such short notice. My father left me something to give to you. A message he wanted you to have."

"Faith, why are you acting like this? Can't we just talk, please?"

She wouldn't look him directly in the eyes. She refused to speak. She simply held out a slim tablet viewer for him to take.

"What is it?"

"The message I told you about. It's on the viewer," she answered, her eyes still downcast.

Chu reached for and took the viewer but held onto her hand as well. She gasped at his touch.

"I feel so badly I didn't tell you how I felt when we were in Miami. Maybe if I had we could have done something different. Maybe K.C. - "

"No, don't!" she cried, trying to pull away. "Don't say that to me. You didn't, so don't talk about it. I helped Daddy distract you and that's all."

Two burly men at the top of the ramp started down towards them like they meant business. Three others appeared from nowhere near him on the dock and were converging on them as well. Chu saw this and let her go.

"Go back," she yelled at the men as soon as he let go, "Leave us alone. I need to talk to him alone!"

The men backed off reluctantly, like excited dogs denied the chase. She turned to him and he could see she was fighting back tears.

"It's part of The Plan. I cannot allow anything to get in the way."

"Whose plan, Faith? Your father's?"

"Not his plan, Derrik," she said shaking her head in earnest. "I'm talking about God's Plan. I hear voices all the time telling me what to do, you know. It's not what I always want, not what I would choose. But if it's part of The Plan then it has to be done. So take this, please. It's information you need. It's part of The Plan, don't you see?" she said, handing him the device again.

He took it and she smiled.

"I must go now," she said.

"Please don't, Faith," he pleaded but she turned her back on him and started back up. "Faith, no matter what, I love you. I don't want to, but I do..."

She stopped and slowly turned around, her eyes looking down at the ramp.

"After you listen to that message get rid of that thing quickly. And get ready to run. I'm sorry, that's as much as I can do. The Plan, The Plan, don't you see?"

Overwhelmed, she turned and ran up the remainder of ramp and onto the ship.

Chu stood and watched her go. There was nothing else he could do. He looked down at the device in his hand and started to walk back along the dock from where he had come.

Chu walked slowly, trying to pick alternate routes he could take if he had to. He knew that right now he was probably a marked man. At first he couldn't get the machine to turn on. Then he saw that it was activated by a thumb print. He guessed correctly that his would work, and it did. The tablet sprung to life, displaying the face of Colonel Sherman Gale. He continued to walk and look for an escape route as it played.

'Hello, Mr. Chu. I am recording this as I wait for your foolish colleagues to arrive. If you are watching this, it means The Plan didn't quite succeed. If so, I'm sure it was largely thanks to you. Congratulations. But things have gone too far to stop now, Mr. Chu.

And although I am dead, I am not quite gone.

Always the good soldier, I devised a Plan B. There is always a Plan B, Mr. Chu, because, as I have told you before, I'm used to getting my way.

But before I go into that I just need to talk to you. I want you to understand why I have done what I've done. I realize it must look like madness to you. But I'm not crazy, Mr. Chu. Not in the least. What would be crazy would be ignoring what God has told me to do. What would be insane would be not to listen to Faith and the word of God she delivered to me. She called me, you know, full of remorse, on her way to deliver the message to you. I told her to remember that our Saviour did something he did not want to do because his Father told him it was to be so. Still, it breaks my heart to know she suffered so.

That you have tried to meddle in my affairs shows that you are an agent of evil. A soldier of Satan. Your abilities are surely inspired by him, and to be respected for sure, but most of all, they are to be defeated.

So I will speak to you as I would to Satan. One who has taken my wife and my son so cruelly from me. I acknowledge you as a powerful adversary, but talk to you now as one who will soon be vanquished as foretold in the Bible. Soon, Christ and all his children will take their rightful place as rulers on earth.

I wanted you to have a part in casting Satan into Hell.

The device you are using to watch me is something much more than a viewing screen. It is a key. By activating it with your fingerprint, you have begun a command sequence that will disable most of the world's computing devices and render the internet useless. The program that you unlocked undermines a Chinese-authored attack Bot, found dormant on computers and servers all over the world. But the code you just initiated makes the program a magnitude more powerful than contemplated and puts it completely under our control.

I hope you take no offence when I say this, Mr.Chu, but the Chinese, they are our true enemy. They've just got too big for their britches. Challenging America both economically and with their military machine. Consider, Mr. Chu, the Chinese are avowed atheists. Inspiring their Godless ways all over the world. While we must continue to battle for souls with the Muslims, at least they have a God and revere our Holy Book.

So this attack, the one you just launched, will be blamed on the Chinese. Their fingerprints, so to speak, are all over it.

Within hours, a state of confusion and mayhem will reign. At the President's request, the military will step in to

*maintain order and good government which will inevitably
include selecting the late Reverend Robert Strong's Vice
Presidential running mate, Ralph Osborn, as President.
Ralph is a one of seven men who worked with me to ensure
God's will become manifest. He is one of the inner circle and
understands what he has to do.*

*Robert's death was necessary, as he couldn't be counted
on. Not when it really mattered. As for the terrible accident
involving your poor mother and grandfather, I am truly sorry,
but I fear I blame you for the death of my son. And, as you
know, it's an eye for an eye and a tooth for a tooth, Mr. Chu.*

*I record this before my last stand, with the knowledge
that my daughter, Faith, was forced to take her own brother's
life because Satan filled him with doubt. What she did, she
did following orders. God's orders. She is a Crusader and
will not falter. She will see that God's will be done. As I
have done.*

In the name of Jesus Christ. Amen.'

He had only gone half way to the main gate by the time
the recording finished. The moment Gale began to say *Amen*,
Chu whipped the device along the ground in front of him. It
skimmed along the decking for less than two seconds, blowing
up in a surprisingly impressive explosion forty feet in front
of him. A ragged hole several feet in diameter gaped, still
smouldering. Chu dashed toward the spot at full tilt. He knew
he was running for his life.

Bullets rained down from sniper fire above, dancing around
him and making strange pinging noises. When he was ten feet
from the ragged hole he leaped forward, tumbled two or three
times and vanished like a rabbit going to ground.

While it looked elegant from above, it proved to be one of the more painful stunts he had ever done. As he fell through the opening, hot embers and splintered wood tore at his skin. He had no idea how far he would fall until it was abruptly halted by landing on top of a large supporting beam. It knocked the wind out of him and jarred his senses. When he went to get up, he found he couldn't move.

After a few seconds he managed to pull himself along the beam a few feet before seeing a narrow service walkway twenty feet below. In the state he was in he doubted if he could make it down to where it ran, but any rational decision-making was removed when shots started ringing out from the hole above.

He pushed himself off the beam and fell. As he did so he twisted his body in an attempt to land on the walkway but missed it and had to catch the railing. It wrenched his injured arm horribly but he hung on and hoisted himself onto the narrow path. Then he began to run, as hard and fast as he could, toward the shore.

High above him, back at the hole, he could still hear them firing shots - meaning they hadn't seen him get away. Giving him hope that he might succeed in escaping. Now he was in running mode nothing else mattered. The blood gushing from his dressing was hardly noticed. The splinters digging into his back, ignored. He was running, and his mindset was that nothing would stop him. Always moving forward.

He got to the end of the service walkway and didn't hesitate when he saw a ladder going down to the water. In fact, he half slid down the ladder using a technique he'd developed back in college. He used to think it was fun in those days to imagine he was being chased. Like his life depended on it. He decided that the real thing was no fun at all.

Pain was beginning creep into his awareness as he climbed over some rocks to where he could see a ladder leading up to the road. Chu was surprised as he crawled up the ladder and looked around. He was on the outside of Victory's dock near the main access road. Without hesitation, he pulled himself up and began to run.

Like lightening hitting him, he felt a sharp bite on his thigh and then a surge of electricity racing through his body knocking him to the ground. He was conscious but paralysed as he saw Hinks moving rapidly towards him holding a Taser.

"Here, let me give it just a little more juice to make sure you don't go anywhere."

Hinks hit a button on the electric gun and Chu vibrated involuntarily with the surge.

"Oh, that looks funny, Chu. You gotta laugh, huh?" he laughed and kicked Chu in the face. Chu couldn't feel it but could taste the blood in his mouth and feel the ragged cuts on his lips and inner cheeks.

"Can't talk yet? Well, I'll wait. We have some time. Those idiots still think you're under the dock," Hinks said grabbing Chu by the face and squeezing it hard, "They don't realize just how tricky you are, do they?"

Chu was still unable to move but found he could talk. He knew he needed to stall.

"Do you realize what you're doing? When your bosses find out..." Chu managed to choke out, stalling for time.

"I only have one boss and that's God. And my *'superiors'* want you dead, anyway. I don't think they'll care how I do it," he said, taking out a skinning knife.

"You think you're working for God? You think this is what He wants?"

"For Satan's agents, yes. You'll burn in Hell, anyway. I can send you there before you're dead."

"You fucking moron, don't you know? *You're* working for Satan."

Chu could feel a tingling in his left foot but he still couldn't move.

"What did you say?" Hinks yelled, grabbing Chu by the collar with one hand and holding up the knife to his face with the other.

Chu didn't respond. He could feel his fingers, they were coming back to life.

"How did it feel when you killed Petersen? Did you enjoy that? Was that doing God's work?"

"That was different. I had my orders and he just wouldn't come around. Kept poking his nose into stuff," Hinks snapped defensively, but moved the knife away from Chu's face.

"So you had to?"

"It was fucking hard, you asshole. But you, you I'm going to enjoy killing. I think I'll start with little cuts to make it last longer."

Hinks stuck the knife deep into Chu's left thigh where the Taser barbs still clung and dragged the blade forward four inches. Blood began to run out from the cut in a torrent. Chu felt a dull ache instead of pain but also a surge of adrenalin that brought his arms back to life.

"What do you say now, tough guy? Cat caught your tongue?" Hinks chided as he twisted the knife deeper into Chu's leg.

Now he felt the pain.

"I have a message for you," Chu grimaced through clenched teeth.

"From who?"

Unknown to Hinks, Chu had grabbed a large, foot-long wood splinter that had been stuck in his jacket and now plunged it with all his might into his assailant's gut, pushing it upwards under his rib cage.

"From Petersen's wife and kids. They want you to go to Hell," Chu said, pulling Hinks close and staring directly into his eyes. Chu could feel the warm blood pouring from the main artery he had hit. Hinks was surprised but didn't say a word. He just slowly went limp, sagging onto Chu with increasing weight, and died.

Chu tossed him off with disdain and tried to get up. He couldn't do it at first, but after a few attempts he got upright and started to head for the road once more. He hadn't gone fifty feet when a large, black car rounded the corner moving quickly. He knew he couldn't get away. That he was done for.

The car screeched to a halt and the door flung open wide. There was O'Reilly, looking as mad as Chu had ever seen him. And behind him was Audrey who now held her hands up to her mouth at the site of him. She was crying.

Chu dropped to his knees smiling, covered with blood.

After they pulled him into the car and sped away, O'Reilly assured Audrey that he was in no danger of dying. Released from worry, she was free to vent.

"Derrik you're a fucking idiot!" she screamed. "A stupid, fucking idiot."

Chu mumbled something in response that only O'Reilly was close enough to hear.

"What did he say?" she sniffled.

"I'm not sure, but I think he told you to watch your mouth."

23 - ARM

Two days had passed since the morning on the dock. Chu was talking with O'Reilly from his hospital bed.

"The information you gave us was invaluable. We managed to shut down most of our network before the program spread. As it is, the President has evoked Martial Law. We're doing better than most places in the world. We were setting up for a very different kind of attack from Gale and his organization. They would have completely succeeded if it hadn't been for you."

"What's happened to Faith?"

O'Reilly winced at the mention of her name.

"Come on, Chu, just forget about her. I would have thought that after everything..."

"I just want to know where she is."

"Shortly after your visit, Victory departed. Destination unknown."

"And Audrey?" he could remember her being there when they rescued him.

"She's been in debriefing for the last two days. Getting to know our organization. The organization I've been working for all along."

"Not the Secret Service?"

"No, it's an organization we established when we saw that a threat was coming to America in the person of Sherman Gale. The American Resistance Movement or ARM for short."

"And Audrey is going to join?"

"Looks that way, yes."

"Are you looking for recruits? Because I'd really like to keep working with her. Is she still mad at me?"

"Let's see now, yes – it's possible - yes. There, I think I dealt with everything."

"So she's still mad."

"More hurt, I'd say."

"Hurt?"

"Chu, she stayed with you at the hospital after you two saved the Gale kids. And then you take off without leaving a word when she steps out for a few minutes. She really," and here he paused, "I don't know how to put it – she has feelings for you."

"Feelings?"

"Yeah, you dumb ass, feelings. And then you go and risk your life to talk to that school-girl psycho."

"Oh, I see."

"So she might not want to work with you. But we'd certainly welcome you joining. You'd be a great asset for us in the fight."

"The fight?"

"The fight to keep us free. To ensure that we live in a democracy, no matter how imperfect it may be. There are lots of things wrong with America but there are a lot of things right about it too. We think it's important enough to try and keep it, so we look at it like a fight. A fight to the death, if need be."

"So, Audrey really likes me?"

"Oh, for Christ's sake. Is that all you think about?"

"No, it's just I didn't know. She always seems so tough. Like nothing matters."

"Let me tell you something, Chu. For whatever reason, you matter to her very much. You should give her a chance. You never know. I was married for twenty-five years before my wife passed away. We fought all the time but now I miss her more than I can tell you. It was she who knew first. Knew that we were going to be together. When you do find somebody who loves you, it's not something to take lightly. You should sit up and pay attention. Anyway, enough of that..."

"Say, O'Reilly, I've been wondering. How did you know I'd be down at the dock? I could've been anywhere."

"It was Audrey. When she saw you were gone and didn't leave any word with her about where you were going she figured you must be going to see Faith. I was sceptical at first but when we found you there, I was pretty impressed."

"Yeah, she's pretty impressive, isn't she?"

"Yes she is," answered O'Reilly, doing a very bad impression of her high, squeaky voice.

They both laughed for a while and it felt good, even though for Chu, it hurt a lot.

———

Chu had just closed his eyes for a few minutes and was now drifting in and out of sleep. He wanted to go back to his dream. It was such a great feeling. He was with Audrey.

He opened his eyes and to his surprise, she was sitting in the chair, waiting for him to wake up.

"Uh, hi," she said.

"Hi."

"You feeling any better?"

"Better than what?"

"You know what I mean."

"Well, at least I'm conscious."

"That's debatable."

The words made Chu grimace.

"Look, Audrey, I know I was an asshole for leaving like that. It's just that Hinks came and there wasn't time..."

"You're going to tell me that it didn't cross your mind that it would bother me if you went to see her? Or are you telling me you were so juiced up at the thought that you didn't think about me at all?"

He sat with a blank look on his face. He was thinking, trying to remember.

"And you just sit there staring at me. What the hell are you thinking? "

"Audrey," he managed to get out, "Audrey, I'm pretty confused right now. I know that may sound lame but it's true. I just want to get the words out right. I want to be honest with you. I like you a lot Audrey, and the more I get to know you the more I like you. I liked taking care of you in Miami – even the kinda gross parts. And I like being taken care of by you."

"And Faith."

"The way I feel about Faith defies me. But it's there. I'm not going to deny it."

"Infatuation?"

"I don't think so. I think it's because I feel she needs me so much. She's so sad, I want to help her. "

"The beautiful damsel in distress."

"She's changed, Audrey. With her father dead she thinks she's fulfilling God's plan now. Gale passed her the gauntlet to carry and she's going to do it. Such a waste. It makes me very sad."

"I can see that."

"Anyway, I guess Faith being so forward made it easier, too. To know she liked me. Or at least pretended to."

"You need overt signals?"

"Yeah, I guess I do. I just don't see why anyone would be interested in me. Even before my girlfriend dumped me in college I was never any good with girls. And after that, it was just a disaster."

"Poor baby," she said patting his arm.

"Ouch," he said, playing it up a bit.

"Oh, Derrik," she said, shaking her head and looking at him sadly, "Just look at you. Look what they've done."

Chu was a mess from head to toe. The burns and bandages made him look like a survivor from Hiroshima.

"Too ugly to love, huh?"

"Almost," she replied laughing, "Almost."

"And Audrey, O'Reilly told me it was you who knew where to find me. I owe you my life. Thanks."

"It was my pleasure," she said truthfully, looking at him directly in the eyes, "And it's also my pleasure to go and get an old friend of yours. The children wanted to come but the doctors said it would be best to wait."

"Until I'm looking a little more presentable?"

"Let's just say, until you're in a little better shape. I'll go get Mrs. Strong, okay?"

She stood up to go and then stopped.

"I've got to know her a bit and she really is something else. Just like you said."

"I can't wait to see her. I'm just so sorry about Robert."

"A lot of people are. It's caused a huge uprising in the Coalition of Christians movement. Something ARM is counting on using."

"It's really started, hasn't it?" he asked.

"What has started?"

"The second Civil War."

She was gone only a minute. When she returned she was followed by a concerned looking Doris Strong.

"Oh, dear! They told me it was bad, but I had no idea!" she exclaimed as she walked into the hospital room.

"It's not as bad as it looks," Chu replied bravely as she inspected him at close hand, clucking all the while. She stood with shining eyes, looking intently at him and smiling.

"You saved our babies. I heard you were magnificent."

"Audrey, too," Chu replied, looking over at Audrey and smiling.

"She told me about you having to camp out in a hedge for a whole day. That you wouldn't give up. You're my hero!"

"I'm just so sorry I couldn't help save him too, Doris. I feel so incredibly bad."

She looked sad and weary suddenly at the mention of her husband.

"It is such a loss," she admitted, "It tears me up, especially when I think about the children. They'll miss him so. And so will I. So will I. As you will miss your dear mother and grandfather. I hear they were victims of this madness as well."

"I wish there was something we could do. Words seem so useless."

They held each other as best they could, united in their sadness. Audrey watched, moved to tears.

24 - New World Order

It was a warm and still evening as Victory ploughed her way through the waters off Bermuda. She had been loosely circling the island for days in a holding pattern, waiting for committee members to arrive. They trickled in over the course of the day until all seven were on hand for the first meeting of Gale's Executive since his death.

The group had agreed to the meeting when they last convened on board the very same ship two weeks before. Gale had stated that his successor would be revealed. The man chosen to control the hundreds of billions of dollars in assets owned by Gale Enterprises, command the formidable Gale Security Division and hold the key to the most complex malicious software program the world had ever seen.

Ralph Osborn assumed it would be him. Gale and he were both military men, they had been close friends in the Gulf, Gale had chosen him to be Strong's running mate and it was looking more and more like he would become the next President. It was logical. Most of the others around the table had made this assumption as well but that didn't stop several of them from secretly hoping it would be them.

Osborn had the floor now, summing up his argument for accelerating his appointment as President.

"If we wait, we're just playing into the hands of our enemies. They are not constrained by political processes that delay decision making. They can move as soon as they see it is to their advantage to move. We are losing valuable time.

The American people are angry at this attack and want immediate action to deal with it. The Chinese are still trying to figure out what hit them. If we follow the timetable, the earliest I'll be sworn in is more than two months away. All that time wasted with a lame duck President who's main mission is to fight us."

"But Ralph," the Chief Justice, and legal council for the group, noted, "If we don't follow the law we will lose millions of supporters and half of the military. The Marines and Navy are on board with an earlier date, but the Army and Air Force won't have anything to do with us if we break the law. And that's what it would be. Breaking the law. No, I believe you must continue to push for the early transition in the media."

"Even if it means letting the Chinese get back on their feet again? Losing strategic advantage?" Osborn countered.

"I suggest you get very public about what you would do right now. Try and make the President do something with pressure. We're doing a very good job there. The alternative is too dangerous. We need to take power legally or we will be accused, quite rightly, of a government overthrow. At least, that's the way I feel."

Several others around the table nodded in agreement.

"So, do we put it to a vote?" the legal man continued.

"We never voted before. It was always Sherman who would decide after discussion. I think we should stick with that way of doing things. It's the most effective," stated Osborn, more sure than ever it would be him that would run things. Gale had done many things that were not supported generally by the group and he was prepared to do the same thing. It was both the prerogative and pitfall of leadership.

"Then I suppose it's time to find out who Sherman picked," suggested the media mogul thoughtfully, "Do we know how to determine that?"

"There's a video clip to play. Sherman sent it to me the day he martyred himself," the Chief Justice said stoically.

Up on the big screen loomed the face of Colonel Sherman Gale. He was dressed in his battle fatigues and looked very tired.

"Today we agreed to meet to find out who will be taking over. I know many problems and issues have come up in the past two weeks. I wish I could be there to help make things work. To that end I want to lay out the Master Plan I have been working to all along. Some of you know much of it, others hardly anything at all. Nobody knows the complete Plan.

"To view the Master Plan you must first unlock the computer console at the front of this room. That is done by palm print and voice recognition. Whomever can unlock the machine is my successor."

"A bit dramatic, don't you think?" offered the industrialist as the clip finished playing.

"I like it," disagreed the media man, "The drama I mean. Who goes first?"

Ralph Osborn looked at him like it was obvious. He stood up and walked over to the computer terminal and sat down. He put his palm on the reader and stated his full name.

"Ralph Tiberius Osborn," he said.

Nothing happened, so he tried again, almost shouting. Still the machine remained dark.

Clearly rattled, Osborn got up and stepped aside.

"Who's next?"

All of them tried in the end, one by one. It was interesting to see in what order they went. This gave any perceptive observer the opportunity to gauge the pecking order within the group. The last to try was the senior career bureaucrat Gale had recruited. When he failed to make the computer come to life there was general sigh of relief.

"Either a bad joke or some kind of malfunction," Osborn stated with authority, ecstatic that none of the others had succeeded.

"We're just going to have to decide among ourselves."

"I'm not sure it works that way, General Osborn. My father was quite specific about orders."

It was the first time she had spoken since the meeting started. At first they didn't know why she was present. After a while they had simply forgotten about her being in the room. She sat where her father used to sit, dressed in the white dress uniform of a Gale Security Commander.

"Pardon me, Miss Gale. I know that you have chosen to join us today, but I'm not sure it's appropriate for you to get involved in discussions, the significance of which you can't possibly comprehend."

Faith smiled when she heard this, apparently not bothered in the least by the patronizing tone.

"Why did you think I was here, sir?" she asked sweetly.

"Well, I thought it was a..." he stumbled, trying to respond gently to the teenager, "Well, to be frank, I thought it was best for us just to humour you."

Faith laughed. Not derisively or in a mean way, but a true and hearty laugh.

"Well, you do humour me, General Osborn. You really do."

Osborn was back on his heels, unsure what to do. Faith looked at him smiling. He could feel her challenge.

"Well, I'm sorry to say that somebody has to be in charge, young lady, and for right now that looks like me."

Without saying a word she got up from her chair and went over to the terminal.

"Faith Patricia-Anne Gale," she said softly after laying her hand on the reader. The monitor immediately sprang to life.

"I'm sorry to correct you, General Osborn, I really am," she said turning to face him, "I prefer to think of this as a cooperative venture, but if there's anybody who's 'in charge,' it's me. And I think we should stick to the timetable as planned. The last thing we want to be accused of is treason."

They were all in shock but she forged on anyway.

"Now then, any objections to hearing what my father has to say?"

25 - St. Pierre

The supply ship had finished unloading its precious cargo of Bordeaux wine, aged cheese and other fine comestibles from France. Twice a year the little ship would make the gruelling passage across the Atlantic to refuel the hearts and souls of the little French outpost of St. Pierre on Canada's doorstep.

She would return to France later that day laden with fish and lobster. Out with the tide. The homeward trip that would take up to a week and at this time of year she was most certainly going to encounter some heavy seas. It was only left to determine how heavy.

Unknown to most of the sailors crewing the ship, they would be carrying a cargo more valuable than seafood back to their native land. This trip, they would be taking a woman and her two young children with them.

Normally, Doris Strong would never have considered taking such a voyage, let alone taking her children with her. But these were strange times and strange things were bound to happen. One of their most valuable witnesses, ARM command determined she was at too high a risk to stay in the country.

The French offered secrecy, sanctuary and protection for her and the children, keeping up a long-time tradition of taking in those who America rejects. There was speculation that the French President's wife had insisted that her husband extend the offer after being requested to do so by his US counterpart. She could only imagine what it had been like for the poor woman.

The Strongs were accompanied by two newly recruited ARM agents, Audrey Kunitz and Derrik Chu. They were sitting in a cafe, watching the ship unload.

"Is it my imagination or is the coffee better here?" Doris asked.

"I'll say, and how about the pastries? I've eaten three already," Chu said, his mouth half full.

The kids nodded enthusiastically as they drank their hot chocolate and ate chocolate croissants.

"Audrey?" asked Doris, "Would you mind taking the children for a little walk when you're done? I need to talk to Derrik for a few minutes."

"Yes, of course, Mrs., I mean, Doris." No matter how hard she tried, she kept reverting to formality, "Sorry."

"That's perfectly fine dear. You must have had manners put into you something fierce when you were little."

"Yes, ma'am, you could say that."

"Well, it could be a lot worse."

They all laughed and kidded some more before Audrey bundled up Marcus and Angela and took them outside. It was cold outside with a bracing wind and Doris knew they wouldn't last long.

"I just wanted to take this chance to say goodbye. And to thank you for all you've done."

Chu started to protest but she stopped him.

"No, please, let me say it. Thank you from the bottom of my heart."

"Please know it has been my pleasure. I can truly say that you and your husband were so kind..." Chu said, choking up at the end, thinking about him. They both paused a moment for reflection. At last, Doris summed up her feelings.

"Robert was just the finest person I have ever known. I will miss him every day until the moment I die."

"And you have faith you'll see him again?"

"I do, Derrik. I know I will."

She was so earnest, it was compelling.

"Now what are you going to do?" he asked, changing the subject.

"Try and keep my children safe. What else can I do? I've told O'Reilly everything I know. If Osborn gets power I don't know what will happen."

"O'Reilly seems to have a pretty good guess."

"And..?"

"Isolation of America. Trade barriers. Annexing Canada and Mexico. Holy war..."

"America won't be someplace I want to be if that happens. But we'll just have to wait and see."

"You can, but I'm not just going to wait. Sherman Gale said he thought about me as Satan. Well, that's just what I'm going to be to them. Satan. I told O'Reilly I'm not going to rest until they're defeated or I'm dead."

"Derrik, please. I didn't want to talk about that, it upsets me so."

"I'm sorry, Doris. I just get carried away. I'm just so angry."

They sipped at their coffees half-halfheartedly, letting things settle.

"How about Faith? How do you feel about her?" she asked suddenly.

"Every time I think I've stopped thinking about her, she comes back. I really don't want her to, but she does."

"Have you told her?"

"Finally, that day by the dock. But she said it was too late and I think she's right."

"That little girl has had problems from the day her mother died. She went through hell and it marked her. She and her father, unfortunately, they're cut from the same cloth. I don't think she can be saved, Derrik."

"I've pretty much come to the same conclusion. But she's still there. Still inside me."

"Me, too. I held her when she was a baby. Took care of her before I had my own children. She'll always be special to me." She paused, thinking before adding, "And you and Audrey?"

"Well, we're seeing how working together goes. She doesn't want to be more than friends while I've got a thing for Faith, so..."

"So frustrating, yes? I'll bet she doesn't play up to you like Faith."

"No, not at all."

"Well, maybe you should try playing up to her."

"I don't think she'll go for it."

"All you can do is try, Derrik. Take a chance. Sometimes you fall, but you'll never know unless you take the leap..."

And on those words, Audrey and the kids burst back into the cafe, all steaming with freshness and cold. Audrey was talking to a local in perfect French. Apparently another language in her repertoire.

Doris just smiled at Chu and patted his arm.

———

They watched as the boat sailed away over the choppy waves. It was bitter cold as the wind whipped from the east.

"I'm going to miss them," Chu said, watching the boat grow smaller and smaller as it steamed out of the harbour.

"They're great kids. Too bad they don't have a father," Audrey replied.

"We're going to do something about that, right?"

"Still won't bring him back."

"No, it won't. Nothing will. But she believes she'll see him again. Truly believes."

"I'd like to too. I hope it's like that."

"Hey, you sure you didn't want to go with them? O'Reilly said he offered it to you."

"He did, but I have other plans."

"I'm glad you didn't," he said putting his arm around her to help keep her warm.

Instead of pulling away she snuggled into him and he held her closer, and together they watched the boat disappear over the horizon and into the great ocean beyond.

Epilogue – Modern Madonna

Spring had come at last, and in the past few days had melted the remaining snow cover away. Faith stood alone on the hill behind the house, just before sunset. The sky promised another blazing glory tonight, its golden disk descending steadily towards the mountains.

She looked down at the site where they had buried her mother. It now contained three grave markers. Her brother and father rested on either side of her mother's original grave. It made Faith happy to know that they were together, waiting for the End of Days to come. She longed for the day when she could join them again.

She spoke to each one of the graves in turn. She told her mother that she missed her and loved her so dearly. She told her brother that she was sorry, so very sorry, and that she prayed for him every day. She told her father that The Plan was still unfolding as God had ordained.

Though there was still no tell-tale sign to give her condition away, she held her belly and sang to the growing babies in her womb. Part of The Plan. The part she found the hardest to understand when her father had told K.C. and her about it only months before. It was then she had learned that she and her brother had been conceived in vitro, and that two frozen embryos remained – identical twins of both K.C. and herself. A fact that haunted Sherman Gale since his wife died. Now they had a home. A home in which to grow and thrive.

It seemed beyond belief, she was carrying her parent's offspring. Two more souls to join them at Rapture when the time came. A time she yearned to come. The culmination of The Plan.

HOLY AMERICAN EMPIRE

Follow Agent Chu in his battle against tyranny and
temptation in the sequel, *Holy American Empire*
(2012 release)

Proof

13718906R00190

Made in the USA
Charleston, SC
27 July 2012